FOUR ON THE FLOOR

A JOHN TYLER THRILLER (#4)

TOM FOWLER

For Lisa and Isabel.

1

<hr>

John Tyler watched over his daughter Lexi's shoulder. "It's just Excel, Dad," she said as she entered a bunch of numbers. "It's kind of a glorified calculator."

"I could use it if it were," Tyler said. "There's a lot of voodoo in this program."

Lexi grinned. "Even though we don't use much of it, it has good power under the hood. I figured you could appreciate it."

"Don't compare this blasted app to a car." Tyler pointed at a cell in the bottom right. "Am I profitable?"

"So far," Lexi confirmed. "I hope you're not planning a long vacation with the proceeds, though."

"It's a start." He patted her shoulder. "Thanks, kiddo."

"You're paying me for this, right?"

"Will I still be in the green?"

"Barely," Lexi said.

"I'll take it." Tyler looked at his watch as the door chime indicated someone entered Special Operations Car Repair. "This must be my interview."

Lexi gave him a funny look. "You're going to hire an employee?"

Tyler nodded. "I'll be able to organize work and get things done faster." He waved his hand toward the monitor. "Your little cells in Excel will appreciate it in time."

"I hope so." She stood. "I'll clear out." Lexi left the office, and a moment later, a man knocked on the door frame. He was a Latino with a light brown complexion and short dark hair which he wore a bit spiky on top. Definitely not a style he could have sported in his active duty days. The man stood about five-ten—the same height as Tyler—and looked a little more slender than his potential boss. His only remarkable features were the top of a tattoo peeking above the top button of his white shirt and a prosthetic lower left leg. Tyler couldn't see it, but he could discern it from the sound it made on the floor, and he'd heard about it when asking around about his prospective employee.

"I'm David Ortiz," he said, extending a hand.

"Thanks for coming in." Tyler shook the man's hand. He could boast of a good grip. "John Tyler."

"Good to meet you." Ortiz said. He gestured to a chair and dropped into it when Tyler nodded. "Glad I got here before the storm."

Tyler glanced outside the window. The sky had grown grayer throughout the day, and a strong wind blew the trees in the median strip of nearby Northern Parkway. He was no meteorologist, but it seemed the recent cold snap intensified. "Me, too. I . . . uh . . . look, I've never really interviewed someone for a job before. I used to work in a shop not far from here. Now, the owner there works for me." This all happened because a drug cartel burned Tom "Smitty" Smith's business to the ground a few months ago. Ortiz didn't need the information up front, however, and Smitty would be unlikely to tell him. "I heard good things about you from the people in the garage at Fort Meade."

"Lot of guys come in there and don't really know what they're doing." Ortiz shrugged. "I helped out where I could. I was a ninety-one bravo."

A wheeled vehicle mechanic. Tyler enlisted under the same MOS over thirty years ago. Despite four tours with special operations, he'd kept his mechanic skills up. "Me, too . . . when the army didn't tell me to go shoot the Taliban instead."

"I know." Ortiz flashed a brief and awkward smile. "I looked you up when you asked me to come in. You're kind of a legend."

Tyler scoffed. "I'm a guy who did his share for his country in twenty-four years of service. Plenty of us out there. A bunch of men and women did more than I ever could."

"I made it to staff sergeant. Only saw one combat tour." Ortiz frowned and rubbed his left knee.

"IED?" Tyler asked.

"Yeah. Once I got hurt, I went back to fixing things until I didn't re-up. Though I guess my days of driving a stick are over."

"You could probably still beat the more famous David Ortiz in a foot race."

"He's won a few more World Series trophies than me, though," the former sergeant said with a grin. "Plus the Hall of Fame thing."

Tyler asked Ortiz about his experience working on cars and found the answers satisfactory. Years of fixing army Jeeps and scavenging for parts tended to make decent mechanics. Tyler knew this from experience. "If I offer you the job," Tyler said, "how many hours a week could you do?"

"Probably three or four days." Ortiz shrugged. "I'm flexible. You need me to come in, I probably can."

"Great. Can you start tomorrow?"

The shop's newest employee smiled. "You got it. Thanks, Mister Tyler."

"Just Tyler is fine." The two men shook hands again, and Ortiz left. Tyler noticed the chill in the air while the door lingered open. It had probably dropped ten degrees from the morning, which wasn't exactly balmy. The third week of March seemed late for cold and snow, but Baltimore weather took on a mind of its own.

Lexi walked back into the office a moment later and sat opposite her father. She pushed her dark auburn ponytail back behind her head. "You hire him?"

"Yeah," Tyler said. "Good guy. I think he'll do well."

"Smitty will be glad for the extra help," Lexi said. She paused and frowned. "Dad, you remember Stacy?"

"Sure. One of your first friends I ever met."

"Right. She's coming back into town for spring break. I offered to go get her at the airport and go out for a girl's day. The weather forecast is bad, though. I don't want to leave her hanging, but it's hard to arrange transportation for her now."

"Someone in an SUV is bound to drive for Uber," Tyler said.

"She was looking forward to me picking her up. It's been a couple years since we've seen each other." Stacy went to college a year before Lexi did. The transition from living with her mom to living with Tyler had been jarring even if she rarely mentioned it. Lexi glanced at the window. "I'm not sure what to tell her. She'll be landing in a couple hours . . . weather permitting."

Tyler tossed Lexi a set of keys. "Take my car home. I'll drive the Tesla and pick her up. Make sure you put it on the charger before you go. Maybe you two can have your girl's day tomorrow. The weather should be better."

"Yeah, I guess." Lexi stared at the round and square keys

—one for the ignition, the other for the doors and trunk. "Wow. You're actually letting me drive the Four-Four-Two."

"She's pretty big and heavy, and she's rear-wheel drive." Tyler's dark green vintage Oldsmobile 442 sat in the lot near his daughter's Tesla Model X. He'd spent a lot of time restoring the car, and while he trusted Lexi as a driver, he'd never let her sit behind the wheel of it before. "I'm sure you'll do fine. I'll pick up Stacy."

"Dad, I can—"

Tyler put up a hand. "I have decades more experience driving in bad weather. All-wheel drive or not, experience matters when the snow piles up. You get home safely. I'll drop your friend off at her house. I'm sure the two of you can spend hours video chatting until tomorrow."

"Thanks, Dad." Lexi smiled. "I'll try not to dent her up too badly."

"I'm taking any repairs out of your paycheck."

"What paycheck?"

"The one you won't get until the body work is finished," Tyler said.

THE BLACK SUBURBAN scoffed at the snow even as it deepened on county roads. The identical vehicle immediately behind it did the same. As the weather grew worse, the number of other cars on the road plummeted along with the temperature. The team hadn't seen another vehicle for about ten minutes. Large flakes fell in front of the headlights, and the wipers worked furiously to keep the windshield clean. Poor visibility forced the lead driver to set a slower pace.

No matter. They would still be on time.

A large stone sign marking *The Manors of Rock Run* indicated they were in the neighborhood. The driver made the next left. Palatial houses dotted both sides of the road. They must have been at least four thousand square feet. The significant distance between homes meant each probably sat on an acre of land. Even in remote Cecil County much closer to Delaware than to Baltimore, properties like this could command a million dollars.

The twin Suburbans eased to a stop in front of the fourth house on the left. Both sets of headlights winked out right away. A few windows were lit up inside the house, which sat at the end of a driveway as long as a football field. Hedges barely getting their leaves back lined both sides. It would make hiding easier, but the team would need to traverse the entire length on foot. Driving so close to the home could alert the residents. A mailbox at the curb told anyone on the street the Chaplain family lived here. The front seat passenger's cell phone rang, and he answered.

"Are you in position?" their boss asked.

"We just arrived. We'll be moving in shortly."

"Excellent. You know what to do. Let me know when you've finished." He clicked off.

Each man slipped a small earpiece into his ear. "Comms check," the driver said. "This is Adam. Over."

"This is Baker," the other front occupant answered. "Over."

"This is Charlie," the man sitting in the second row said. "Over."

"Donald in vehicle two," added the man behind them. "Over."

Next, all three in the lead SUV slipped thin black gloves on. They took out their pistols, examined the magazines, and racked the slides. Identical black ski masks went over their faces next. They matched the shirt, pants, jacket, and shoes each member of the team wore. Four doors opened as the quartet slipped out of the Suburbans. Each man was close in height, so the four would be indistinguishable if anyone happened to see them. They bent low and walked up the driveway. About three inches of snow lay on the asphalt, and it quietly crunched under each man's feet.

A couple minutes later, Adam, Baker, Charlie, and Donald put their backs to the garage door. "We'll take the rear," Charlie said. "Wait for me to tell you we're in position." He and Donald padded off. Adam and Baker kept low and approached the front entrance. A couple minutes later, Charlie's whisper sounded in their earpieces. "In position at the back door."

"All right," Adam said. Baker's other hand held a snap gun to bypass the lock quickly. "We'll breach on my signal. Remember we have a target we need to bring out alive. Kill everyone else, and let's get clear. No mercy. We go in three . . . two . . . one."

2

———

Large snowflakes bounced off the Tesla's windshield. It started with a full charge as Lexi remembered to plug it in before she left. Tyler felt glad he'd sent her home. He didn't want her driving in this mess. He didn't really care to be out in it, either, but he'd told his daughter he'd pick up her friend. The sudden snow left the state unprepared. They normally did a good job of pretreating highways and major roads, but reduced notice meant the interstate was slushier than normal. Tyler kept his speed in line with the rest of the cars on the road. He'd get to the airport a little late, but Stacy's flight would probably be delayed because of conditions on the runways.

Sure enough, Lexi texted him a short while later. The message displayed on the electric SUV's center screen. *Stacy's flight is late. Expected to land in about forty-five minutes when there's a break in the weather.* At first, Tyler hated the large display. He remained a fan of analog gauges in an increasingly digital world. Over time, he'd come to appreciate some of the Tesla's quirks in comparison to the classic cars he loved. She followed with another message. *Be careful, Dad.*

Trouble has a way of finding you. Tyler dictated a reply—something he'd never imagined himself doing up to a few months ago. "It's a simple trip from the airport. We'll be fine."

The sure-footed all-wheel drive made the ride uneventful even if it wasn't easy. Other people were still on the road, and some of them had no idea how to operate a vehicle on anything other than dry pavement. Tyler avoided them when he could, speeding up long enough to get around a couple erratic drivers. He didn't want to push it too hard, though. There was no rush. He could even park in the garage and plug the Model X in for the drive to Cecil County.

About forty minutes later, Tyler took the left exit off of the airport loop and collected a ticket for the hourly garage. He found the EV spots and left the Tesla to charge. An elevator ride and skywalk connected him to the terminal, where he found the departure and arrival boards. Stacy's plane made it to the gate. Many were delayed, and a few were canceled. He headed downstairs to baggage claim. Tyler had never seen a major airport so empty, and his many travels over the years forced him to fly at odd hours. A few minutes later, a carousel number got added to the plane's information displayed on a large screen. He texted Lexi. *Does Stacy know I'm meeting her instead of you?*

The reply came quickly. *Yes. She'll be looking for you while managing her disappointment. Thanks, Dad. Drive safely.*

Tyler eschewed a wooden bench nearby. It would force him either to sit with his back to the door or contort himself into a pretzel to keep an eye on it. He didn't like either option, so he remained standing. Not many people came in or left the area, but a blast of cold air always followed them when the doors slid open. A line of passengers filed into the area from behind the security checkpoint. Tyler spotted Stacy near the back.

She'd always been easy to find as she was Lexi's tallest

friend. Stacy stood an even six feet. She played volleyball in high school and was also one of Lexi's track teammates. Even though she was a year ahead, the two remained friends. Stacy smiled and waved when she saw Tyler. In addition to being tall, she was also very pretty. Stacy had light brown skin and wore her long black hair pulled into a ponytail. She hugged Tyler when she approached. "Thanks for coming. It's so good to see you."

"You, too. I didn't want Lexi to drive in this mess."

"She told me. I get it. I think we're going to hang out tomorrow instead." She chuckled. "A flight delayed by snow. Some spring break, right?"

"Doesn't really seem seasonal," Tyler said as they waited at the carousel. A buzzer sounded, and the belt moved. "How are your parents?"

"Busy as always," Stacy said with a slight wag of her head. "Nothing turned me off from going into academia faster than growing up with two administrators. It's just so time consuming."

"They've done really well, though."

"I guess." She shrugged. "I was kinda hoping they'd slow down. Maybe they want me to finish college first . . . get the expense off the books."

Tyler nodded. "I can tell you firsthand it isn't cheap. Lexi has a partial scholarship and commutes, and it still feels like usury."

"My folks would probably agree." Luggage slid onto the belt, and a few people plucked their bags as they came around. "That's me." Stacy moved toward a large black suitcase. It looked like a lot of others except for her name in bright purple paint across the front.

Tyler cut in front of her, grabbed the bag, and heaved it off the carousel. He expected it to be heavy and wasn't disappointed. Stacy offered to take it, but Tyler declined. He wheeled it into an elevator, along a corridor, and then down another elevator to the garage. As they approached the Tesla, Stacy whistled. "Lexi mentioned a Tesla. Wow. You must be doing all right, too."

Tyler put the suitcase in the back and climbed into the driver's seat. "I . . . acquired it from someone. It's kind of a long story." The SUV originally belonged to Kent Maxwell, a toady for disgraced colonel Leo Braxton who commanded both men in special operations. Maxwell worked for Braxton again in his vendetta against Tyler. They both died—along with several other bootlickers—and Tyler kept the Model X as spoils of war. Getting it retitled and registered in his name proved a bit of a challenge, but he knew some army red teamers and lawyers who helped. Lexi drove it more than he did, and it showed when he tried to use the electronics.

"We have a long drive to Cecil County," Stacy said as they exited the garage. "You always told interesting stories. I wouldn't mind hearing this one."

Snow fell softer now, though it still covered the roads. Tyler hoped the highways would get better as the state road crews continued to work on them. They'd need the help heading northeast. "Maybe some other time," he said.

THE LOCK YIELDED to Baker's snap gun quickly. It wasn't a silent process, however, and the same scenario played out at the rear entrance. Anyone close to the doors would hear something. Adam kept low and moved inside. A powder room was the first thing he saw, and he quickly cleared the tiny space. Three carpeted stairs led to a large living room full of sofas, chairs, and a massive TV mounted on the wall. A teenaged boy looked up in alarm.

Adam put two bullets in his chest and a third in his head.

The body slumped to the side as blood poured onto the tan leather couch. While the shots hadn't been completely silent, the suppressor did a good job of soaking up a lot of the noise. Adam and Baker moved through an archway and entered a large dining room. Charlie and Donald arrived from the rear.

A balding white man approached the front while the rest of the family sat at the table. He was the father. A laptop remained on the table where he'd been working. Adam put a hand on the man's chest and steered him back to his spot. The mother, a slender black woman, also toiled away on a similar-looking computer. A girl of about fourteen regarded the intruders with wide eyes. Another young woman glared at them. She was the target. Adam frowned. One more daughter was supposed to be here. "Where is it?" he barked.

"What are you talking about?" the mother asked. Her lips trembled, and her eyes darted around the room. For having four muzzles in her face, she wasn't doing too badly. "Where's my son? Where's Jackson?"

"Dead," Baker said. "If you don't want to join him, you'll tell us where it is."

The father stood again. Charlie shot him in the head, and his body crumpled to the floor. Cries went up around the table. Adam brought the mom back to the here and now by pressing his gun right up to her tear-streaked face. "Please," she shouted. "I don't know what you want."

"Files," Adam said.

Baker grabbed the oldest daughter by the hair and stuffed the barrel of his pistol in her ear. "She should know where. Tell us where you keep everything, and we'll be on our way."

The girl grimaced. Pain and grief played out on her face. "Who the hell are you people? I don't know what you want."

"Tell them, Kacey!"

"How am I supposed to know what they want?" Her eyes

flicked to her dead father. "They're just going to kill us anyway."

"You're almost right," Adam said. He aimed his gun lower and shot Kacey's mother four times in the torso. Blood splattered onto both of her daughters, but the youngest didn't get much time to react. Donald put three rounds in the center of her chest. Kacey bawled and wailed as Baker hauled her to her feet.

"Tell us where your files are," he ordered. She sobbed and offered no reply.

"Charlie, Donald, search upstairs," Adam said. "Bring any computers. See if the other daughter is up there, too. Kill her if she is."

The two men left the area. Kacey sputtered and wiped at her face with her sleeve. Baker still held her in the chair with a strong hand on her shoulder. Adam crouched and got in her face. She stared back at him. "You know who we work for?"

"I can guess," she said.

"Your sister here?" Kacey said nothing. "Is she?" No response. "We'll find her if she is." Adam looked around at the large table. Blood and bits of bone dotted the laptops. The team would take them, though they were unlikely to have the right files. Kacey's mother's body remained slumped in the chair, her eyes staring at nothing. Adam grabbed her cell. It was a newer iPhone, and he held it in front of her face to unlock it.

"Leave her phone alone," Kacey said.

"Shut up," Baker told her.

Adam opened the mail app and browsed messages. He found a confirmation email for Stacy's flight. "She flew in this afternoon." He opened Google and entered the airline and flight number. The plane had been delayed but landed a half-hour ago. "Probably on her way from the airport now."

"Unless she was waiting for Mom and Dad," Baker said. He turned toward Kacey's dead father and spat on the corpse. "Race traitor."

"Save your Klan crap for another time," Adam said. "We have a job to do."

Charlie and Donald returned carrying two laptops and an iPad. "Nobody up there," Charlie said.

"The other daughter just flew in." Adam pointed at Donald. "You take the girl." He jerked his head toward Kacey. "The rest of us will wait nearby. We don't want the SUVs to draw attention here. People might notice in a neighborhood like this. When Stacy returns, we'll kill her and go."

"Leave her alone!" Kacey shouted. Tears ran from her eyes again. "She has nothing to do with anything. Don't you hurt her."

"Get this girl out of here," Adam said. Donald hauled the protesting young woman to her feet and ordered her to put shoes on. She punched at his arm to no effect.

"We're going to walk outside," he told her in a quiet voice. "Your neighbors ain't close, but they might hear you scream. Be quiet if you don't want to end up like them."

"You'll kill me anyway," she said through her cries.

"You're a pretty woman alone with four men. We don't have to kill you right away." She paled. "Now . . . you gonna be a good girl and not make a fuss?" Kacey offered a small nod. "Right." Donald grabbed her arm. "Let's go."

3

"You're quiet," Tyler said as he guided the Tesla north on I-95. The storm must have been hanging over the highway. Snow stayed constant as he drove, and even a couple trucks from the state road crews only made minimal difference. There was no rush, however, and Tyler kept the speed at about forty. Traffic around him was light but moved at around the same pace.

"Sorry." Stacy looked up from her phone and showed an awkward smile. "Am I normally a talker?"

"When you're a single dad used to army life," Tyler said, "all teen girls are chatterboxes."

"Lexi and I weren't even teenagers when we met." Stacy grinned. "We were definitely chatterboxes, though."

Tyler remembered. He'd recently left the army for good and hadn't seen his daughter in close to a year. Despite the dissolution of his relationship with Rachel, Lexi always wanted to see him and tell him things about her friends. She would have been nine at the time. "Fourth grade, right?"

"Fifth for me," Stacy said, "but yeah." She went back to her phone. Tyler focused on the road. They passed through

Baltimore and neared White Marsh in the county. In normal driving, Stacy's house would be a half-hour or so away. In the current slushy conditions, closer to fifty minutes. Maybe an hour if things got worse the farther north—and away from Baltimore—they got.

The Tesla lapped up the miles without complaint. Its all-wheel drive seemed unbothered by conditions on the highway. Salt trucks made occasional appearances. Even with the snow staying steady, the drive improved a little as they reached Harford County. "Weird," Stacy said as they approached the Bel Air exit. "I can't reach anyone at my house."

"Were you able to earlier?"

"Yeah . . . I texted my mom when I landed and again when we were leaving. She had my itinerary. My dad's gone quiet, too."

"It's a bad storm," Tyler said. "Power could be out. Maybe they're trying to conserve their batteries."

"Maybe." Stacy sounded skeptical. Tyler didn't blame her. He knew his suggestion was weak, but he didn't want her to worry. There were many reasons why someone would become unreachable via phone or text. The problem was a lot of them were bad. Stacy's parents worked in academia. The only people who would have it in for them were students who got poor grades, and they tended not to kill people. Stacy frowned as she tapped on her phone. Tyler sped up a little. He hoped everything was all right, but his years of experience already made him prepare for the worst.

~

ALEX ANNE FINISHED STRUMMING her guitar with a flourish. "There's the music," she said. "I haven't written the lyrics yet, but I will."

"It sounds great," Lexi said. Via FaceTime, she chatted with the singer she'd befriended a few months prior. "I think people will want to hear you play instruments, too."

"Probably. It seems like that kind of record." Her voice deepened for a moment. "Really serious and with a message."

"You can't sing radio-friendly pop songs forever. Besides, I listened to the words on all your songs. You've been getting heavier for a few years."

Alex Anne grinned. "I have. This . . . is different, though. It's one thing to say I'm a little older now, I've been through more, and what I write is going to reflect that. It's another to survive a sex trafficking ring. Not too many songs written about it."

"I know." Alex Anne survived thanks to Lexi's dad, who rescued a plane full of girls before they could disappear to the dark corners of the world. Even Lexi found herself wrapped up in it, as the main smuggler's nephew recruited a friend to grab her, too. She'd had to shoot both of them outside of her car on the University of Maryland campus. At her dad's urging, both Lexi and Alex Anne saw therapists to help them process everything. "Clue people in right away. Call your album *The Therapy Recordings* or something like that."

As she set the guitar down, Alex Anne laughed. "Maybe I will. Except, my dad might not like it."

"He's your manager. That means he works for you."

"He's also my father," Alex Anne said. "But you're right. It's my album. I'll call it what I want. We'll see how supportive the label is when I hand them the tapes."

"Are all the songs going to be about . . . what happened?"

"Probably." Alex Anne's ponytail bobbed as she nodded. "Anyway, I still want to write something with you. What you went through would be really powerful in a song."

"I know." Lexi sighed. "I'm still thinking about it. It's one thing to talk about it in therapy. It's another to . . ."

"To put it into words?"

"Yeah. Especially words I won't sing." She paused and smiled. "And you know you don't want me to sing."

"I remember." Alex Anne smiled, too, and it was good to see. "You're pretty good on the sax, however. Hey, when this album is finished, I want you and your dad to come over and listen to it. We'll have dinner, but I want to play the record for you."

"I'd love to," Lexi said. "I'm pretty sure my dad will find it weird, but whatever. Old people are strange."

"Don't be too rough on him," Alex Anne said.

"I know. He's actually picking up a friend of mine at the airport now. Didn't want me to drive in the snow. I . . . when I first came to live with him, I wasn't happy about it. I didn't hate him or anything, but it was a big change, and I was bitter at my mom for going to jail." She let out a mirthless snort. "Now, I can't imagine not being here the past couple years. He's come a long way from his army days . . . even if he does still shoot people sometimes."

"Sounds like talking to a shrink is going well for you, too."

"Yeah. I don't talk much about it, but it is."

"Good," Alex Anne said. "Therapy BFFs?"

Lexi grinned. "You know it."

DONALD GOT the older sister away without incident. Adam followed him out and then left the large SUV on the side of a nearby street. They could see the only road into the Chaplains' development. The whole community was poorly designed. One way in and out created a single point of failure. Rich people never considered the downsides of their exurban fantasies. Adam fidgeted in the driver's seat as they waited. "You're sure her flight landed?"

"Positive," Baker said. "It touched down fifty minutes ago."

"All right. So it takes her a few minutes to get off the plane. A few more to get her bags. She's coming home for spring break, so she definitely has luggage. Her parents didn't pick her up, so she either got an Uber or arranged for someone else to be there."

"I can't see too many drivers trying to make money in a blizzard," Charlie said.

"There are probably a few," Adam said. "I think you're right, though. She knew her folks weren't coming and arranged a ride. If whoever was already there, it took her ten minutes . . . maybe fifteen . . . to get into a car."

"Better hope it's an SUV," Baker added. "Roads are lousy. Even the highways are probably slushy and slippery." He looked at his watch. "On dry ground, they might make it here in forty-five minutes."

Adam scoffed. "You'd need to be hauling ass to get from BWI to here in forty-five. It's at least fifty. In these conditions, I'm sure it'll be an hour or more. We might have a little wait in store for us." He turned the engine on to get some heat into the cabin.

"Still nothing coming," Charlie said from the back. He sat sideways to keep an eye on anything approaching from the rear, even if Adam would see headlights in his mirrors. They lapsed into silence. A few minutes later, Adam killed the engine. In case another vehicle approached, he didn't want to give away the fact someone remained in the Suburban. The dark windows and generally bad visibility would prevent most people from seeing in.

A pair of headlights appeared in the driver's side mirror.

"We got something," Adam said. He slid a little lower in his seat.

"I see it," Charlie said. "Can't tell what it is yet." The approaching vehicle drew closer slowly. It went down a hill, briefly breaking visual contact before emerging again. "Looks like a truck." As it neared their position, Adam confirmed it was a large pickup. It rolled past the street leading to The Manors of Rock Run. False alarm. Adam sighed and sat up again.

He turned the engine on again a few minutes later and let it run long enough to blow the chill out of the cabin. A short while later, another vehicle approached. "I think this is an SUV," Charlie said. "The headlights make me think Tesla."

"Fits in up here," Baker said. "Bunch of rich assholes."

The other vehicle neared their spot. As it passed, Adam looked to his left. The passenger was a pretty woman with light brown skin and long black hair pulled back. Even seeing her for a moment, Adam could tell she bore a strong resemblance to a woman and a girl the team killed earlier. "It's her."

"I think you're right," Charlie added.

"Let's go," Baker said.

"Let's wait a couple." Adam cautioned. "There's no rush. It'll take a few minutes to get to the house and get inside. They probably haven't seen many other cars. We don't want to be obvious about following them."

"And she'll see her family dead and call the cops."

"She'll be stunned. She's a college girl." Adam shook his head. "She won't know what to do. Let's use these couple minutes to be ready to roll in and kill her . . . her driver, too."

"Last Uber ride he'll provide," Charlie said with a snort.

The trio checked their comms and weapons and slid masks back over their faces. With everything in place for the second round of the operation, Adam started the Suburban and pulled back out onto the main road.

4

———

The snow eased as they entered Cecil County. Once off the highway, however, road conditions worsened. Most were a single lane in each direction, and the short notice for the storm meant no one salted them in advance. Tyler kept both hands on the wheel as he followed the center screen navigation and guided the Tesla along the route. As they approached Stacy's neighborhood, a Suburban sat on the side of the icy asphalt. Not unusual in such bad weather. Even if the vehicle could traverse the roads, the driver might prefer to wait for conditions to clear.

Rock Run Road was basically a large loop full of massive houses. Stacy's family moved in when the development first sprang up. They were the first people Tyler knew to move beyond Harford County. Since then, Cecil joined it in being full of suburban sprawl. As Tyler approached the house, he noticed tire tracks. Two sets. Snow filled them in part of the way, but they remained noticeable. They pulled to the side of the street in front of the Chaplain home. "You expecting any guests?"

"No," Stacy said. "Maybe my folks got a delivery."

The impressions were at least as wide as the Model X's tires. It meant two large vehicles. No delivery required those. A bad feeling buzzed in Tyler's head, and he reached for the pistol he kept in a custom holster on the door. His hand came back empty. The Sig remained in his 442 which Lexi drove back to Baltimore. "Maybe," he said to go along. No need to put Stacy on edge. Tyler tended to presume the worst. Perhaps an innocent explanation would reveal itself when they walked inside the house, and he wouldn't need a gun after all.

They climbed out of the Tesla. The precipitation had tapered off, but flakes still fell. Tyler immediately spied four sets of footprints heading up the driveway. Like the tire tracks, the snow falling since they'd been made partially obscured them. Each looked like a men's size 11 or 12. Stacy didn't seem to notice them. As they approached the house, Tyler kept an eye on the tracks. Two split off from the rest at the garage. They probably went around to the back. A pair of large vehicles. Four men approaching, then two breaking from the pack to go around to the rear.

This wasn't a delivery. It was a hit squad.

"Maybe you should wait in the car," Tyler said.

Stacy frowned. "What are you talking about?"

"Tire tracks near the curb. Two large vehicles . . . probably bigger than mine." He gestured to the snow-covered driveway. "Four sets of prints. As we get closer to the garage, two of them break off from the rest. If we follow them, my guess is they'll lead to your back door. This is no delivery, Stacy."

She shook her head. "My parents are college administrators. No one's trying to kill them. Don't look for threats everywhere, Mister Tyler. Let's go in."

He couldn't dissuade her, and he wouldn't force her back into the Tesla. "Fine. At least let me go first." She bobbed her head. They walked up four steps. A black iron railing framed the porch. The dark wooden front door looked heavy. A brass knocker hung not far below Tyler's eye level. The lock bore a few scratches. Tyler pointed at them. "My guess is someone bypassed this lock recently."

Stacy's eyes widened. "You really think someone came here before we did?"

"I don't know. All the signs are there. You might tell me I'm looking for threats. I'm telling you if I wanted to storm your house with a four-man squad, all the evidence I've seen is basically how I'd do it." Stacy bit her bottom lip. "Now, let me go first and see how things are. If I'm wrong and it's all good, you can come in, too. We'll try the easy way first." Tyler used the brass knocker. It thudded into the door three times. If anyone were awake—or alive—inside, they would've heard it. No response came.

"What does this mean?" Stacy asked with a tremor in her voice.

"I won't lie . . . it's probably not good. Give me your keys." Tyler wondered how he kept finding trouble. This was supposed to be simple. Drop his daughter's friend off, say hi to her folks, and leave. No matter. Keeping Stacy safe became the priority. If whoever came here realized they'd left a family member alive, they could circle back. Tyler took Stacy's keys and undid both locks. He twisted the knob, stood to the side, and pushed the door open. Nothing happened. No hail of bullets. After waiting a few seconds, Tyler walked inside.

The smell of copper greeted him. Blood. Probably a lot of it. "Shit," he muttered under his breath. The powder room immediately inside the entrance was clear. Tyler walked up a few steps into the living room. A teenaged boy's body lay on the couch. Most of his blood seeped into the leather and dripped to the floor. Two bullet holes dotted the center of his chest, and a third was right in the center of his forehead. A professional hit.

"Jackson! No!" Stacy shrieked and ran toward her dead brother. Tyler held her back, and she struggled against his grip. "Let me go!"

"You can't do anything for him. I'm sorry, Stacy."

She stopped fighting, and Tyler let her go. Stacy capitalized by sprinting from the room. She yelled again a moment later. Tyler followed her. Her parents and younger sister were also dead, each shot at least a couple times. Stacy sobbed and pounded the tabletop as her shoulders shook. Tyler looked around. A few spiral notebooks littered the table. So did two power cords. No computers, though. Whoever shot Stacy's family took their equipment. Tyler walked through the dining room into the kitchen and mud room. The rear door remained unlocked.

Two teams, each with a pair of men. The brother probably died first. Stacy's parents and sister would have been easy marks from there. Houses here sat pretty far apart. No need to be too friendly with the neighbors. Suppressors would have dampened the reports enough. Someone was missing, Tyler realized. Where was the older sister? He returned to the dining room. Poor Stacy clutched her mother's corpse and bawled, sputtering something incoherent. He was about to say something when he heard an engine out front.

Tyler walked to the living room and crouched at the window. A dark Suburban pulled to a stop. He remembered passing one near the development as they approached. Three men got out. Where was number four? Did he leave with Stacy's older sister? No time for questions. Tyler moved back to the murder scene. "Three men are here. You need to get upstairs."

Stacy stopped crying long enough to ask, "What?"

"Three men are here. I'm guessing they knew you were

gone, and they came back to finish you off. Get upstairs. Hide in your room and find something to use as a weapon."

"What are you going to do?" Stacy wiped her eyes.

"Try not to let them get to you. Go. Don't come down unless I call for you." She nodded and took off for the second floor. Tyler walked into the kitchen, grabbed the largest knife he found in the block, and assessed possible hiding spots. The attackers would likely split up again. It worked last time. Probably one guy to the rear door this time. He'd enter through the mudroom. A long counter made for a good place to hide. Tyler crouched and waited.

LAMONT WILLIAMS APPROACHED HIS UNOFFICIAL BOSS' office door. As usual, it was closed. Before he could knock, however, he overheard the senator and his wife engaged in an animated conversation. A good assistant would walk away. Lamont didn't have a formal title in this gig, but he'd never call himself an assistant. Despite this, he knew he needed to look out for the man's best interests even at unexpected times. If he heard something juicy, maybe he could profit from it later. Lamont put his ear closer to the wood and listened.

"What do you mean you're going back?" the senator asked.

"The other daughter returned," a voice said over a speakerphone. Lamont shook his head. Behind closed doors, his boss tended to put calls on speaker even when it might be to his detriment. "Someone was driving her. We're almost back to their house."

"Remember the real objective," his boss' wife said. "We want the flash drive. Maybe she knows where it is."

"I don't care if she knows," the senator added. "Really,

Miriam. There are only so many places a girl could hide something. Besides, the one who hid it is on her way back here. Kill the other daughter and whoever's driving her."

"Yes, sir."

"Tear the house apart when you're done. In case our interrogation doesn't bear fruit, I want to cover all the bases."

"And we need what's on the drive," the wife said. "Once you have it, we won't need to keep anyone alive."

"Understood," the unknown man said. "We're approaching now. Baker, Charlie, and I will deal with the people in the house, and then we'll recover the item."

"Get back here right away when you do," the senator ordered. "I want to minimize the chances anyone will see you coming and going. There's not going to be much traffic now. People are home. They might get curious and look out their windows."

"We'll be careful." The call ended.

"For Christ's sake, Richard," the senator's wife said. "I hope this works."

"It will. Either they find the drive now, or the girl tells us where it is when we question her." They were both silent again. "Don't act like this wasn't as much your idea as mine. You know what's at stake."

"I'm aware," she said. "It will all be worth it in the end."

Lamont backed away from the door. He felt ambivalent. His boss clearly used the information Lamont gave him. He didn't think people would die, but could he really be surprised? The only way to make real progress in the world was to pave your roads with blood. Considering the senator's plans for the future, Lamont would soon be looking at an official title, bigger office, and bigger payday. He'd finally get the recognition he deserved. Like a good employee, he would maintain he didn't hear anything he wasn't supposed to.

5

S oft footsteps moved along the side of the house. If the Chaplains were working at the table before their grisly demises, they might not have heard. Tyler remained quiet and listened so he would know when the enemy approached. At least Stacy was upstairs. The footfalls progressed along the rear of the home and softly crunched the snow outside the back door. A muted voice said something Tyler couldn't hear but presumed was a confirmation of being in position. The door swung open a second later.

If whoever walked in were observant, he would know someone pushed the door shut after the hit squad left. It meant the intruder would need to waste a few seconds clearing the mud room first. Tyler adjusted his position slightly. He'd still be impossible to spot behind the counter, but being a couple inches closer to the end left him in a better position to strike.

A soft squeak told Tyler a man entered the kitchen. Careless. He should have made sure his soles were dry. He probably didn't expect to face active opposition, but failing to plan was planning to fail. The assailant crept closer. Tyler's grip tightened on the handle of the knife. He held the tip pointing downward and waited to attack. The toe of a black boot entered his field of vision, and he uncoiled.

Even behind the ski mask, Tyler saw surprise on the other man's face. He needed to finish this quickly. The other two couldn't be allowed to reach the second floor. The combatant before him wore a standard-issue ballistic vest over a black shirt and matching pants. They'd be invisible in low light or the prevailing gloom outside.

Tyler's left arm swept a Glock pistol toward the ceiling. His right followed it, and he slammed the knife under his opponent's chin, burying it to the hilt. The gunman's grip wavered, and Tyler snatched the pistol. No point wasting a shot. The kitchen knife had a long enough blade to do the job. Tyler eased the body to the floor, padded to the wall of cabinets, and flattened himself against it.

"Charlie, do you see anyone?" a voice called from the living room. "Over." Tyler didn't reply. He eased his way toward the dining area. At least one other man would be coming toward him. Maybe two. They'd both be wearing vests. Based on the size of their boots, the remaining men were likely to be at least six feet tall. Quiet footsteps moved closer. "Charlie, do you copy?" A pause. "Charlie?" Another pause. "I'm coming your way. Baker, you check the second floor."

"Copy," another man said.

Tyler again couldn't lose time. He moved in to the dining room and crouched against the right-hand wall. Whoever came in from the other side would see the table and left side of the room initially. His position would give Tyler a very brief advantage. Sure enough, another attacker came around the wall, his gun barrel leading the way. When his body cleared the corner, Tyler lined up his head. The man's eyes flicked in his direction. Tyler fired once, and the black-clad assailant dropped like a rock.

"Adam?" the remaining man called. He wasn't even trying to be quiet anymore. "Adam, do you copy?"

Adam, Baker, and Charlie. "What a bunch of assholes," Tyler whispered to no one. He debated whether he should answer Baker. If he did, the man would come and find him. Which was fine. If he remained silent, Baker could decide to finish the mission no matter what. Even if Stacy found the best baseball bat in the world, she'd be up against someone with a pistol and some training on how to assault a house. Not ideal. "Adam's dead, you prick."

"Who the hell are you?"

"Come find me and see for yourself."

Tyler liked his position in the dining room. Unless Baker left the house and re-entered via the back door, he couldn't assault it from behind. He'd need to come through the living room. The corpse of his compatriot would be a deterrent to an all-out engagement. He'd be cautious. Maybe even smart. Tyler would need to be smarter.

He tipped a chair onto its side, the top pointing toward the entrance to the dining area. Baker descended the steps. Tyler set another chair on its side near the head of the table. Closer to the body of Adam. Baker would see it first. He might presume someone hid behind it and waste a split-second shooting it. It would be all the time Tyler needed. He stretched out behind the other chair, braced his forearm atop it, and waited.

Baker approached. He didn't try to keep his movements quiet. No point anymore. "Jesus," he whispered as he neared the fallen Adam. "Who the hell are you?" He took another couple steps. His gun barrel came into view. It angled down toward the other chair. Two shots rang out. Baker advanced. Tyler exhaled.

When he saw his opponent, Tyler sighted his head and fired. The shot took Baker an inch above the ear, and he pitched forward, falling a couple feet from his teammate. Tyler stood. He didn't hear anyone else, but he cleared the rest of the first level to be sure. While in the kitchen, he grabbed Charlie's earpiece and popped it in. Silence. For now at least. He rifled through Charlie's pockets and found a wallet and phone. The other two guys carried the same things—even their billfolds were identical, though Adam also carried a set of car keys.

"You can come down," Tyler called up the stairs. "They're not going to bother anyone again."

Footsteps slowly descended the stairs, and Stacy emerged into the living room a few seconds later. "You got them?" Tyler nodded. She walked near the dining room and stopped. "Holy shit. You weren't kidding."

"There's a third in the kitchen." Tyler opened the first wallet. He pocketed the two hundred in cash. The only ID belonged to a company called Elite Security Services, and it identified the bearer by the single name of Baker. No other name. Not even a photo. Tyler grabbed Adam's wallet next. Other than the different mononym on his company ID, he carried the same setup. Charlie made it three for three. Tyler remained in the kitchen long enough to find the junk drawer and carry a hammer back to the dining room.

Stacy spat on the corpse of Adam and kicked it in the midsection. "You bastard! You bastard . . . you killed my family."

Tyler set their three identical phones on the table. "You want to let off a little steam?" he asked.

"What?"

He held the hammer handle first toward Stacy. "For their phones, not their skulls." He paused. "Once we break their comms, though, I don't care what you do to the bodies."

Stacy lined up the first cell, drew the mallet back, and slammed it down onto the screen. The loud crash produced a large crack. She whacked it again and again until it got reduced to a pile of unrecognizable plastic and glass. The second received the same rough treatment. Before Stacy could smash the third one, however, it rang. *UNKNOWN* showed on the display. She stopped with the hammer drawn back and ready to strike. Tears rimmed her eyes. "What should I do?"

"Save it for the moment," Tyler said. "We'll use it to call the police once we're out of here. Right now, you should go pack a bag. We need to leave."

6

———

To be certain the house was empty, Tyler searched the upper level and basement while Stacy packed a bag. There were plenty of rooms in the large home for someone to hide, but other than the two of them, it was unoccupied. Stacy came down the stairs. Her eyes were red and puffy. Tyler tried to offer a reassuring smile even though he knew it wasn't really in his skill set. "Let's hit the road. There could be another team on the other end of the phone call."

Stacy nodded, and Tyler led her toward the kitchen and the rear door. She paused for a final look at her family before walking with him. She soon averted her eyes and wiped fresh tears from them. "Why are we going this way?"

"In case they have someone out front. I didn't see anybody a minute ago, but I want to be sure." Tyler stopped at Charlie's corpse and collected his two spare magazines.

"You think you'll need more bullets?" Stacy asked.

"I didn't think I'd need a single one when the day began," Tyler said. "Better to have too many than not enough."

They moved along the back of the house. Snow still fell,

though its pace slowed to small and occasional flakes. Tyler looked around the corner, didn't see anyone, and they headed toward the front. He did his best to step in the footsteps of Charlie and another man. If anyone came later, let him wonder what happened. No one waited for them on the street side. Tyler and Stacy climbed into the Tesla, and he quickly got them out of the neighborhood. He used Charlie's phone to dial 9-1-1 and report the gruesome scene, trying to keep his descriptions minimal for Stacy's benefit.

When he ended the call, Tyler checked the road. No cars approached in either direction. He wiped the device down, tossed it out the window, and then ran over it a few times before moving on. He wondered where they would go. Keeping Stacy safe was the priority. Whoever killed her family came back for her once, and they could persist in trying to finish the job. His passenger took out her phone and tapped on the screen. A few minutes later, she said, "I can't reach my older sister."

Tyler realized he'd forgotten about her. He'd only met the rest of Stacy's family a few times. "Was she supposed to be there?"

"Yeah. We were texting this morning while I was waiting for my flight."

"She's out of college, right?"

"A couple years now," Stacy said. "She tried to get her own place, but it didn't work out. She's lived with our parents again for at least a year."

"What does she do?" Tyler wanted to know.

"Are you just making conversation to keep me from thinking about how terrible today has been?"

"Partially. She's missing, though, and . . . I know this will sound indelicate . . . not dead with everyone else. It's unlikely she left on her own due to the weather."

Stacy rubbed her forehead. "You think whoever killed my family kidnapped her?"

"It's a possibility," Tyler said. "Knowing what her job is could make it more or less likely."

For a few seconds, Stacy remained quiet. Then, she sighed and said, "Kacey is an investigative journalist. She started at her college newspaper. John Hanson. Exposed a booster and a coach when there was a scandal they were trying to keep quiet. The whole thing blew up. I don't know if she wanted to do it before, but it gave her a taste, and she went after it. She's worked for a local outfit for a couple years . . . since she graduated."

"Journalists are common targets."

"Do you think someone did all this just to abduct her?"

"I don't know," Tyler admitted. "Those kinds of investigations really aren't in my wheelhouse. For now, we need to get you away from here. We'll figure out our next move soon."

"I'm worried about my sister." Stacy's voice cracked. "She's all I have left now."

"I know. Keep trying to reach her."

"I will."

Tyler figured it would be futile. Someone wanted to abduct Kacey, and they covered the crime by murdering the rest of the Chaplain family. Stacy represented a loose end, and she would until this whole mess concluded. Tyler gripped the wheel tightly and blew out a deep breath. A simple trip to the airport turned into a shootout and a battle against an unknown adversary. Despite how bad things looked now, Tyler knew they would get worse before they got better.

∼

ANOTHER CALL WENT TO VOICEMAIL. The senator seethed and slammed his phone down. "I can't reach the team," he grumbled. "They told me they saw the girl headed back to the house. They were going to wait and take care of her. Now . . . nothing."

"Was she alone?" his wife asked.

"No. She was the passenger in an SUV. We don't know who the driver was. Could have been an Uber."

"Nevertheless, the troublemaker is on her way?"

"Yes," the senator said. "One of the men left with her while the other three waited."

His wife shifted in her seat. She flicked a stray lock of brown hair—the finest color his money could buy—over her ear. "Think about it, Richard. There's been bad weather all day. Maybe they had a problem dealing with the girl and whoever drove her to the house. Maybe the storm is messing with cell reception."

"I doubt it." He checked a note on his desk. "I'm going to ask the second team to investigate. This all needs to be behind us." He made another call, and Edgar picked up right away. "Are you near the house we discussed?"

"Not far, sir. What do you need?"

"The first team seems to have hit a snag. Now, I can't reach them. I want to confirm the mess there has been cleaned up. Can you stop by and check on them?"

"We will," Edgar said. "We're about fifteen minutes out."

"Drive fast," the senator said. "Call me back when you know something." He broke the call. "I guess we wait."

"How far away are our man and the girl?" his wife asked. A quick text with Donald revealed the answer: about twenty-five minutes. "I think we'll get what we want soon either way. Don't worry so much, Richard. Even if something happened, the men are replaceable."

"The expense of hiring them isn't, Miriam."

The senator read a few emails while he waited. With the state's annual three-month legislative session coming to a close soon, his daily grind would get easier and allow him more time to focus on the next office. A national one. Holding a high state office was fine, but the real power lay in Washington. With it, of course, came greater access to money. Only fools went into politics for noble reasons, and the senator was no fool. Neither was his wife, and together, they'd carved out a nice empire. It could expand soon, and it would be smoother with the reporter and her family out of the way.

A short while later, his phone rang. "We have a problem, sir" Edgar said. "The place is swarming with cops. I left before we got too close."

"County or state?"

"Looked like locals to me."

"Not so big a deal," the senator said. "They'll have to process the scene. I'm sure it'll be a couple hours. I'll see what I can do to tamp down their enthusiasm for the investigation. Are you still in the neighborhood?"

"More or less," Edgar said. "We left, but we didn't go too far."

"Remember, you have a special ID in the glove compartment. It's too early for me to ask a lot of questions without drawing attention. I'll need you to be my eyes and ears for a while. Let me know when the deputies are finished."

"Will do. Do you want us to move in when they're gone?"

"Someone is coming soon who will be able to help us answer your question," the senator told him. He checked his watch.

Twenty-two minutes.

Tyler eased the Tesla into a parking spot. They pulled into a rest stop off I-95 a short ways outside the city of Aberdeen. Stacy needed to use the ladies' room, and it was a good time to regroup and figure out their possible next steps. Before Stacy left the car, Tyler slipped her one of the twenties he'd taken from the security guys. "Get yourself some food. Me, too. Whatever you pick is fine."

"I'm not hungry."

"You need to eat," he said. "We don't know where we'll be going from here. We have a few minutes to get some food. Might as well use it."

"All right," Stacy said in a resigned tone. She hopped out of the car and walked into the main building. Tyler got out also, and connected the Model X to a charger. He popped inside to avail himself of the facilities and returned to the SUV. By now, Lexi would be wondering where he was. Tyler wanted to talk to his daughter before Stacy did. He hopped back into the Tesla and called her.

"I was starting to worry about you," she said.

"Save your concern for Stacy," Tyler said. "It's . . . been a hell of a day."

"Dad, why do I think trouble found you again?"

"We got to her house, and I could tell we weren't the first ones there. Two SUVs and four men got there before we did."

"I don't like where this is headed," Lexi said.

"I went in first." Tyler took a deep breath and lowered his voice even though he doubted anyone could hear him. "It was a hit squad. Four dead. Stacy's parents, her brother, and her younger sister."

"Jesus. She must be destroyed."

"She's keeping it together somehow. Doing pretty well, all things considered. Three of the guys circled back while we were still there. I . . . dealt with them. Then, we left and called the cops."

"You all right?"

"I'm OK. I'm a lot more concerned about Stacy. Her older sister is missing, and I think she's focusing more on figuring out what happened. It's probably helping to keep her mind off . . . everything else, but it's all going to crash down around her at some point."

"Kacey's gone?" Lexi asked.

"She was supposed to be there," Tyler said. "No sign of her. I told Stacy whoever stormed the house must have taken her. She might even have been the target. The guys who came back seemed like they were there to finish the job. Stacy was a loose end. I guess I was, too."

"You need to ditch your phones."

"I doubt they know who I am. No one would have seen me for long."

"Still," Lexi said. "They'll be able to track Stacy's phone. It's probably only a matter of time before they tie you to her. What did you always tell me? Presume your enemy is capable."

Tyler smiled. She was right. He learned the lesson first-hand in Afghanistan. American leadership—both civilian and military—underestimated the Taliban. A similar story played out in Iraq. One of the reasons Tyler's special operations unit saw so much success was their more realistic presumption of the enemy's capabilities. "All right. We'll replace them both. Should be some places nearby to do it." He paused. "I'm also not sure where I should take her. She can't stay with family even if she has any left. I don't want to bring her home."

"Couldn't you turn her over to the police? Some kind of protected witness?"

"Maybe. I'm a little leery of county outfits, though. I think deputies could've done more against the cartel a few months ago. I'll talk to her. See what she wants to do. For now, I'm fine to hole up in a hotel."

"It might be your best choice in the short term," Lexi agreed.

Stacy moved toward the exit door inside the main building. "She's coming back," Tyler said. "I'll check in when I can."

"Let me know if you need any help."

"I will. Thanks, kiddo. Love you."

"Love you, too, Dad. Be safe."

"I'll do my best." Tyler broke the connection. Stacy climbed into the Model X a moment later.

She handed him a Burger King bag. "Thanks for lunch." She opened her own and pulled out a chicken sandwich. "I still don't want to eat, but I know I need to."

"We'll need to figure out where we're going from here, too," Tyler said. "I'm hesitant to drop you with the cops. We don't know who we're up against and what his reach might be."

"Where does that leave us?" Stacy asked.

"Trying to lie low. Let's eat and then we'll need to get back on the road and find a place to hole up."

Stacy's eyes welled. "Are we going to get the men who killed my family?"

"We will," Tyler said. "My first job is making sure you're safe, though. You're a loose end to them. It's why they circled back to try and kill you. If they get the chance, they'll make another attempt. From here, we'll ditch our phones for burners."

"Right now, I just want to eat a mediocre lunch."

Tyler checked the Tesla's battery level. He wanted as much charge as possible. So far, he'd seen no sign of anyone coming for them. They probably had a little time.

KACEY CHAPLAIN REMAINED quiet in the passenger's seat of the large SUV. The man driving—who hadn't identified himself yet—told her to sit there and stay silent. Don't alert anyone to what happened. Considering the brutality she'd witnessed a short while ago and the threat of sexual violence against her, how could she not comply? Kacey wiped her eyes for what felt like the millionth time. She hoped Stacy was still alive. Right now, it was the lone piece of hope she could cling to.

She glanced down at her gray hoodie. Blood from her mother still dotted it. She couldn't bear to wipe it off. If she kept the sweatshirt when this ordeal was over, it would remain stained forever. The driver pulled off the highway at exit 80. He turned into the Riverside Shopping Center. "You hungry?" he barked.

"How could I eat right now?"

He stopped the SUV in a parking spot. "I don't know how much chance you'll have later. The people I work for want information from you, and they might not be inclined to feed you for a while." He shrugged. "Your call. I'm getting McDonald's."

"Fine," Kacey said. "I'll take whatever you're having."

He pulled into the drive-through line. Two cars waited ahead of them. "Keep quiet," he said. "Don't yell while I'm ordering. Don't try to signal anyone. This can go pretty easy for you if you let it."

"You assholes shot my family and abducted me," Kacey said. "I don't feel the burden is on me to be nice."

"Have it your way. Just don't be stupid."

"I don't even know your name."

He frowned and shrugged. "Call me Donald."

"All right, Donald. I'll be a good girl for now. I want to meet the man who's signing your paycheck. Might as well know who I'm going to take down . . . even if I already have a guess."

To his credit, Donald didn't take the bait. His job was grim, but he seemed like a professional at it. He inched the large vehicle forward and rolled his window down. Kacey kept her word and didn't try to alert anyone. "Can I have two twenty-piece nuggets, two large fries, and two chocolate shakes?" Donald said into the microphone. The cashier told him a total, and he moved up to pay. A few minutes later, they sat in a parking spot and ate. If she weren't crushed by grief over her family, Kacey might have laughed at the absurdity of the situation.

Kacey couldn't eat all the food. She didn't offer any to Donald, however, and he didn't seem interested in her leftovers. When they finished, Donald tossed their trash into the back of the SUV. He fished out a black bag. "Put it over your head."

"What?"

"Put this over your head," he said. "You're not gonna see where we go." Kacey glanced around. "Tinted windows. No one's going to notice. There aren't a lot of people around, anyway."

Kacey took the sack and put it over her head. Donald tightened the strings at the bottom. She could still breathe, but taking the bag off would be a challenge. He started the SUV and pulled away. Even without being able to see, Kacey tried to keep track of where they went. It felt like he got back onto Route 543 which ran along the front of the shopping center. From there, they banked right. Was he getting back onto I-95 North?

They soon picked up speed. Kacey couldn't see anything, but she knew they drove pretty quickly, and she felt sure Donald went north. Maybe he was taking her back to Cecil County. If her guess as to the team's employer proved correct, it would make sense. Kacey practiced slow breaths to manage her anxiety. It grew stuffy with her head and face covered. She did her best to remain calm and keep her wits about her. If Donald wouldn't tell her where they went, she'd need to figure it out for herself.

THEY'D ANTICIPATED the cops getting involved at some point. Contingencies needed to be accounted for. Each team carried a single comprehensive fake police ID in their vehicle. Edgar reported he would use it to gain access to the Chaplain house. He provided updates while there. The place teemed with deputies moving from room to room. The coroner's staff milled about the bodies and conducted various onsite tests. No one questioned Edgar's credentials, but this early in the response, there wasn't much information to share.

Edgar soon reported he was leaving, and the team would make contact from nearby. The senator paced the floor waiting for the call. He could handle the state police. The locals represented a wild card. Despite being elected, sheriffs sometimes liked to play hardball with politicians. "What are we looking for, sir?" Edgar asked once he finally called.

"First, I want you to clean things up," the senator said. "I know it'll take the coroner a while to move the bodies and the deputies to roll out. Don't leave the place a mess. Word is going to spread, but we don't want to attract attention. Make it look like a normal house again, not a shooting gallery."

"Understood. Are we looking for anything while we're there?""

"Yes. Any files the girl might have are still missing. She's young, so they're probably not in hard copy, but check anyway. Look in her room. An office if there is one. The basement. Anywhere she might have stashed a folder, a disc, or a flash drive."

"You know you're talking about most of the house, right?" Edgar asked.

"Of course I know," the senator said. "There are two of you. You should be able to get it done." He clicked off and walked into the next office. Gustav, the security company's tech wizard, sat at a desk staring at three large monitors. Other than an email client, nothing else on the screens made sense. "Were you able to get into their comms?"

"Of course," Gustav said, sounding a little insulted.

"And?"

"At the moment, they seem to think it's a botched home invasion. I don't know how long the theory will prevail, but we probably have some time before they come up with something better."

"I've been on law enforcement committees for years," the senator said. "Time of death usually gets down to a window of a few hours. If it's the best they can do, they might never come off their hypothesis."

"Here's hoping."

"Did you find your missing phones?"

"Yes," the slender guy said. "Two of them stopped sending a signal within the house."

"Turned off?"

Gustav shook his head, and his glasses slid down his hawkish nose. "I think it's worse. My guess is the phones were destroyed."

"None of those men would destroy their comms."

"I agree."

"Text the other two," the senator ordered. "I want to know if they find anything which might be two broken mobiles."

Gustav did it from his computer. "The third made it about a mile from the house." He tapped on the keyboard. "It made a 9-1-1 call. Its location has held steady ever since."

"Tossed out a window?"

"Probably." He paused. "Deputies are talking about a pair of smashed-up Android devices."

"The younger daughter came home," the senator said. "Someone drove her. They went inside. Alpha team minus Donald pulled up." He spread his hands. "The girl and her driver took out three trained professionals? Who the hell is this guy?"

"I can try to get a line on their escape," Gustav said. "It'll take a few minutes."

"Do it."

The colorfully backlit keyboard looked silly, but Gustav's fingers flew over it. New windows popped up on his monitors, and he dragged them into whatever position he wanted them. It took the promised time, but the hacker said, "I think I have something." He pointed at the far right screen, and the senator leaned closer for a better look. "One of their neighbors has a video doorbell. Default credentials." He snorted. "Anyway, they pull up in a Tesla SUV. The Suburban follows about five minutes later." Gustav fast-forwarded the feed from there. "Next thing we see is the Tesla leaving again." He paused the playback on a shot of the electric SUV driving away. "The windows are too dark to get a look at the driver."

"Can you follow its movements?"

"Being in Cecil County helps. They're going to want to get out of here. It's either north into Delaware or farther south into Maryland. Looks like they chose the second option." Another still photo of the Tesla filled the screen. "I'm still waiting for a good shot of the license plate. It's hard to see on what I've found so far. Even so, I'll figure out who her driver is."

"Good," the senator said. "Let me know the second you do."

8

Gustav worked on the most recent problem. Over the years, he'd gotten used to new challenges cropping up while working on a project. He could even handle micromanagers despite not liking them. One jackass saw his credit rating go into the toilet afterward. Served him right. Gustav had pondered ruining him further, but the man learned his lesson. The senator was worse than any of them. Such were the dangers of freelancing, Gustav figured, even with a skill set as in-demand as his.

The mystery man rolled up in a white Tesla Model X. Nice ride. Even filtering on color, there were enough of them in the state to require more data. Tapping into the Maryland Department of Transportation's camera and toll system proved easy. States did the worst job of securing their systems. Gustav hadn't seen a clear shot of the license plate yet, so he needed to monitor toll facilities and highway cameras. It wasn't a needle in a haystack, but knowing the plate made finding a vehicle about a hundred times easier.

It took a few minutes, but he found it. This time Gustav got a good view of the tag. The Tesla hadn't followed a predictable path. What was the driver doing? More importantly, who was he? The state's system resolved the plate to a man named John Tyler. Gustav looked him up and soon realized why things went so wrong at the house. Tyler spent over two decades in the army and left as a decorated Green Beret. He worked in private security for about eight more years before two ventures into classic car repair. "My boss won't be happy to hear about you," Gustav whispered to the screen.

He checked on the Tesla's current location next. The last camera to pick it up was on an exit ramp coming off I-95 headed toward Bel Air. Gustav knew the area. It was rural enough in spots, but plenty of houses, strip malls, and shopping centers made for excellent places to hide. A man like Tyler could disappear here even carting a civilian around. He looked for likely destinations in Bel Air and found some surveillance systems he could tap into easily. The Model X passed a major plaza on Route 24, and he saw it approaching in another camera.

Gustav called Edgar. "Where are you?"

"We left the scene," the other man said. "Didn't want to attract attention. We're back near the bridge."

"Good," Gustav said. He hoped Edgar meant any of the bridges connecting Cecil County to Harford across the Susquehanna River. "I have a location on the girl and her driver."

"Send it to me."

"I will." He paused. "Edgar, be careful with this one. He was a soldier."

～

LEXI KEPT an eye on the small digital clock in the lower right corner of her screen. She'd postponed the virtual therapy session once already and didn't want to do it again. These were far from typical circumstances, however. Her father again found himself embroiled in some pretty serious shit. Worse, one of her best friends got caught up in it, too, and lost most of her family as a result.

Kacey Chaplain must have been the key.

Despite meeting the woman a few times, Lexi didn't know her well. She was a few years older than Stacy, so she wasn't around much when the girls were younger. Lexi knew Kacey went to college and got a job, but her knowledge basically stopped there. She grabbed her dad's old company laptop. Patriot Security issued one to each of its operatives. Despite leaving the company and pissing off the owner, her father kept the laptop. Of course he did. It proved useful many times since, and Lexi became quite adept at using some of its more interesting red team capabilities.

She began with simple research. After graduating in the top three percent of her high school class, Kacey Chaplain went on to attend John Hanson College. She graduated a semester early and worked as an investigative reporter for a little over two years. Her first big story involved a scandal with the basketball program and a corrupt booster at JHC. Ever since, she'd shown a knack for solid reporting and not pulling punches. It earned her a nice local reputation, but it also made her a target.

Lexi couldn't uncover any pattern in the kinds of stories Kacey pursued. Tales of corporate or government malfeasance and shafting the little guy covered a broad swath. The clock showed five minutes until her appointment, and an email reminder made her phone vibrate. Lexi ignored it. Stacy might know what her sister worked on, but she'd just been through the wringer. She might shut down. Even if she didn't, Lexi knew her dad didn't exactly possess a ton of people skills. Coaxing information out of a grieving young woman was way outside his skill set.

Another couple minutes ticked by. Lexi didn't have much to go on. Kacey must have been working on a story which compelled someone to come after her, but there were no online breadcrumbs. The online paper she worked for hadn't focused on anyone or a particular area recently. Stories of the Maryland legislature increased, but this was typical during their three-month session.

The witching hour arrived, and another notification hit Lexi's inbox. She kept going. Her therapist would simply need to wait.

TYLER TOOK A SOMEWHAT meandering path from Cecil County. Stacy needed time to process everything. Once they made their way into Harford County, he exited toward Bel Air. "We're in a different jurisdiction now. If you want me to drop you off with the local deputies, I will."

Stacy shook her head and remained quiet for a moment. Eventually, she said, "I don't know who I can trust."

"We're not in your county anymore," Tyler pointed out.

"I know. My sister investigated a lot of people, though." Her voice cracked as she continued. "She was never afraid of money, status, or power. She went after college boosters, politicians, the cops . . . even the current mayor of Baltimore." Stacy glanced at Tyler. "Kacey might have a long list of enemies."

"I don't see how Harford County's deputies could be on the list."

"You rescued me." Stacy's voice was small. "I'd be dead if not for you. Please . . . don't leave me with anyone else now. You didn't seem like you wanted to get rid of me."

"I don't. You're an adult. If you wanted me to drop you off with the deputies, I would. You're making the right call."

Tyler's one interaction with the LEOs up here proved indifferent. The snow had stopped falling here, but a layer of slush still covered Route 24. Tyler knew a bunch of shopping centers, eateries, and even a mall lay ahead of the red light where they waited. If Stacy didn't want to go to the police, he didn't know where he would take her. Her family's house would be a crime scene and inaccessible. He wouldn't risk using his home. In case whoever targeted the Chaplains put two and two together, Lexi would be in danger, too. They would need to hole up somewhere . . . maybe for more than one night. It meant they would need supplies and something passing for a plan.

Tyler looked at the Tesla's range. It was down to about forty percent. He'd need to charge it before they headed anywhere outside the area. "All right," he said. "I know this is going to be tough, but if you're stuck with me for a while, I'm going to need to know. You told me your sister's investigated a lot of people. Any of them have the means and desire to kidnap her and kill your family?"

Stacy stared out the window. "I don't know."

"You need to think about it. I can't keep you safe if I don't know who might be coming after us. Based on what we've already seen, it must be someone with a good bit of money . . . or at least the right connections. Hit squads don't work for just anyone, and they're not cheap to hire."

"She's been at it a couple years," Stacy said.

This wasn't the question Tyler asked, but at least she told him something. "Do you know everyone she's gone after?"

"Probably not."

Tyler steered the Model X onto a side road. It connected to a large shopping center ahead. Maybe he'd even find some electric vehicle spots where he could plug the SUV in to charge while they bought supplies. "Work with me here,

Stacy. Who would come after her like this? It has to be a small list."

"I don't know," she said again.

Talking with people would never be counted first among Tyler's skills. He didn't have much of a knack for it even when they were cooperative. It was hard to blame Stacy considering what she'd been through today, but her reticence didn't help the situation. Every war featured some unknowns, but being in the dark about the enemy's identity would be a new one. Tyler was about to say something else when he noticed a pair of headlights coming up behind them.

Based on the ride height, he pegged it for another SUV. And it approached at ramming speed.

9

———

Lexi spent another thirteen minutes on research without a solid lead. Even with the Patriot laptop's expanded capabilities, she couldn't find anything indicating what Kacey currently worked on. Her current story could have been the one to land her in trouble. If so, she took care to hide it from prying eyes. It made Lexi wonder how she ended up on the radar of someone so dangerous. The situation her dad described would only be possible when going against a powerful adversary with a lot of resources. A few of Kacey's prior article subjects fit the bill—most notably Vincent Davenport, the present mayor of Baltimore—but Lexi found plausible reasons to disqualify them all. Especially Davenport. He would lose the office he sought and won.

Without anything strong to go on, Lexi set her dad's laptop aside and opened her own. She tried to join her therapist's Zoom room, but she ended up waiting a few minutes with no results. He'd been a stickler about being on time before. Did he just ignore the virtual room after a few minutes? She dialed the office, and his secretary picked up.

"You're late for your appointment, Miss Tyler," the woman said in a matronly tone. Lexi felt she was being judged.

"I know. I was helping a friend."

"You made a commitment."

"So did Doctor Janishefski," Lexi said.

"He waited for you," the woman said. "After a few minutes, the doctor finds a better use of his time."

A better use of his time? The hell with this practice. "Like I said, I was helping a friend." Lexi tried to remain diplomatic, but she heard the anger bubbling over in her own voice.

"I can reschedule you. Is there a time you think you could keep?"

"What would happen if I were coming in person and got a flat tire?" Lexi said. The receptionist didn't reply. "Would the doctor still need to find 'a better use of his time?'" No response. "I can hear you judging me. You know what? Tell Doctor Janishefski to go to hell, and you can enjoy the ride with him." Lexi ended the call and spiked her mobile onto the bed. She'd find another therapist. It took her dad a while to discover one who worked for him. Maybe the next one would be a little more reasonable. It wasn't like Janishefski led her to a major breakthrough. Lexi picked up her phone and called Alex Anne.

"My therapy BFF," the singer said. "What's going on?"

"I'm going to find a new provider."

"Plenty of them out there. I'm okay with mine for now."

"Good," Lexi said. She paused. "I'm . . . worried about my dad. He's landed himself in a mess again. This time, it might be my fault."

"I'm sure it's not," Alex Anne said.

"I wish I were." Lexi sighed. She relayed the story about Stacy flying into town, her dad stepping in to make the airport run, and the grim discovery which waited for them in

Cecil County. "He insisted on doing it, but it was a commitment I made. Hard to think I'm not responsible."

"Your dad is going to do what he does. I'm a beneficiary of it, so maybe I see it differently than you do. I witnessed how relentless he is when he's after something, and I also got to see him in action. It's . . . actually kind of amazing that he can flip a switch and go from father to killer and back again when he needs to."

Lexi stewed on her friend's words. Alex Anne was right. Her father wouldn't let something go once he got involved, especially if he could protect someone at the same time. "I know," Lexi said after a few seconds. "I don't want to change him. He's who he is, and there's a lot of him in me. I know that now . . . especially these last few weeks." Maybe her shrink hadn't been useless after all. She paused for a steadying breath. "He's turning fifty-one soon, though. I know he's not *old*, but how many times can he go up against a bunch of younger goons and walk away?"

"It's a fair question," Alex Anne said. "It's one you should ask him."

"I already know what he'll say." Lexi affected a deeper masculine voice. "I'm more experienced. I've done this stuff before. I'm macho. I'll be fine."

"He probably will." Alex Anne paused, and Lexi didn't fill the gap in the conversation. "I know you're worried about him. Want to hear another song I've been working on?"

"Hell yes." Lexi felt her mood brighten right away.

"All right. Hang on a sec." The line went quiet, and Alex Anne came back on a short moment later. "You're on speaker now. Can you hear me?"

"Yes."

A few guitar notes came through the connection. "I don't have any lyrics yet. For anything, really. They're . . . still in progress. I'm working through a lot." Alex Anne cleared her throat. "Anyway. You know all that shit." She played a quiet song at medium tempo. Lexi knew enough about music to hear the chord changes and appreciate her friend's skill. Alex Anne hummed over some of the music, but she didn't ad-lib any words. The tune changed a few times—probably for the bridge and chorus—until it ended after about two minutes. "It's not finished yet," Alex Anne said. "What do you think?"

"I like it," Lexi said. "It's less poppy than some of your earlier stuff. More . . . singer-songwriter-y. More mature."

"I hope the label likes it."

"The hell with them if they don't."

Alex Anne laughed, and Lexi was glad to hear it.

TYLER GOT BACK on the accelerator, and the Tesla surged forward. Even with its battery far from fully charged, the instant electric torque helped him evade the SUV. Stacy sat bolt upright in the passenger's seat. "What's going on?"

"I think the men from earlier found us," Tyler told her. "They're probably here to try and finish the job."

"They want to kill me?" Stacy's voice sounded small.

"Don't feel too bad. They probably want to kill me, too."

Stacy didn't react. Tyler stayed ahead of the other vehicle while keeping an eye on it in the mirrors. Someone leaned out a window on the driver's side, extended a pistol, and fired. The bullet whizzed past the Model X and buried itself in the snowy ground. "They're shooting at us!" Stacy said. She held onto her seat bolsters with a white-knuckle grip.

"I noticed," Tyler said. He looked around the area. He didn't know Abingdon and Bel Air very well. Still, too many houses dotted both sides of the road for a firefight here. Shooting a moving target was hard enough without doing it in an SUV bouncing on a county road. The odds of a stray bullet flying into a nearby home were too great for Tyler to shoot back. Another report sounded behind them, and another round whistled past. The men on their six did not share Tyler's objections.

Tyler cut the wheel hard and made a left. Another residential street. The SUV behind them slid a little but remained in pursuit. The same guy leaned out the window and fired again. This time, the bullet found its mark, striking the Tesla somewhere in the rear with a metallic twang. "They hit us," Stacy said.

"I'm aware."

"Are you going to shoot back?"

"You see all the houses around here?" Tyler said. "I have no problem taking out a few assholes, but I don't want a stray round to go through a wall and kill someone." As if on cue, another bullet tore past them. "These clowns don't seem to care."

"How are we going to get away?" Stacy asked.

"I'm working on it."

The road ended a short distance ahead. Tyler made the right at speed, and the all-wheel drive system capably gripped the road. The vehicle following them slid a little again. The current road was two lanes in each direction, though houses and shops still lined each side. Tyler spotted a few cross streets ahead. According to the center screen, going to the left would get them away from the residential area and into a more rural section.

Tyler jerked the wheel to the right and stomped on the brakes. The Tesla skidded but clung to the slush-covered asphalt pretty well. The large SUV tailing them moved past. No one on the passenger's side had a gun ready to go. Once the Suburban cleared their position, Tyler got back on the throttle. He backed off a little to ease the Tesla into position right behind it. Ramming it would be a complicated maneuver. He needed to do it hard enough to push the larger SUV where he wanted it to go but not with enough force to deploy the airbags.

The Model X's nose nudged the big Chevy's rear bumper. Tyler floored the accelerator. Despite pushing a heavy load, the Tesla gained speed. The intersection on the left neared. Tyler pushed the Chevrolet a little farther before backing off the throttle. The larger SUV's wheels skidded as it kept going. Tyler stepped on the brake and made the left hard enough to slam himself and Stacy to the right through the turn. They steadied quickly, however, and Tyler gave the Tesla more speed. He checked the rearview mirror.

The Suburban wasn't there anymore.

10

Edgar tried to control the Suburban in its skid, but it was a big, heavy beast and getting pushed by another vehicle didn't help. The brakes failed to get a lot of purchase on the road. "They turned, dammit," he heard as he got the large SUV under control a couple hundred yards past the intersection. He was able to bring it to a stop at the side of the road.

"What the hell?" he said.

Francis climbed from behind him into the passenger's seat. "I told you they turned. Made the left back there."

"They have a big head start on us, then."

"You think sitting here is the answer?" Francis scoffed. "We going to hope this guy's dumb and drives by again?"

"No," Edgar said. "I'm going to be smart about it. We'll never catch them even if I take off now and drive as fast as I can. Too many places they could go ahead of us." He pointed to the map displayed on the Chevy's screen. "We could get lucky and guess right, but I have a better idea." He called Gustav, who answered right away. "I need their position again."

"He gave you the slip?" Gustav wanted to know.

"More or less. Son of a bitch is a really good driver. I got the plate if you need it."

"I've had it for a while." Gustav sounded like he was about to laugh. Edgar didn't find anything about the day's events funny, but he kept quiet. "It looks like you're on a side road."

"Yeah," Edgar said. "I think he's headed more for the sticks, but there are a lot of ways he could go. Probably not many cameras back here."

"Those are only one way to keep tabs on them." The sound of rapid key taps came through the speakers as Gustav lapsed into silence to do his job. "They're in a Tesla. People love all the online stuff, but it comes with a downside."

"You can track it, I hope."

"I can," Gustav confirmed. "The tag gets me the VIN. From there, it's not hard to find a bunch more information. I'll have something for you in a minute." He went back to typing.

Francis made a slash over his throat, and Edgar muted his phone. "You think this guy can find them just because they're in a Tesla?"

"I think he could get their location in a lot of modern cars," Edgar said. "Probably the GPS. My brother's pretty good with all this computer shit. I've heard more than I care to about it from him."

"Got something," Gustav said.

Edgar turned his mic back on. "Good. Where are they?"

"Your guess about heading for the sticks was good, but it's not far from downtown Bel Air. They're moving slowly on a narrow road." He paused. "I texted Francis the info." The passenger checked his mobile and nodded.

"Thanks. We'll get after them." Edgar took the route the Tesla turned onto a couple minutes ago as Francis plotted a course. He showed Edgar the screen. "Four minutes?" Edgar gave the big Chevy more gas. "We'll do it in three."

WITH THEIR TAIL gone for now, Tyler eased the Tesla down a rural road. The battery showed thirty-six percent. He didn't like driving it below half and hated running it below a third. Once their pursuers were gone for certain, he'd need to plug it in. It was the downfall of electric vehicles in his mind. If he needed gas for a car, the process took maybe three minutes. Charging an EV took ten times as long and still left the battery well under full.

"Where'd you learn to drive like that?" Stacy asked.

"Fort Bragg, mostly. Also got some practice at Bagram Air Base."

"You think they're gone?"

"I'm not going to presume," Tyler said. "We'll keep moving. They seem pretty determined. I don't think one maneuver is going to dissuade them."

Stacy nodded and sobbed quietly. Tyler couldn't find anything to say. Anyone who walked into her home and saw nearly her whole family slaughtered wouldn't comfort easily. He drove along, keeping one eye on the speedometer and the other on their charge level. Off the main drags, plows didn't come regularly, and several inches of snow still covered the asphalt. The Tesla seemed unbothered, so Tyler maintained ten miles over the suggestions on the speed limit signs. They passed a farm on the left. White powder lay on a wooden split rail fence. If Tyler cared about photography, he might've stopped for a picture. He stored the image in his mind in case he wanted to paint it later. He would need a session with his watercolors after this mess.

A pair of headlights swung around the bend behind them. They approached at high speed. "Shit," Tyler muttered, and he pressed the accelerator harder.

"They're back?" Stacy asked. She turned, looked to the rear, and blanched.

"They're persistent. Whoever signs their checks really wants you out of the way."

"How do you think they found us?"

Tyler glanced at the map displayed on the large center screen, and the answer became obvious. "This damn thing has a GPS. We were careful about using them in the military. They make it easier for people to find you if they know how." He slowed a little to navigate a curve and then got back on the throttle. "These assholes must have a tech guy in their operation."

"We need to get rid of this car?" Stacy said.

"Let's not get ahead of ourselves," Tyler said. "We need to get away from these guys first."

The Suburban's passenger leaned out the window and fired. The bullet cut the air to the right of the Model X. In a more remote area like this, the odds of a round making it into a home were almost nil. Tyler took out the pistol he'd confiscated at the Chaplain home. "Grab the wheel," he told Stacy.

"What?" She looked at him with wide eyes.

"Grab the wheel. Hold it as steady as you can." It took her a couple seconds, but she did. Tyler lowered his window and unbuckled his seat belt. He leaned out, extended the pistol, and fired three shots. The first whizzed past the Suburban, but the second and third blasted holes in the windshield. Neither hit the men inside, but the driver backed off. He found his courage again soon, however. When the passenger leaned out, Tyler aimed for him and fired. He hit the exterior mirror and the A-pillar. The man leaned hard back inside the cabin.

So far, Tyler proved the better shot, but he only had one gun and a limited amount of ammo. Both men in the Chevy would be packing. Only one might do the shooting, but they could keep it up long after Tyler ran out of cartridges. He needed to stop their ability to continue pursuit while not exposing Stacy to unnecessary risks.

The Suburban got its power from a large-displacement Chevy V8. It was a modern engine but traced its lineage back to ones Tyler had worked on. A few well-placed shots through the grill would take out the radiator, and the engine would soon overheat. "Keep her steady," he said to Stacy as the Suburban approached again. Tyler leaned out the window, held the front sight in the rear notch, and emptied the magazine into the big SUV's grill. A metallic clang followed each bullet as it blasted through the plastic.

Smoke soon poured out from under the Suburban's hood. Tyler settled back into the driver's seat, took the wheel back from Stacy, and pushed the accelerator harder. They opened up a large lead on their pursuers. Stacy turned her head and looked to the rear. "Did you kill them?"

"No. Too hard to hit. I disabled the engine."

"Could they fix it?"

"Sure," Tyler said. "They'll need the right parts and some time. I doubt they have either."

Stacy offered a tentative nod. "What's our next move?"

"I have two immediate goals—keeping you safe and figuring out who's trying to kill you. Before we do much more with those, though, we need to get out of this car. They'll only find us again." Tyler made a turn and headed toward the more populous areas of Bel Air.

"What are you going to do?" Stacy said. "Steal a car?"

Tyler bobbed his head. "Among other things, yes."

11

―――――

Tyler wanted to abandon the Tesla, but they needed to get somewhere with more signs of civilization first. Disabling the pursuing Suburban bought them some breathing room. Even a resourceful adversary would need time to deploy another team. He guided the electric SUV down Route 22 and into Bel Air proper. Homes gave way to businesses and strip malls on each side of the road. Tyler made a right into a parking lot featuring a couple chain restaurants and national retailers. A similar setup waited across the street. He parked the Model X at the end of a row. "We'll leave it here."

"You sure you want to?" Stacy asked.

Tyler shrugged. "It's the right call. This vehicle is a liability right now." He paused. "On two fronts, actually . . . the GPS and the battery. Besides, Lexi drives it way more than I do."

The trace of a smile played on Stacy's lips for a second. "What are we going to do?"

Tyler took out the cash he confiscated from the trio of killers at the Chaplain home. He gave Stacy half of it—three hundred dollars. "The first thing we're going to do is walk across the street. There's a place over there we can use for everything. If the assholes chasing you find the car here, let them spin their wheels looking in all these shops." He swept his hand at the many storefronts ahead of them. "Anyway, you'll buy us a couple prepaid phones. We'll leave ours somewhere around here, too. Maybe get some snacks while you're at it. We'll need to eat and stay hydrated." He waited a second while Stacy offered a slow nod. "In the meantime, I'm going to find us a different ride. Hopefully, an older one we don't have to worry about some geek tracking from his keyboard."

"All right," Stacy said.

"Wait for me in the store when you're done," Tyler told her. "I want to minimize the time you're exposed." She bobbed her head again, and they climbed out of the Model X. Tyler took Stacy's phone and walked with her as she approached the shops. He veered off once they reached the sidewalk and moved to the far end. Thanks to the weather, the plaza wasn't crowded, but Tyler still wanted to avoid prying eyes. He walked around to the side of the last shop, a fast casual restaurant, and tossed her mobile onto the roof. He'd ditch his after he used it next.

He continued around to the rear. A road ran there, probably for deliveries. Each store's green back door featured its name in bright white lettering. A few dumpsters sat against the curb. Tyler made his way to the dumpster of a second-hand clothing store and liberated an abandoned wire hanger. As he made his way back to the front, he undid it and formed it into an improvised slim jim.

Once Tyler had what he needed, he headed across the street. Normally, a dash across Business Route 1 would be foolish. Thanks to the weather, it was easy. On a normal day, there would be more people about and a greater number of vehicles to choose from. The downside would be the increased odds of someone seeing him break into a car and hotwire it. He wanted a truck or an SUV because of the weather, at least for the next day or two. Depending on how long he kept Stacy with him, they'd need to change vehicles again. The more visibility a stolen car got, the greater the odds someone spotted it.

Halfway across the asphalt expanse, Tyler found a good candidate. A gray S10 Blazer sat several spots removed from the nearest car. It looked like a late 'nineties or early 2000s model. Reliable V6. Probably four-wheel drive. Best of all, no GPS chip to be tracked. Tyler concealed the slim jim in his sleeve and approached. A woman climbed into a nearby Corolla, and he waited for her to pull away before padding to the SUV.

Popping the lock was a cinch. Tyler inserted the wire hanger between the window and the door and pulled up on the locking mechanism. He checked for people in the area, didn't see anyone, and climbed in. No alarm went off. To the left of the steering column, Tyler removed a plastic panel. He pulled two wires out, put them together, and twisted their ends as the engine turned over.

The owner coming out of a shop could ruin their plan before it got off the ground. Tyler drove off to the left, swung the Blazer to the top end of the shopping center, and kept an eye on the entrances.

THE SENATOR PACED the room as Edgar and Francis returned. They'd given him a brief rundown over the phone, but he was too disappointed in their failure to listen to the whole story. Why was this one girl so hard to kill? Alpha Team accomplished their objectives without delays or problems. The reporter would tell them what they needed to know soon enough. Bravo, on the other hand, brought nothing but excuses. Someone knocked on the door. "Come in."

Edgar and Francis entered. They were smart enough to close up behind themselves without being told, at least. Edgar cleared his throat. "Sir, we--"

The senator cut him off with an upraised hand. "One girl. Other than the older sister, she's the only one left. This should be easy. Why do you keep failing me?"

"It's the guy who's with her, sir," Francis said. "He gave us the slip once. Sort of rammed our SUV from behind, and we went into a skid. After we reacquired him, we were in a rural area, so we tried shooting at them."

"We hit the Tesla once," Edgar added while the senator pondered their loose usage of "reacquired." They'd enjoyed a fair bit of help. "The guy driving leaned out and put a volley into the grill. He ended up drilling the radiator and disabling the engine. We were dead in the water until Francis called for a repair."

"It'll need a real fix at some point, but—"

"I don't care," the senator broke in. "We can always get another goddamn car. You guys are supposed to be the best. Maybe I should recruit the man driving Stacy around." Neither operative said anything. It didn't matter. "While you were getting your Suburban fixed and coming back here, Gustav got a new hit on the Tesla's location. It's been stationary for a while now."

"Could be a ruse," Edgar said. "They might have abandoned it."

"I know. You'll need to check it out, anyway. If they're gone, we'll have to find a new way to track them while we interrogate the nosy one."

Edgar nodded. "We'll leave right away." He and Francis exited the room. They were probably right. By now, Stacy and her savior must have known they were being tracked. Only a fool would remain stationary in such circumstances. Still, the team might learn something about where they went. Maybe their trip wouldn't be a total loss.

The senator left his office. He wanted to know if the reporter talked yet. They'd been nice to her so far. Further silence would force a change in tactics.

STACY FOUGHT tears as she walked into the store. It was a local chain who sold a little of everything, sort of like a large convenience store. Despite the events of the day, she felt hungry. The rational part of her brain told her she needed more food at some point. She puttered along the first of the snack aisles. Most things on the shelf were full of chocolate and sugar. In the past, Stacy would reach for things like these when something happened. A bad breakup was the most common time. It didn't seem right today. Some jerk didn't decide he'd rather be with someone else. Most of her family lay dead, and her older sister was missing.

"Miss . . . you all right?" A kind-looking older man with a round face frowned in concern. Stacy realized she'd stopped, leaned on a shelf, and was crying. She offered a quick smile and wiped her eyes.

"Yeah. Thanks. Just . . . a rough day is all." *The roughest I've ever had.*

"All right." He moved along. Stacy took a deep breath and tried to focus on what she came in here to do. Mister Tyler would find them another car. She needed to buy snacks, drinks, and prepaid phones. Despite feeling hungry, eating was the farthest thing from her mind. They would need food later. Candy seemed a poor choice. Stacy browsed the area and made some better selections. She grabbed two bags of beef jerky, a small loaf of bread, a jar of peanut butter, and a box of assorted cutlery. It all left her hands full, so she grabbed a basket from near the entrance before adding a few liters of water and two bottles of Gatorade.

The phones remained. Mister Tyler didn't tell her which ones to buy. The store kept a few models behind the long counter. Considering his concern about the Tesla's GPS, she scanned for older units. Most smartphones could be tracked. The place still carried a classic flip model with a small screen and no letter keys. They were a lot cheaper than any of the Android models, too. Stacy didn't feel comfortable going to the police. She was stuck with Mister Tyler for now, and either of them using an ATM would give away where they were. Whatever cash they had would need to last.

Stacy fought the urge to cry as she got in line. She knew people would look at her strangely like the old fellow a few minutes ago. No one here would understand what she'd been through in the last few hours. If it weren't for her friend's father, she would have been found lying dead on the floor near the rest of her family. Minus Kacey. What the heck happened to her? Did she get away before the shooting started? It was a nice thought. If she did, she should've reached out by now. Whoever shot her parents and siblings held her sister now. Stacy was sure of it. She wished she could brainstorm an idea how to get Kacey back.

The cashier, a slender Chinese man, cleared his throat, and Stacy moved up. She asked for two of the older phones. He rang everything up and frowned at her hundred-dollar bill. Before he could say they didn't accept them, she said, "I'm spending ninety-seven dollars. Just like it's seventeen, and I handed you a twenty." The clerk's expression didn't improve, but he agreed enough to take Stacy's money, give her change, and put everything into two bags.

She collected her purchases and moved toward the door. Two large men in dark coats and black pants came in, and her breath caught in her throat. Were these the pair who chased them earlier? They were both white and fairly young. Neither made any move toward Stacy as fear rooted her in place. Both men furrowed their brows as they looked at her. Did they recognize her as a target? What happened to Mister Tyler? Her hands clenched as one of the men reached inside his jacket.

12

———

While he waited near the front of the store, Tyler set his phone on the center console and called Sara Morrison. He dialed the main number for the Pentagon and asked to be connected. They'd dated for several months now, ever since Tyler rescued her from a group of killers tied to his former commander. Sara worked as a senior executive at the Pentagon, and despite his general disdain for defense department civilians in his active duty days, Tyler loved Sara. She loved him, too, and she put up with his moments of acting as a knight-errant as she liked to call him. "Hey, handsome," she said.

Tyler smiled in spite of the situation. "You must not have gone for your annual eye exam yet."

"A few weeks ago, actually. What's going on?"

"I . . . need a favor."

Sara sighed. "Let me guess. Someone landed in the soup, and you feel like you need to help get them out of it."

"Yes," Tyler said. "One of Lexi's best friends, actually. I picked her up at the airport earlier today. Didn't want Lexi to drive in the bad weather. Anyway, we get to the girl's house, and four members of her family had been shot and killed."

"My god," Sara said in a hushed tone. "Is she all right?"

"As much as she can be, I guess. We dealt with the hit squad coming back to finish the job, too. It's been a hell of a day."

"Sounds like it. What can I do?"

"It's kind of a long story. The girl's older sister is missing. Probably kidnapped. She's a reporter. Stacy doesn't want to go to the cops because she's not sure who she can trust. I said I'd stay with her, but we need a place to hole up."

"You want me to get you a hotel room?" Sara asked.

"If you could," Tyler said. "I have some cash, but I can't use a credit card or ATM. These guys already tracked the Tesla by its GPS. We're in Bel Air. I'm sure plenty of places around Aberdeen offer the government rate. It doesn't need to be fancy." He considered they could be tracking his phone. He'd be rid of it soon, and a call to the general number— what the army used to call the main switchboard—at the Pentagon wouldn't reveal anything about the person on the other end.

"I'll do it. I'll attach a name to the reservation and say you won't need to provide ID. It's a protocol we use for protecting certain intelligence sources." She paused. "Please be careful. It sounds like this has gone south already. I don't want anything to happen to you."

"I will."

"Should I text you the details?"

"No," Tyler said. "I'm ditching my phone after this. I'll ping you when I have a new one."

"All right. Try not to get killed at the hotel. Or kill anyone else while you're there. I don't want a massive cleanup bill on my government credit card. SECDEF might not sign off on it."

"I'll be sure to consider the burden to the taxpayers if I'm being shot at."

"Good. Love you."

"Thanks," Tyler said. "Love you, too." No sign of Stacy yet. He reached across to the passenger's door and rolled the window down by hand. Tyler gave his phone a final look before pulling the battery and tossing both out into the roadway as hard as he could. A few seconds later, the mobile crunched under the tires of a car.

~

EDGAR TURNED the Suburban into the lot. The Tesla sat about a hundred yards away. "It's here," he said.

"Of course it is," Gustav said over the Bluetooth connection. His nasally voice played through the SUV's speakers, and Edgar wished it didn't have the upgraded audio system. "Right where I told you it would be."

He pulled closer. The Model X looked empty. If Stacy and the man left, they could be in any one of twenty stores or eateries. "OK, smart guy. Where are our missing people? I got a lot of choices here."

Tapping keys were the only sound for a few seconds. "Looks like she's still there. Some kind of restaurant at the end. It's where her phone pings from. As for her rescuer . . ." Tap-tap-tap. "His last signal came from the middle of the street."

"Sounds like he ditched his phone, then," Francis said. He looked over his shoulder. "No one's standing anywhere near the road."

"I knew it would happen eventually," Gustav said. "One of them should have figured out how you kept finding them. Anyone who's watched *NCIS* could have a clue."

"We'll fan out here and look around," Edgar added. "I

doubt the girl's in the Italian place. They probably left her phone in the trash or something. We'll find them if they're nearby."

The senator spoke next. "Remember, the girl is the objective. If you can't get rid of her there, take her someplace you can. Same for the guy with her."

"Understood." Edgar broke the connection, and both men climbed out of the Chevy. "I'll start at the right . . . might as well see if either of them are really there. You go left. We'll meet in the middle unless we see them first." Francis nodded and trotted off toward the far end of the plaza. Edgar headed for the eatery. As he suspected, it wasn't crowded. The interior looked like a hundred other small Italian places he'd walked into over the years. Two people shared a large pizza in a booth. Other than the employees, no one else was in here.

Edgar went to the counter. An older man approached. "I'm trying to find my friend," Edgar said. "I can't reach him, and I think he might've come here." The other fellow shrugged. "He's older than me . . . probably fifty or so. White. He would have been with a college-aged girl. Black, light complexion."

"Haven't seen them," the employee said.

"You sure?"

"Look around. I ain't had nobody in here most of the day. Damn snow. The pizza those two are eating is the first one I sold in hours."

Edgar put his hands up. "All right. Thanks anyway. I'll keep looking." He wondered how the girl's phone showed as being in here. If she or Tyler never came inside, they couldn't have thrown it in the bathroom or a trash can. Edgar returned outside and walked the perimeter. He didn't see a mobile anywhere. Maybe Gustav got it wrong. They hadn't worked together much. Keyboard jockeys held their value only as long as they were right.

He checked the next few places. No sign of the girl or Tyler. Edgar dialed Gustav. "Dead end," he reported when the computer guy answered. "No sign of the girl or her phone."

"It's definitely there," Gustav said.

"I'm telling you it's not. I've looked all over the place. No one's even seen these people. It's like they left their stupid Tesla here and disappeared."

"Maybe you should look harder."

"Maybe I should strangle you with your keyboard cable."

Gustav snickered. "It's wireless. What am I, forty-five?"

Edgar sighed and clenched his fist. Maybe he could bludgeon Gustav to death with his precious wireless keyboard when this was all over. It would take a few whacks, but Edgar would enjoy it more. Francis approached and offered a quick wag of his head. "Francis hasn't found shit, either. They're not here. We need another plan."

"Do you have one?" Gustav asked.

"What about the guy? We're focused on the girl because she's the target. You said the man with her was a soldier. What else do we know about him?'

"Give me a minute." The tapping of keys dominated the connection. A short while later, Gustav said, "John Tyler, retired Green Beret. Twenty-four years of active duty. Four deployments to Afghanistan with special operations. He's been out about nine years now."

"I knew most of this already," Edgar said. "What else? Address? Family?"

"He lives in Baltimore. Pretty decent drive from where you are now. Has a daughter in college who lives with him. His father lives in some adult community in Bel Air."

"Not far, then."

"He won't be there," Gustav said. "This guy's smart. He's not going to lead you to his dad's place right away." He paused. "This is all public records stuff. The senator doesn't want me breaking into the army's networks . . . even though I'm sure I could. He owns a car repair shop. It's too far from your current location."

Edgar shook his head as Francis tried to listen to the call. He didn't want to put it on speaker. "And he probably wouldn't lead us there, anyway."

"Like I told you . . . look harder."

"We need some ideas," Edgar said. "Francis and I are happy to search, but I'm pretty sure you get paid for data. Right now, you're not really providing much."

"I've just given you a lot of relevant details," Gustav said. "It's not my fault we're up against someone smart. If the other team took him out, we wouldn't be having this conversation."

"Call back when you know something." Edgar broke the connection. "Prick."

"We're in the dark?" Francis wanted to know.

"Basically. He just read the soldier's file. Nothing we can use right now. Maybe we can visit his old man or his daughter later. For now, I think we need to stick to the area. They ditched their car and phones recently. They couldn't have gotten far yet. We'll do a good old-fashioned low-tech search."

Francis nodded. "Good. I'm down. Let's find these two and deal with them."

"Once we do," Edgar said, "I'm killing the goddamn geek, too."

13

———

Tyler looked at his watch. Stacy had been in the store long enough. Buying two phones and a bunch of snacks didn't take much time, and the weather would keep foot traffic down. He guided the Blazer around the perimeter of the lot and curbed it in front of the shop. Stacy stood near the door. She edged around two men in dark clothes. Tyler put a hand on his pistol before they walked harmlessly into the aisle. Stacy ran to the SUV and climbed in, tossing the plastic bags down at her feet. Her eyes looked red and puffy, and her voice was small when she spoke. "I thought they were the guys from before."

He pulled away while she buckled her seat belt. Getting out of the area quickly in a stolen vehicle would be important. He got back onto the main road headed toward Aberdeen. "I can see how you'd think they were. Any other problems?"

"No," Stacy said. "I got us each a flip phone. They're older, and I figured they can't use a GPS to track us like they could with a newer model."

Tyler nodded. "Good call. Can you set them up? I want to call Lexi."

Stacy unpacked each phone and snapped their batteries in place. They were identical models, and she handed one to Tyler. "Where are we headed?"

"Aberdeen. I have . . . a friend who was able to get us a hotel room. It'll be anonymous. Not traceable to you or me. We need a place to hole up while we figure out our next moves."

"All right." Stacy paused and frowned. "I'm not sure I want to talk to Lexi. Don't get me wrong. I really like her. Hell, we were supposed to be doing a girl's day right now. It's just . . ."

"I know." Tyler opened the phone, dialed his daughter's cell, and put the call on speaker. "This is my new number," he said when she picked up. "At least for now."

"Is Stacy there?"

"I'm here."

"Oh my god, I'm so sorry about what happened," Lexi said. "I know you're not all right, but . . . I hope you will be."

"Me, too," Stacy said in a small voice. She wiped at her eyes.

"We're up against some savvy people," Tyler told his daughter. "They tracked the Tesla by its GPS. Found us twice. We're in another vehicle now." He pondered how much to tell her. By now, he presumed the hit squad and their bosses knew who he was, meaning the killers finding Lexi only took another second or two. They could be spying on her calls. He didn't know how exactly, but if they could pinpoint the Model X, eavesdropping had to be right in the wheelhouse. "Headed to Edgewood." If anyone were listening, they would go in the opposite direction of Aberdeen. Stacy remained silent.

"What do you want me to do?" Lexi asked.

"By now, they have to know who I am. I want you to be safe. Go to your grandfather's until this is finished."

"Again?" She sighed. "You know they'll have his information, too, right?"

"Sure," Tyler said. "But he lives in an access-controlled facility and owns enough guns to hold off a thousand men. I think it's a better place for you to be right now."

"All right." Tyler heard disappointment in Lexi's voice. He understood—he wouldn't want to stay with his father, either. In the end, however, it was the right call. It worked out well when Tyler went against a drug cartel a few months before. They'd gone after his house in Baltimore but left his dad's place alone. "I'll head up there soon. This time, I'll give him a little advance notice."

"Good. I'll talk to you again when I can. Might need you for research and all."

"I'll take along the good laptop."

"Thanks, kiddo. Be safe. Love you."

"I love you, too . . . even when you send me to Grandpa's." She ended the call.

"She's salty," Tyler said, "but she understands."

"Your father sounds interesting." Stacy smiled for the first time since she walked in on her family. It was nice to see.

"Retired navy master chief. I'm pretty sure he's got the run of the place where he lives. It suits him."

They lapsed into silence for a few minutes. After they left Bel Air, Business Route 1 reverted to being Route 22. Tyler turned the heat on and reached for the ancient radio to find an FM station. It still featured a cassette deck. Even Tyler abandoned tapes for CDs ages ago. He still had them plus a bunch of vinyl records. Lexi embraced streaming, but Tyler couldn't go along with her. Music sounded better when it came from a physical medium. After a short while, Stacy said, "What are we going to do?"

"Our main objective is to hole up and keep you safe."

"And then?"

"It would sure be nice to know who took your sister. I can't get her back until I know who might want to grab her."

"You think you can find her?"

Tyler shrugged. "Maybe. A lot of it's going to depend on what you're able to tell me. Someone wanted her alive, so we should presume she'll stay so for a while. How likely is she to talk?"

"Kacey's a hardass," Stacy said. "She won't break."

"Everybody breaks. It's a matter of biology."

Stacy crossed her arms and frowned. "It'll take her a while, then."

"Good," Tyler said. "I hope we can find her quickly. Whoever snatched her might reach out to you. Offer a trade." He glanced at her new phone. "If they can figure out how to reach you, I guess. Anyway, I need to know if they do."

"All right."

They approached Aberdeen. Sara scored them a room at the Hilton Garden Inn. Tyler remembered the area well enough to find it. The hotel sat behind a Tractor Supply Company off Beards Hill Road. It was close enough to eateries and the main road but would require a little bit of effort to find. The perfect spot. Tyler was grateful for the accommodations but hoped they wouldn't need to stay here long.

AFTER STAYING with her grandfather during the cartel mess a few months ago, Lexi kept a bag mostly packed in case it happened again. Her dad would piss someone off again, and he'd ask her to leave the house in case they tried to get to him through her. Lexi understood. It happened with Braxton and his men, so the threat was there. She got kidnapped, and her dad rescued her as part of ending it all. At least they got the Tesla out of it.

This time, the goal would be keeping Stacy alive.

Lexi wished she could help. Her dad would ask her to look things up on his old work laptop, and she could. He sort of understood it, but she'd become quite good at using its many programs. He'd never ask her to do more, though. Right now, she couldn't. They ditched the Tesla, so she couldn't try to track them with it. Ditto their phones. As much as she didn't like it, Lexi would have to be on standby and wait to help.

She tossed another day's worth of clothes in the suitcase, added a bag of toiletries, a pistol with a couple spare magazines, and closed it up. Last time, she dropped in on her grandfather unannounced. He'd been happy to see her, but the whole thing felt awkward at first. This time, she'd call and give him a heads-up. He didn't answer his landline, so she called his cell, which he picked up. "Hi, Grandpa."

"Lexi! It's nice to hear from you. How are you?"

"I'm all right. Listen, Dad's wrapped up in something again, and—"

"You need to come here, right?" he asked.

"Yes. At least you have some notice this time."

"You know you're always welcome. Your father is, too. He might need a reminder."

Lexi winced. Her dad and grandfather didn't really get along too well. "I'll tell him."

"Wouldn't do any good. At least he came for my birthday." The old man paused. "Roads are still pretty crappy. Be careful. No need to rush up here."

"I'll be all right, Grandpa. My Accord has front-wheel drive, and I'll stick to the main roads as much as I can."

"All right," he said. "See you soon."

"Thanks, Grandpa." Lexi clicked off the call. She grabbed her bag, took it to the front door, and looked out through the window. Nothing out of the ordinary. Lexi opened the door, locked it behind her, and walked to her car. She didn't see anyone who shouldn't be here. After tossing her suitcase in the trunk, she backed out of the driveway and left the neighborhood as quickly as the road conditions would allow.

THEY DROVE a lot longer than Kacey expected. She couldn't see past the hood over her head, but it didn't feel like Donald spared the accelerator. He'd taken plenty of curves and turns. Maybe he was getting off the highway and back on to throw her off. At some point, she heard his phone buzz, but he never spoke to anyone. Kacey remained silent. No reason to anger the man who was delivering her to wherever they were headed.

A short while later, the SUV moved slower. A residential area? Donald made a few turns. Kacey heard a motor ahead of them and what sounded like a garage door being raised. The SUV inched along, stopped, and then the noises repeated themselves. A loud thunk came at the end. Definitely a garage, she figured. But where? If they remained in Cecil County after all Donald's driving around, it would likely point to a newer home.

"Wait there," Donald ordered. He got out, closed his door, and came around. The hood remained over Kacey's head as he grabbed her arm and herded her through a door. "We're going down a set of stairs." He walked in front of her and didn't object when Kacey put a hand on his shoulder to help her descend. She hated the thought of touching a man who shared responsibility for the deaths of her parents and siblings, but tumbling down the steps wouldn't do her any good.

Once they reached the bottom, Donald grabbed her arm again. He shoved her into a hard chair. "Finally," another man said. Kacey recognized the voice. It matched the face she saw a second later when he pulled her hood off. State senator Richard Raburn glared at her from above. He was in his fifties but looked older thanks to his full head of gray hair. He'd sported it for years and leaned into it rather than dye it. A few wrinkles creased his face, and crows' feet surrounded his eyes. He was unimpressive physically, but he wielded a lot of power in Maryland politics.

And he was the target of Kacey's current investigation.

Very few people knew about it. She wondered how Raburn got wind of it. "Miss Chaplain," Raburn said.

"Screw you," Kacey said right before spitting in his face. "You had my family shot."

The senator used a handkerchief to wipe his cheek. "You forced my hand."

"It's about time people knew you're dirty. How much money did you make on that shady land deal no one reported?"

Raburn flashed a wolfish smile. "How nice of you to mention it. You've found out a lot about me. I talk to the press when I need to, of course. Every politician does. There are plenty of things I've never told them, however. Yet here you are digging them up and putting them in your story." He leaned closer to her. "I want to know where you got your information."

Kacey spat on him again. "I'll say it again . . . screw you. I'm not telling you shit."

Raburn backhanded her across the face. The blow turned her head, and her cheek burned. "You have no idea what you've stumbled onto, girl," he said. "I have plans . . . plans beyond this state. I'm not going to see them derailed by some nosy bitch." He turned to Donald. "Tie her to the chair. Then, get the supplies." The other man nodded. Kacey struggled, but Donald proved too strong. He lashed her wrists behind her back and bound her ankles to the legs of her uncomfortable seat. She squirmed and struggled, but it was no use.

Donald left the room and shut the door behind himself. Kacey looked around. The floor and walls were bare concrete. A small drain sat to the left of her chair. She turned and saw a sink behind her. A couple minutes later, Donald returned. Kacey couldn't get a look at what lay beyond her immediate area before he locked up again. He carried a towel and two large jugs of water. Kacey's pulse quickened. "What are you going to do?"

"You have information I need," Raburn said. Donald grabbed her chair and leaned it back. Her neck rested against the edge of the sink. The white towel went over her face. "One way or another, you're going to tell me what I want to know. How much you suffer and whether your other sister lives are up to you."

Kacey's reply died in her throat as water filled her nose and mouth, and she felt as if she were drowning.

14

___

The check-in process went smoothly. The clerk didn't ask Tyler for ID once Sara Morrison's name came up. In lieu of a credit card, Tyler handed over a hundred-dollar bill to cover any incidentals and demanded a receipt. He collected two keycards and led Stacy to their ground floor room. Two would have been ideal, but any awkwardness in shared accommodations got dwarfed by the greater ease in keeping Stacy alive should something bad happen.

The interior looked like many places where Tyler stayed over the years. The bathroom lay a step or two inside the door on the right. The size of the shower impressed Tyler. Two identical queen beds occupied a lot of the floor space. A dresser, desk, office chair, and recliner took up the rest. A TV about the size Tyler owned sat atop the dresser. He spent a few minutes checking for cameras and bugs and came up empty.

"I need to lose the SUV," Tyler said once they'd settled in. "I don't want it traced here."

"What are you going to do?" Stacy asked as she sat on the right-hand bed.

"Leave it nearby."

"What about the next time we need to go somewhere?"

Tyler shrugged. "I'll find something else. It's important we don't get run in by the police at this point." He handed her the pistol. "You ever use one of these?"

Stacy looked at the Glock like he tried to hand her a cobra. "I've been to the range a couple times. Doesn't mean I like guns."

"You don't have to like them. Just point and squeeze if someone other than me tries to come in. You don't need to look for a safety because it's in the trigger. Pressing it makes it ready to shoot, so keep your finger off until it's time to fire. When I come back, I'll knock three times, then twice, then once. If anyone else comes, try to get rid of them. If they make it inside anyway, don't hesitate to shoot."

"Will you be gone long?" Stacy said.

"I doubt it." Tyler headed for the door. "Remember—three knocks, then two, then one." She bobbed her head. He left the room, made sure the door locked behind him, and returned to the stolen SUV. It would take a while to trace it here, but they remained in the same county where the theft occurred. Ditching it would be the smart play. Tyler started it again and drove it to a nearby shopping plaza. He parked it far away from other cars, walked into a dollar store, and bought a pack of disinfectant wipes.

It took a few to do a thorough job, but Tyler removed all traces of himself and Stacy from the interior. He wiped down any surfaces they might have touched on the outside, left the old Blazer where it sat, and walked back to the hotel. He rapped on the door in the pattern he told Stacy and then used his keycard to open it. After he locked up, she lowered the pistol. "No problems?" he asked.

"All quiet," she said. "How did it go with the car?"

"Even if they find it, they won't trace it to us."

"That's good, I guess." Stacy yawned. "I don't know why I feel tired."

"You've been through a hell of a lot," Tyler said. "This has probably felt like the longest day of your life. Get some rest."

"But the people who killed my family are still out there."

"They will be until we do something about it. Our odds of success go up if we've gotten some sleep and eaten something."

"I want to do everything I can to find these people," Stacy said. "Not take a nap."

"Doing everything you can doesn't mean going full speed twenty-four-seven. It means being at your best as often as you can. To do it, you need to eat and sleep when you can." She frowned. "Trust me," Tyler added. "It kept me alive a lot of times in Afghanistan. When you're tired or hungry, you can be distracted. Weak. A step too slow. Any of those by themselves can get you killed. Start adding them together, and your odds just get worse."

Stacy sighed. "All right. That makes sense." She stacked two pillows, fluffed the top one, and lay down. "You going to rest, too?"

"Eventually."

"What about the speech you just made?"

Tyler grinned. "I'll get some Zs. You've dealt with more today than I have. You go first."

It took about ten minutes, but Stacy drifted off. She snored softly on the other side of the room. Tyler dragged the recliner closer to the window, sat in it, took out his burner phone, and dialed Lexi. "We made it to the hotel," he whispered. "She's finally sleeping, the poor kid."

"I can't imagine what she's been through," Lexi said.

"Me, neither. You at your grandfather's?"

"Yeah. He appreciated a little notice this time."

"I'm sure he did," Tyler said, keeping his voice low as Stacy slept about ten feet away. "Do you know any more about Kacey?"

"Some," Lexi said. "She's a reporter. Takes it seriously as far as I can tell. She's big into calling herself a journalist. Her work shows some freelance history, but most of her stuff is for *The Investigative Voice*."

"Never heard of it."

"It's a local online paper."

"Sounds kind of like a blog."

"Wow, Dad. I'm impressed you know what a blog is."

"I looked it up on Tweetbook," Tyler said.

Lexi groaned. "Anyway, I'm pretty sure I know who her editor is. Doesn't do me a lot of good, though. Nothing I could find tells me what she might be working on."

"It's pretty likely someone she wrote about went after her and her family. Maybe a past target."

"I agree," Lexi said. "I don't think anyone she's covered before has the reach. They're all assholes, but they're small time. A guy who owns a couple shops. A high school coach. You said pros were involved, right?"

"Yeah. Doesn't seem like those people could hire one. We'll have to work out who was in her crosshairs . . . and how they found out."

"I'm ready to help. Not a lot else to do up here."

"You could play shuffleboard with your grandfather," Tyler said. "You'd be the youngest person there by about forty years."

"Hard pass, Dad." They said their goodbyes, and Tyler ended the call. He wondered how much Stacy knew about her sister and the people she wrote about. Despite the trauma of today, Tyler would need Stacy's help. He couldn't ask anyone else in the family, and Lexi's talents with the computer couldn't reveal everything. For now, she needed to rest. Tyler rummaged through the snacks, tore open a small bag of honey roasted peanuts, and ate a few as he kept watch.

KACEY BREATHED in huge gulps as the men left the small room. They locked the door behind them. She remained tied to the chair by her wrists and ankles. Her face, hair, and upper body were drenched, but at least she could inhale and exhale without feeling like a raging river pulled her under. She understood why people called waterboarding torture. She'd managed to avoid saying anything, but there were dozens of moments where she questioned her decision to remain strong. Professional soldiers caved when their captors did this to them. Why should she be able to hold out longer?

Whatever the reason, she did . . . at least for now. Raburn and his attack dogs would be back before long. They could waterboard her again. How much more could she endure? Even if the logical part of her brain told her she wasn't drowning, every other part of her body felt like she sank in the ocean. If she didn't tell them what they wanted to know, what would come next? She was a young woman imprisoned with a bunch of men, and it didn't take long for her to imagine the worst things they could do to her.

They wanted her story. She'd spent weeks researching Richard and Miriam Raburn and the network they built around themselves. After a few days, she got the impression something sinister lurked behind the smiling veneer and years of public service. She was right, and the people of Maryland deserved to know. Rumors abounded that Raburn would seek national office of some sort, and if her story bounced him from the ballot, she would count it as a win.

The ambitious senator and his upwardly mobile wife, however, would not.

She still wondered how they found out. Kacey's editor knew of the investigation but not a lot of the content. She'd also told her parents, but she held back most of the details with them, too. Recently, Kacey started dating Lamont Williams. He worked for a political consultancy firm in Annapolis, so she shared only the bare minimum with him—not even her quarry's name. How, then, did the news come across Raburn's desk?

The ropes holding her arms and legs immobile didn't budge. She struggled until her limbs ached. The knots were too far up her wrists for her to reach. This was hopeless. Kacey reasoned not telling Raburn anything would buy her some time. Time for what? Her family was dead. Stacy's flight being delayed bought her a reprieve, but a man like Richard Raburn would send someone back to finish the job. As if on cue, the senator and Donald walked back into the room. They didn't say anything, so Kacey spoke up. "I'm still not telling you shit."

"How noble," Raburn said in a mocking tone. "I'm going to give you a choice even though you don't deserve it. Tell me what I want to know, and your younger sister lives."

Stacy was still alive? How did she avoid getting caught in all this? "You're a liar," Kacey said as her brain turned over the possibilities.

"As much as you may hate me, I'm a man of my word."

"How do I know she's not already dead?"

"She got away from us at the house," Donald said. Raburn's sour expression confirmed it. "It's just a matter of time until we find her."

"A limited time, as it were," Raburn said. He turned to his goon. "Check the house again. Tear it apart if you have to. I don't care how it looks anymore. Find what I need." He regarded Kacey with cold eyes. "If my men recover what I want, there's no reason to keep you alive . . . or to spare your sister."

"And if I talk?" Kacey wanted to know. "If I give up the details, you kill me and Stacy?" Raburn frowned but didn't say anything. He'd gotten used to dealing with the regular reporters who covered state government. Someone asking real questions put him on his heels. Kacey kept her eyes on the senator, though she knew all the supplies they'd used to torture her were still in the room. She could hold out. Her life and her younger sister's depended on it.

Besides, there was no way a few hired tough guys would find anything at the house. Not where she hid it. At some point, Raburn would need to offer a better deal.

15

———

Yellow tape covered the doors and windows of the Chaplain home. After parking the Suburban across the street and a couple hundred feet farther along, Donald and Edgar walked back. They checked for any eyes on them, saw none, and headed around the garage. The cops marked off the entrances in the rear, too, but a knife and a basic lockpicking set got them inside. "I don't think we searched the basement before," Donald said when they stood in the kitchen.

"If we did, it was brief."

"I'll go upstairs. You take the main floor. We'll do the lower level together."

"Sounds good," Edgar said.

"Let's keep the lights off, too," Donald added. "We don't want the neighbors thinking anyone's here."

Edgar nodded his assent, and Donald climbed the stairs. He checked the hall bathroom first. People often hid things in the toilet tank by taping them to the lid. Nothing. He searched the cabinets and behind the vent and came up empty. Next came the linen closet. After a few minutes sifting through sheets, towels, and toilet paper, Donald came up empty-handed. He moved on to a bedroom.

Sports posters dominated the wall, and a Lego set took up much of the desk. This must have been the son's. A few sports trophies—basketball and football, matching the wall hangings—sat on the main shelf in the large closet. It took Donald a few minutes to conduct a thorough search. Among a hidden porn collection, music, and movies, he came up with an unlabeled flash drive and three homemade DVDs. Probably nothing. Why would the oldest sister hide her stuff in her brother's room? Still, he put it into a bag. Let Gustav sort through it. If the discs held porn, it might do the uptight man some good.

The parents' large master suite held a bunch of nice furniture. Much better than the stuff at Donald's house. If he found something like a Rolex, he resolved to keep it. Raburn wouldn't care, and Donald could use the money he'd get from hocking it. Despite the size of the room—it must have been twenty by twenty-five—it didn't hold much. The attached bathroom was a dud, too. The spacious walk-in closet turned up a flash drive on a shelf near the mother's shoes. Another unlikely place for sensitive data to be stashed, but Donald bagged it and moved on.

The last bedroom belonged to the missing girl. He wondered if Gustav ever reacquired her and her savior. They'd vanished in Bel Air yesterday. Probably knew they were being tracked and followed. The guy with Stacy took out each member of the alpha team. Donald couldn't underestimate him. They'd turn up at some point. Raburn might need the girl, and he could try to convince her to save her older sister. Then, the senator could be rid of the whole family, and Donald would split a nice windfall with the remaining team members.

He didn't find much to sift through. The girl lived on

campus, so she didn't keep much in the house. Donald walked back to the main level and found Edgar waiting in the kitchen. "Anything?"

"Not much." Edgar shrugged. "A couple discs with no label. Might be blank, but we'll leave them to the geek."

They headed downstairs to the finished basement. Here, a sprawling living room and fireplace took up most of the space. A quick search of the laundry and powder room revealed nothing. The storage area held a bunch of boxes, many of them still taped shut. None of the open ones held anything of interest. Edgar searched the sectional sofa and chairs while Donald took the entertainment center. It looked a bit old-fashioned in such a modern house. The dad owned an impressive music collection. There must have been four hundred CDs on various racks. Donald didn't uncover anything. Despite expecting to find nothing, he looked in the gas fireplace and wasn't disappointed.

"I got nothing," Edgar said.

"Same here," Donald said. "Not much of a haul." They returned to the main level. "It's a big house. For rich assholes, they don't hide a lot of shit."

"Maybe they don't have much to keep from people like you and me."

"I guess." Donald frowned as he heard a siren. He walked to the front and peered out the window. Two pairs of red and blue lights came closer. "We gotta go. Out the back."

They left in a hurry, padded across the yard, and hopped the fence. The two men stayed low and moved farther away. At the third house, they stopped. Donald peeked through the boards and saw two cops nosing around the Chaplains' backyard. He gestured for Edgar to keep going. The next house showed no lights inside. They couldn't hop the fence without being seen. Edgar popped the gate, and they moved through it. Once they cleared the garage, both men stood and walked to their SUV at a normal pace. The cops were less likely to harass people who looked like they belonged.

Donald and Edgar climbed into the Suburban and drove toward the police cars. None of the deputies tried to stop them.

~

TYLER RUBBED his eyes and looked at the alarm clock on the nightstand between the beds. Its bright green digits showed 6:30. Stacy still slept. She'd woken up after midnight and stayed awake for a while. Tyler took the opportunity to sleep then. He'd probably gotten about five hours total. It would need to be enough for now.

A peek through the heavy blinds showed the sun shining. The few icicles clinging to the balcony above them dripped water faster than some faucets Tyler used in the army. Weather wouldn't be a factor today. It helped their adversaries as much as them. At least Tyler wouldn't be confined to looking for an old SUV if they needed to steal another car and move again.

Stacy stirred and sat up in the other bed. She looked at the clock and sighed. "Did you get any rest?" she asked in a sleepy voice.

"A few hours."

"You good?"

"I'll be all right," Tyler said. "Today, I want to learn more about your sister. We need to figure out who took her. Once we do, we can narrow down where she might be."

"You think she's still alive?"

"I don't know. I hope so. How easily do you think she'd tell some asshole what he wants to know?"

"Not very," Stacy said.

"Then, we'll presume she's alive."

"You think you can get her back?"

"I've already taken out three guys," Tyler said. "Knowing who we're dealing with will clue us into the size of the operation and help me make a plan. For now, let's say I'm cautiously optimistic."

"What are we going to do first?" Stacy wanted to know.

"Eat. I saw a couple fast food joints on the way in here."

Stacy wrinkled her nose. "I don't really want breakfast."

"Too bad. We both need to have some. There might not be a chance later."

"Fine." Stacy stood. "I'm going to the bathroom."

Tyler waited a few minutes for her to emerge. When she did, he set the pistol on the nightstand. "Same thing as before. I'll knock three times, then twice, then once. Don't open up for anyone but me. If you need to use it, aim for center mass and keep pulling the trigger until they stop twitching." Stacy offered a small nod after regarding the gun with a sour expression. Tyler slipped his coat on, turned the collar up, and walked out of the room. He made sure the door locked behind him.

Despite walking a circuit of the entire floor, he saw no one in the hallways. A couple men used treadmills in the small fitness center. Two clerks worked the desk. Tyler took the side exit and made for the rear of the building. He kept an eye out for vehicles sitting and idling or anyone who looked like they didn't belong. His sweep came up empty. Maybe their disappearance in Bel Air worked better than he thought. Being farther away would still be better, but this was good enough for now.

Tyler crossed the street. Lingering slush still dotted the sidewalk. The closest fast food restaurant was close to a mile away. Tyler didn't want to leave Stacy alone for so long. He changed plans and walked to a nearby 7-Eleven. He could refill their snacks, but the real factor was the superior coffee they brewed. Tyler took a basket when he walked in. He headed down the first aisle and pretended to look at the first aid supplies as he surveyed the interior.

A man fixing himself a cup of decaf concerned Tyler. He was dressed well. Jacket, tie, short hair, clean shave. He could have been a professional on his way to work. Or he might be one of the killers sent to dispatch them. Tyler slipped into the next aisle and picked up a large can of soup. He could throw it if he needed to, and it would make a fine bludgeon at close range. The well-dressed man paid for his unleaded brew, got into a nondescript Japanese sedan, and drove away. He never looked at any of the other customers.

Tyler put the can back and waited for a few people to leave the coffee area before pouring two tall cups. He grabbed a few hot breakfast bagel sandwiches and a day's worth of food. Plenty of cash from the three dead operatives remained. Tyler took care not to present his face to any of the security cameras in the store. The high collar of his jacket helped, and he kept his head angled down. He left with two full plastic bags, the pair of large coffees, and the hope Stacy didn't need to use the gun.

STACY FIXED a fascinated gaze on the black pistol. She'd left it on the nightstand once Mister Tyler left. A thousand thoughts raced through her head. She sat on the edge of the bed and stared at the door. He'd only been gone a few minutes. She remembered seeing a McDonald's on their drive to the hotel. If he went there on foot, it would take him at least fifteen minutes each way. It seemed like a long time to leave her alone.

What were the odds anyone would find them here? They'd been careful. Both their phones were gone. The Tesla sat in a Bel Air parking lot. The older SUV Mister Tyler stole couldn't be traced to them. Someone else made the hotel reservation. Whoever tracked them should have hit a wall yesterday. Still, Stacy didn't want to let her guard down. Her parents weren't expecting a hit squad.

She got up and paced the cheap carpet. Each time she walked toward the door, Stacy looked at the gun. She'd seen their handiwork up close. The blood from her brother on the wall and sofa. Her mother, father, and younger sister strewn around the dining room table, the tile around them more red than beige. A shudder ran down her spine. Stacy knew she'd never be able to shake those images from her mind no matter how long she lived.

What if she needed to use the pistol? Four men executed most of her family. Three of the killers got their comeuppance already. Mister Tyler seemed okay with it. He'd been in the army a long time. Stacy didn't like the thought of people having guns much less using them. She sat on the bed again. The weapon felt heavy in her hand. She turned it over and looked at it. The letters LOCK stood out on the side surrounded by a stylized G followed by the number 19 and AUSTRIA, then 9X19. She only recognized the name of the country in Europe. Stacy held it toward the door, stared over the sights, and imagined training the business end on a stranger walking through the door.

It repulsed and excited her at the same time.

She wondered if these twin feelings were what drew people to guns in the first place. Stacy set it back down on the nightstand. No one approached. If someone did, she would pick it up again and hope for the best. A few minutes passed, and she felt hungry for the second time since walking in on the scene in her house. Despite figuring it was futile, she took out her burner phone and dialed Kacey's number from memory.

A thought gripped her before she hit the green call button. This was a disposable phone. It couldn't be associated with her. Still, if someone held her sister captive, they would have her mobile. They'd see the incoming call. Could a tech-savvy person figure out where she called from? Even if they couldn't get her exact location, a radius would be bad. There were only so many places they could be up here. Stacy flipped the phone shut without calling.

Footsteps approached. She glanced at the clock. Too soon for Mister Tyler to be back already. Stacy picked up the gun and pointed it where she figured someone's center mass would be. Her pulse thudded in her ears. A second later, three raps came from the door, then two, then a final one. The lock whirred as Stacy set the pistol back down. Mister Tyler walked in, his arms full of bags and two cups of coffee in a cardboard carrier. She saw the 7-Eleven logo on one of them. "Didn't go to fast food?"

"This was closer," he said. "I didn't want to leave you alone for too long. Besides, they have better coffee."

"Is that really a factor?" Stacy asked.

"It should be for everyone. All things being equal, go with the place who can brew a better cup." He held one out, and Stacy took it.

"Thanks, Mister Tyler."

"Just Tyler is fine." He dropped onto his bed. "I got us a couple breakfast sandwiches. The rest is water and snacks to last another day. I hope we won't need them."

Stacy let out a deep breath. "Yeah, me, too."

16

The senator watched as Edgar and Donald set a pile of discs and a flash drive on Gustav's desk. "Excellent!" he said, clapping his hands. "Let's find what we need on here. Then, we can get rid of the girl."

Gustav took a deep breath before engaging with his colleagues. "Where did you discover these things?"

"All over the house," Donald said.

These men did not have eyes or memories for the important details. "Such as?"

"The brother's room," Edgar said. "The parents'." He shrugged. "I dunno. We saw something maybe important, and we grabbed it."

"Any from the reporter's room?" the senator asked.

"No," Edgar admitted.

Gustav rolled his eyes. He already suspected this would be futile. A careful reporter wouldn't hide something in a place she didn't control. What if it got discovered? Or discarded? Or overwritten? No, she would take care to keep it away from men like Donald and Edgar who ransacked houses and found the obvious things. "I'll check everything, but I doubt what we need is here. I'd like you all to leave while I work."

Donald and Edgar shrugged but moved toward the door. Only their benefactor remained. "I'm paying you. I want to know what's on there."

"I'll let you know if I find something good," Gustav said.

"But I—"

"Out!" Gustav pointed toward the door. The senator glowered for a few seconds, but straightened his tie and headed for the exit. Finally. He tolerated the senator lingering while he worked because the man signed the checks. Working alone remained his preference. Data didn't lie. Ones and zeroes held no biases. Given the choice, Gustav would prefer his computer to his colleagues even though he'd worked with the other men for a few months now.

He popped the first disc in to the external DVD drive. It held a bunch of songs. Gustav never heard of most of them. He scanned the files but didn't find anything out of the ordinary. The next was the same save for a new collection of songs. The third held a bunch of movie files. It only took a few seconds to realize they were all pornographic. Probably from the brother's room. He was the right age to be into shit like this. Even though he figured it would turn up nothing, Gustav ran another automated check of the files. Nothing unusual turned up.

The rest of the haul gave similar results. Gustav discovered years' worth of photos and tax documents. They could prove useful against the Chaplains if they were still alive. With the family dead except for two daughters, however, the data held little value. Gustav sent a text to the senator, who returned to the room a couple minutes later. "Anything?"

"Nothing we can use," Gustav said. "You're not going to get the girl to talk over some pictures and tax returns."

The senator crossed his arms. "What if she thinks we have more?"

"She's smart. Smarter than the guys you send out, which isn't saying much. I don't think she'll fall for a simple ruse. You either need to break her or find her sister and give her some incentive to talk."

"We'll keep working on both," the boss said. "I want this whole mess behind me as soon as we can get it there."

IT FELT like the start of an interrogation. Tyler was no specialist in the area, though he'd taken the same training his fellow soldiers did. The army often brought in experts when the stakes were high. They would typically open by building rapport. Offering a drink. Trying to be friends. Things often went downhill from there—including the "enhanced" sessions Tyler despised—but the beginnings were the same. When Tyler set the bagel sandwich and coffee on the desk for Stacy, he got a brief memory of Afghanistan.

He shook it from his mind as he sat on the edge of his bed. She slid onto the chair. "Thanks for getting food," Stacy said as she unwrapped the meal. Tyler picked up two identical bacon, egg, and cheese bagel sandwiches.

"Let's hope it's the last meal we need to eat in a hotel room," he said.

Stacy's head bobbed slowly. "Would you do this again?"

"Do what?"

"This." She gestured around the room. "Stay in a hotel another night . . . maybe even a different one."

"Yes."

"Why? You don't even know me very well."

"You're Lexi's friend," Tyler said. "If I needed another

reason, there's what we walked in on yesterday. I couldn't leave you to fend for yourself."

"She used to complain about the time you spent away," Stacy said. "Even after you retired. I think she missed you."

Tyler felt the words like a punch to his gut. "I certainly missed her. I know I wasn't around for a lot of things while she grew up . . . even if you leave out the situation with her mother and me."

"Lexi's been my friend for a while." Stacy frowned. "I think she didn't like what you did. Not just that you went away. It was the whole army thing." A tiny smile formed on her lips. "Like it or not, all the stuff you did in the army is what's keeping me alive right now. It's the only hope I have to see my sister again."

"The things we do are hard for people to understand," Tyler said. He figured Lexi didn't like the idea of him flying off to war when she was a young girl. She'd grown up a lot since. "Some soldiers never really get it. They're the ones who struggle most when they try to go back to their old lives." He put his hand up when Stacy started to say something else. "Enough about me. We need to figure out who took your sister and where. You're the key here." Tyler knew some of it already from what Lexi told him. His daughter only had second-hand knowledge and whatever she'd researched, however. It might have been good intel, but Stacy would be a better source.

They both ate a little of their sandwiches and drank coffee. Tyler figured Stacy needed some time to go into everything. "She's a reporter."

"I know. I'm not coming into this blind. I need you to tell me the things I can't find on Google."

"She freelanced for a while. More recently, she's had a steady gig. At least a year now."

"Who's she work for?"

"*The Investigative Voice*," Stacy said, confirming Lexi's intel. "They're all online. Articles, commentary, even some vlogs." She paused a beat. "Sorry, do you know what a vlog is?"

Tyler grinned. "A year ago, I would've said no. Lexi's taught me a few things about the online world . . . even though I don't really want to be a part of it."

"Some days, I don't blame you." Stacy sipped her coffee, and Tyler followed suit. "I don't know her editor's name offhand. They get along well, though. He gives her assignments sometimes, but he also trusts her to find and deliver good stories."

"You know what she's been working on recently?"

"Not exactly," Stacy said. "She hit on topics at random before. I think her editor tried to focus her." The young woman paused again, and her eyes flitted up and to the left. Searching a memory, as Tyler learned in his interrogation training. Whatever she added was extremely likely to be true. "Kacey told me something about state government. I know she spent time in Annapolis."

"State government is a pretty big umbrella," Tyler said. "Between politicians, appointees, and aides, you're looking at a few hundred people."

"I know." Stacy's shoulders slumped. "I wish I could tell you more."

"Me, too," Tyler admitted. "It's a start, at least. I rarely got all the information I needed in the army."

"So what now?" Stacy wanted to know.

"My first objective is to keep you alive. I'd also like to know who targeted your family and get your sister back. The trick is how to do them without losing sight of the main priority."

"Can't you just bring in someone else?"

"We should presume our adversaries know who I am,"

Tyler said. "By now, they've done a full workup on me. They know who I'll try to call and where I might turn up. I'm not saying we're all alone, but we need to be judicious."

"All right. What next?"

"Do you think there's anything at your house?"

"I don't know." Stacy blew out a breath. "Wouldn't the assholes have already searched it?"

"Probably," Tyler said. "My guess is they were planning to kill you and take the place apart when we stopped them. Since then, cops would've been all over it. Maybe they haven't seen a chance to go back yet."

"I don't know if Kacey would've hidden anything there," Stacy said. "When we were younger, we'd pass messages at the fireplace. One of the stones was loose, and we'd hide notes for each other under it." She smiled as she recounted the memory. "Mom and Dad never found out . . . or they never said anything if they did. Kacey has a work laptop. She can back things up to the cloud, and I'm sure she does. Her boss probably requires it. They use encrypted email and everything."

Tyler nodded. "Let's try to chip away at the Annapolis angle, then. If we can narrow the suspect pool, we can figure out who's responsible for all this."

"What will you do when you find out?"

"Kill them," Tyler said.

17

———

Lexi checked her watch. Five minutes before ten. She drank her second cup of coffee and sat at her grandfather's kitchen table. The old man put groceries away from his recent trip to the store. Lexi offered, but he refused. For a man of seventy-six, Zeke Tyler sure got around well. He didn't seem slowed by age. Lexi wondered why he needed to live in an active adult community which doubled as assisted living when he didn't need the help. Her dad's theory was loneliness, and he was probably right. Her grandfather was the most extroverted member of the family by a healthy margin.

A minute later, someone knocked on the door. "Who the hell?" Zeke said. He opened a small drawer and pulled out a pistol.

"It's all right, Grandpa." Lexi stood. Her grandfather keeping a gun in every room of the house didn't surprise her. Where else would her dad have learned it? "I invited someone over. Hope it's all right."

"You coulda told me," he grumbled. "It's not a boy, is it? I ain't putting this gun away if it is."

"No." Lexi opened the door. Alex Anne smiled, and the two embraced. "Come in." Her friend walked in, and Lexi closed up. Alex Anne didn't look the part of a pop star in her faded jeans, plain black hoodie, and Nike high tops. "Grandpa, this is my friend Alex."

Zeke offered a polite smile. "Nice to meet you." His eyes moved back and forth between them. "Lexi and Alex, huh? Wow. You even look a little alike."

"She got caught up in that mess Dad took care of at the airport," Lexi said.

"I'm sorry to hear it," the old man said to Alex Anne. "You need anything?"

"A few more years of therapy," she said while trying to summon a grin.

"I can't help much there."

"Actually," Lexi said, "I think we both can." Two confused expressions served as responses. "I figured we could all go to the range and do some shooting."

Zeke clapped his hands. "I never need an excuse to go. I'll pack a few guns." He walked out of the room.

Alex Anne frowned. "I don't know. A gun range?"

"I didn't want to go the first time my dad took me," Lexi said. "I was eleven. He'd retired a few months before. I hated the idea of him flying off to war in someplace I couldn't even find on a map." She took a deep breath. "Later, I'd realize that was my mother's influence. My first time at the range was . . . interesting. I was the only girl there and easily the youngest person." She remembered her dad talking to her for several minutes about gun safety before letting her pick anything up. "I ended up really enjoying it. Couldn't tell my mother, though. I think it was the day I really started to become my father's daughter."

"You think it could help me?" Alex Anne asked.

"I don't know what you went through, but I'm sure you

felt helpless. Powerless." Alex Anne's downward gaze confirmed it. "Holding a gun in your hand and firing it is the total opposite. It's power. It's a rush of excitement. It's knowing you'll be able to do what you need to when shit hits the fan."

"All right." Alex Anne wiped a tear from her eye and smiled. "You talked me into it. I'll go."

"It'll be good for me, too," Lexi said. "I'm between shrinks. I could use the outlet."

Zeke returned with a duffel bag which clanked when he walked. "Got a variety here, including a good pistol to learn on. I'm not sure what I'm in for with the two of you, but I won't turn down some time at the range."

Lexi squeezed her friend's hand, and Alex Anne flashed a game grin. "I think we'll be all right, Grandpa."

TYLER AND STACY walked to a nearby discount clothing store. It was about a mile away. They cut through other lots and avoided walking along main roads as much as possible. "We'll get a couple days' worth of clothes," he told her. "Sale racks all the way. We don't know how much cash we'll need later." Stacy nodded, and they each spent about fifteen minutes shopping.

Tyler bought another pair of jeans, a combo pack of white T-shirts and boxers, and a zip-up hoodie. He didn't look at what Stacy chose, but her basket was full. Eighty dollars later, they left the store and walked back to the hotel. "I need a shower," Stacy said as she rummaged through her plastic bag. It bulged at the sides before she took a few items out of it. She walked into the bathroom and closed the door.

Once the water ran, Tyler took out his burner phone. He dialed the general number for the Pentagon and asked to be connected to Sara Morrison's office. Her secretary came on the line next and asked him to hold. After a few minutes, Sara picked up. "Are you all right?"

"So far, so good," Tyler said. "I'm learning more about who we might be up against. Still need to do some work there."

"How's the girl?"

"Traumatized but holding up well." Tyler paused. "I think we might need to extend the hotel. It's a good base of operations. No one's on to us yet."

"I'm worried," Sara said. "I know you're always going to be a knight-errant, but you seem pretty isolated up there."

"There's a major installation a few miles down the road," Tyler said. He'd never been stationed at Aberdeen Proving Ground, though he'd visited a few times. He probably still knew people there. Regardless, his army retiree ID would get him past the gate, and the armed guards there could handle any pursuers.

"You'd still need to get there," his girlfriend said. "You have a car?"

"I had to leave the Tesla in Bel Air. They were tracking it. I . . . can get a vehicle if we need one. We drove here, after all."

"I'll add a couple days to the reservation. You're going to owe me . . . big time." Sara's tone lightened, and Tyler grinned. "And I mean to collect."

"I'll gladly pay," he said.

"Try to get some help, though. Maybe Rollins is available. I'm worried that you're on your own against who knows what."

"I will. Thanks again."

"I love you," Sara said, "even though you're often an enormous pain in my ass."

"Love you, too." Tyler ended the call. He debated calling Rollins. A clever adversary could connect him and Tyler.

Maybe even surveil his house and phone. If he had his normal mobile, Tyler would try an app like Signal. The basic flip model didn't have such capability, however. He took the risk and keyed in Rollins' number from memory. His friend usually answered quickly. This time, he needed four rings. "You're slowing down in your middle years."

"Still younger than you," Rollins said. His voice was quieter than normal.

"What's going on?"

"I'm tied up in something."

"All right. I wanted to see if you were free, but don't worry about it."

"You good?"

"Not really, but I'll manage. Maybe I'll even help you out when I'm done."

"Wouldn't turn it down," Rollins said.

"Let me know if your schedule frees up," Tyler said. "Otherwise, I'll call you when I wrap things here."

"Roger that." They hung up. Tyler sighed as he slipped his phone back into his pocket. Rollins represented his best chance to find help. Other people Tyler might try weren't local. He didn't feel comfortable reaching out to anyone else. For now, he and Stacy were on their own.

STACY DRIED her hair and pulled it into an unruly ponytail. She looked in the bathroom mirror and sighed. Even though it seemed like a lifetime ago, she remembered being excited to come home for spring break. She'd hang out with her family and friends. The school work could wait. Then, the storm hit, and Kacey apparently pissed off someone enough to kill everyone else in their house. Despite sleeping last night, Stacy had dark circles under her eyes. She wiped away a stray tear and walked back into the hotel room. Tyler sat on his bed. After a moment, she said, "I wish I had my phone."

"Someone you need to call?"

"No. Pictures. Kacey often sent some to me when she was working on a story. She never trusted her own eye for photography." Stacy let out a dry chuckle. "I'm not sure mine was any better, but I was happy to help her out."

"Any photos come to mind?" Tyler asked.

"Maybe." Stacy sat on her bed facing his. "Kacey had been going to Annapolis for a couple weeks. She didn't really tell me much about anything, but I got the impression she was onto something big. Like . . . she was even more secretive than usual." Tyler didn't say anything. Stacy kept talking after a pause. "About a week or so ago, she sent me a few pictures of a vacant lot."

"Odd choice." Tyler frowned. "Not really something you'd need a second opinion on, either."

"I know. I asked her about it, but she just wanted to know if the photos looked good." Stacy shrugged. "All I could see was grass and a few trees."

"You think it was connected to what she was writing about?"

"I'm sure it was . . . even if she didn't tell me."

"Do you know who it was about?" he said. "Maybe she mentioned a name in conjunction with the empty lot."

Stacy searched her memory. Having the phone would be easier. She closed her eyes and tried to recall the text thread. Kacey sent a few snaps of the lot. Stacy looked at them. She couldn't tell it from any other random grassy plot. "It was in Cecil County," she said as a recollection of Kacey's answer came to her. "I don't know how far from where we live." Her sister clammed up after divulging the general location. Stacy opened her eyes. "It's all I got. I'll need access to my messages to try and get any other details."

With her phone gone, it meant trying to access her account from a computer. Which they didn't have. Even if Tyler got access to one, he didn't want their adversaries to get a bead on Stacy's location because she logged in somewhere. "If we really need to," he said. "I think it's risky. They tracked us before in a Tesla."

"We could probably do it safely," Stacy said.

"If you can remember something without getting into your account, it would be better."

Stacy sighed and ran her hands through her hair. "I know. I'm trying."

Tyler didn't reply. In his army days, he would have told a young soldier to try harder. Stacy didn't need the reminder. She'd seen the consequences of failure firsthand as they lay dead in her house. Nothing Tyler could say would trump the image.

18

After a couple fitful hours, Kacey actually got some sleep. It surprised her. She remained in the chair, and she'd never drifted off before even in far more comfortable models. What she'd endured must have exhausted her enough. She'd been awake for a while now, though the lack of windows or a clock in the small room prevented her from knowing how long. Right now, she knew she needed to pee and eat something.

Donald opened the door a few minutes later. He untied her and walked with her to the powder room. After her brief restroom visit, he gave her a peanut butter and jelly sandwich and a bottle of water. Kacey nodded her thanks to him and scarfed down the food. She could have eaten two more, but he didn't offer her anything else. Kacey drained the water bottle before Donald tied her to the chair again. "Don't get comfortable," he said as he left.

"No chance of that," Kacey muttered. She struggled against the ropes and found it as futile as before. Raburn hired capable men, at least. He'd probably come down himself soon. Had to eat a nice breakfast and all. Heaven forbid the people he represented got an honest day's work from him. Kacey wondered what else they might do to compel her to talk. Killing most of her family and torturing her were already extreme measures. How much further could they go? Not for the first time, she realized how vulnerable she was as a woman held captive in a house full of men who didn't care about her well-being.

Sure enough, the bastard senator walked in a short while later with Donald in tow. He wore a dark gray suit, and not a hair on his head looked out of place. "Ready to talk today?" he said.

"Go to hell," Kacey told him.

"All I want is how much you know and who told you. It's not unreasonable."

"I'm still not telling you shit."

Raburn shook his head and possessed the gall to try and look sympathetic. He succeeded only in looking constipated. "Have it your way, foolish girl. Donald."

The hired goon leapt into action. He tossed a towel over Kacey's face and leaned her chair back again. The water soon poured over her face. The reporter's logical part of her brain tried to tell her this was torture. She wasn't really underwater. These assholes only wanted her to talk. Her body told a different story, however. She thrashed as much as the ropes would allow, which was very little. Liquid in her nose and mouth convinced her she was drowning. The water kept coming, and Kacey choked and burbled. When she thought she couldn't take a second more, Donald stopped. He let her chair go, and the front legs slammed to the floor, sending a jolt up her spine.

Raburn pulled the wet towel away and scowled at her. "We can do this all day. Make it easy on yourself."

Kacey spat a mouthful of water on his expensive shoes. "Piss off."

"Think of your sister," Donald added. "If you won't save yourself, maybe you'll do it for her." Raburn frowned but didn't say anything.

Stacy was still alive, then. They hadn't found her yet. Donald confirmed it, and his boss didn't look happy at the revelation. They'd done something similar the day before. Kacey wondered how much longer Stacy could stay hidden and if she had any help. Regardless, she would keep fighting as long as someone else in her family remained alive. Raburn couldn't take that from her. "She'd tell you the same thing," Kacey said. "Go to hell."

Raburn's face twisted, and before Kacey could try to react, he hit her with a hard right cross. It snapped her head to the side and sent the chair clattering to the floor. The impact shook her. The left side of her face throbbed. "Don't take it easy on her, Donald," the senator said. "I want this bitch talking. If you can't get anything out of her this way, get more creative."

"Yes, sir," the lackey said.

Raburn stomped from the room. Donald hoisted the chair upright again. "He's right. You should make it easy on yourself."

"I'm not telling you assholes a single thing," Kacey said.

Donald shrugged. He covered her face with the wet towel again and tilted the chair back. As the water poured over her, Kacey wished she could have screamed past the ongoing sensation of drowning.

～

Miriam Raburn welcomed the reporter with the same ready smile she'd practiced many times. "Thank you so much for coming on short notice."

"Thanks for the opportunity," the journalist said. She was a woman in her mid-twenties. Under her winter coat, she wore a sensible sweater and an acceptable pair of jeans. The weather wasn't perfect, after all. The last few inches of her shoulder-length hair were purple, however, and it ruined any semblance of professionalism. It took some effort, but Miriam maintained her happy expression. Appearances mattered. "Is your husband ready?"

"I thought he'd be up here by now. Richard was . . . dealing with something in the basement." Miriam took out her phone and texted the senator. *Reporter is here for an interview. I arranged it last night. We'll be in your office.* She held her hand out toward the stairs. "Would you like to wait with me? Richard keeps an office on the second floor."

"Sure. Thank you." Miriam led the way. Her father refinished the steps and much of the other wood in the house about a decade ago. She'd taken months curating a furniture collection to look modern and refined, putting a spin on the age of the building. The place looked better than it had in a hundred years, and this damned reporter couldn't even make a comment on it. Miriam hid her growing anger in a deep breath as she walked to the left at the second floor. Her husband's office was the first door on the right.

As she sat behind the large mahogany desk, her phone vibrated, and she checked the message. *Seriously? How is this a good idea right now?*

Miriam drafted a quick reply. *Get up here and get this over with. We control the narrative.* "He'll be up in a minute," she said as the reporter frowned.

"It's fine," the young woman said. "I need a little time to get everything set up, anyway." She placed her own mobile on the desk. "Do you mind if I record our conversation so I can make better notes later?"

"Not at all."

She also took out a mechanical pencil and spiral note-book. It took several seconds of flipping to find an empty page. Before Miriam could make a comment on how many stories the journalist worked, she heard footsteps coming up. "Here he is now."

Richard walked into the office a few seconds later. The reporter stood, and the two shook hands. "Thanks for coming," he said. "I didn't realize you were here, and I was caught up in something downstairs."

"It's all right, Senator." Her easy expression turned into a frown as she looked at his torso. "Your shirt is wet."

He looked down. "Ah. I didn't notice. I like to get a little hands-on with some projects."

"I wish I had the know-how." Miriam said nothing as the reporter tapped her phone screen. "This is Lucy Wayne with the *Baltimore Sun*. I'm talking to Maryland Senator Richard Raburn and his wife Miriam in Cecil County."

"Happy to speak with you," Raburn said, showing the quick smile every politician needs in their arsenal.

"Before we get into some of your recent legislative achievements, Senator, I want to take a different tack. We're coming up on an election year. Rumors are swirling around Annapolis that you're going to seek national office. Any truth to them?"

Raburn spread his hands and kept his expression jovial. "I've long thought I could do more for the people of Mary-land than simply serve as a state senator from a single county."

"That's not a denial," Lucy said. "Not really a confirma-tion, either."

"It's a little early for announcements. We're definitely

exploring it. For now, my focus remains on making life a little better for my constituents every day."

"Any time someone makes a move like this, there will be charges of leaving people behind . . . or too much ambition. What do you say to those critics?"

"The same thing I generally say to my critics," Raburn told her. "Look at my record. I've been in state government for two decades, and I'm pretty sure I've never been elected for my looks." He flashed another grin.

Miriam matched it. "I don't like ambition being a dirty word," she added. "Without it, people are stuck. It's what makes us want to do more, achieve more, think bigger. I would question the motivations of anyone who's throwing stones at someone for being ambitious."

Raburn nodded sagely. "My wife raises a good point. She often does."

ALEX ANNE TURNED the pistol over in her hand. It fit well, she had to admit. She didn't like the look of it, but she'd never gotten used to guns. Her father never held much of an interest in them, either, though he had no problem employing men who did. Men like Lexi's father. "I'm not sure about this," she said.

"I was nervous my first time, too," Lexi said.

Alex Anne smiled. She could hear her friend even past the ear protection. "Good to know."

"Of course, I was in middle school." Lexi grinned. "You get used to it."

"That's what I'm worried about. I don't want to get used to it."

"Shooting ain't for everyone," Lexi's grandfather said. Considering he brought an entire duffel bag full of guns, Alex

Anne didn't know how seriously to take anything he said on the subject. "I knew plenty of men and women who loved it, and I even served with a few who only went to the range because they needed to qualify every year. My point is you'll never find out if it's something you like by just standing there and looking at it."

He was right, of course. Lexi told Alex Anne this could be therapeutic. She was willing to try for that reason alone. "All right. I think I'm ready."

"Good," Lexi said. "The gun is a Glock 19. A lot of people say it's a girl's gun. It fits your hand well. There's no conventional safety. Just point, aim, and squeeze the trigger. We'll start you on the fifteen-yard target."

Alex Anne snickered as she stared at the man-shaped white paper target. "I'm not sure I could hit a barn at fifteen feet, let alone something so small three times farther away."

"Don't worry about being accurate right away. Get used to the gun. Feel the recoil in your arms and learn to live with it." Lexi slipped her clear plastic safety glasses on. "Exhale before you fire. Give it a try." In the next stall, Lexi lined up an identical target at the same distance. She exhaled a deep breath and fired. Alex Anne watched as her friend pulled the trigger at a steady rhythm until it looked like her gun broke. "When the slide locks back like this," Lexi said, "you're out of ammo." They both looked at the target. A bunch of bullet holes surrounded the paper man's heart and chest. Any of them could have been kill shots. Lexi had been forced to use her skills already, of course. Alex Anne wondered how her friend felt about even recreational shooting in the aftermath. If it bothered Lexi, she gave no sign.

"All right," Alex Anne said. "I won't be nearly so good, but I'll try." She spread her feet and tried to relax like Lexi's grandfather told her. The gun wasn't too heavy as she held it out. Alex Anne lined up the metal sights and focused on the target's center mass. She exhaled and pulled the trigger. The Glock barked in her hand, and the force of the shot sent it skyward. She held onto it, but it felt like someone much taller tried to snatch it away.

She'd missed the paper villain completely.

"Not bad for your first time," Lexi said. "Try squeezing the trigger faster. You can move your hand and wrist with the recoil once you get used to it. It'll take the edge off."

"All right." Alex Anne set herself again. She lined up the white outline. A breath left her lungs, and she fired. The gun kicked again, but she was ready for it, and it didn't feel so bad. A bullet hole punctured the target. She'd hit the faceless man in the forearm. "I'll take it."

"Good job," her friend said.

Alex Anne imagined the head of Farzaad Durrani, the sex trafficker who ordered and masterminded her abduction, atop the paper cutout. The terrified cries of her fellow captives played briefly in her mind. She felt a sneer curl her lip as she squeezed the trigger again and again. Alex Anne's hand shook as the gun fired its last bullet. Each time, she did a little better. A few holes surrounded the man's outline, but several dotted his arms and midsection. She envisioned Durrani or his hired man Josef shot in the gut and bleeding. It made her happier than she anticipated. "I think I'm starting to like this," she said as her friend clapped her on the back.

"I told you it's therapeutic," Lexi said.

"You're right." Lexi showed her how to eject the magazine —she chuckled when Alex Anne called it a clip—and pop in a fresh one. "They'll call an all clear in a couple minutes. We'll need to put our guns on the tables and point them downrange. Until then, though, try again."

Alex Anne looked at Zeke two stalls down. He held a rifle and took aim at a much more distant target. "You think I could try a bigger gun later?"

"Maybe next time," Lexi said. "You've gotta hit the seven-iron before you pick up the driver."

The golf metaphor sounded like something her dad would say, but it made sense. Besides, Alex Anne liked the Glock. She took a shooting stance, exhaled, and lined up the target again.

19

———

"I don't care how many times you've looked. You obviously missed something important." The senator seethed as he lectured the men who worked for him. "Gustav tells me you brought back a bunch of pictures, meaningless documents, and the teenaged boy's porn collection. None of it helps. I think Kacey hid something in the house. So far, she's not telling us anything." Donald looked down at the floor. "I don't know if she will. Let's make her cooperation irrelevant. Find whatever she's hiding there, and we don't need her anymore."

"We've been already," Edgar said. "Searched the place from top to bottom. We brought back whatever looked important."

"Doesn't matter. You haven't brought anything I need."

"Who says she has a physical backup?" Francis demanded. "Kid's young. She probably uses the cloud. Why don't you ask the geek to break into her Dropbox account instead of sending us on another wild goose chase?"

"Gustav has tried," Raburn said. "So far, he hasn't gotten in. Unlike a lot of people, this damn girl actually does security pretty well. No matter. She's thorough, and her boss is a little old school. He doesn't strike me as the type to trust online storage completely. Kacey isn't going to use a CD or DVD. Her computer probably doesn't even have the right drive anymore. You're looking for a flash drive."

Francis shrugged. "The cops have been there, too, you know. Maybe they already grabbed whatever we needed."

"They haven't. I'm on the law enforcement committee. I have many insights into what the various police agencies across this state do, and people in each are happy to give me information if I ask for it. The sheriff's office is still early in their investigation. They haven't recovered anything significant."

"We've been over the whole place," Edgar said.

"Main floor?" Raburn asked, and Edgar nodded. "Upstairs? Basement?" He bobbed his head again. "Is there an attic?"

"How the hell would I know?" Edgar turned up his hands. "Besides, you think a girl her age who lives with her pretty well-off parents is going into the attic or crawlspace?"

"I think she'll hide a flash drive where she thinks people are least likely to look for it. You two idiots are proving her point." Raburn pointed at Donald. "You go with them. You can't get the girl to talk. Maybe you can find what we need, and we don't need to deal with her anymore."

"Yes, sir," Donald said.

"Bring me back the drive," Raburn said.

IT TOOK A WHILE, but Stacy found a thread to pull on. She contemplated her home county, empty lots, her sister's work ethic, and the kinds of people she often targeted with her stories. Kacey loved exposing abuses of power and station.

She tackled this theme in every industry she could find it. Her favorite was always state government. Stacy smiled at a memory of her sister saying Annapolis sat on the water so the slime had an easy avenue of escape. "I think it's a senator," she said.

"Your sister's target?" Tyler asked.

"Yes. I don't know which one, and I'm not sure she'd even tell me before the story ran. She loved going after local politicians. Delegates often don't stick around long enough. The state senate is where people build careers . . . for better or worse."

"It's a start. Certainly narrows the pool."

"I think she was writing about corruption in our county," Stacy said. "Something regarding an empty lot." She shrugged. "I don't know more than that."

Tyler bobbed his head. "It might be enough to run with."

"I know where we can find out more." Stacy grinned, and Tyler winced.

"Negative. Going back to your house is a bad idea. Whoever we're up against already sent a hit squad twice. He could have someone there casing the place."

"If so, I'm sure you could take care of him."

"Even so." Tyler ran a hand through his short hair. Stacy remembered when it was solid dark brown, almost black. Now, spots and patches of gray intruded. It didn't make him look more distinguished. Instead, it lent an air of danger, and Stacy knew he could deliver on the promise. "It's easy to call in reinforcements." He paused. "Do you even know what we'd be looking for?"

"Not exactly," Stacy admitted. "Probably a flash drive. I can't see my sister using something else. She wouldn't trust online cloud storage by itself."

"I'm no tech wizard, but I know how small a flash drive is," Tyler said. "It's a big house. I'm sure our enemy has already checked the obvious places. Why do you think it would still be there?"

"It's not in an obvious place." Tyler didn't say anything. "We didn't live there originally. My parents had the place built when I was nine. It was one of the first houses finished in the community. We kept a punch list while they worked on the other homes. Did I tell you about the downstairs fire-place? One of the stones was loose. Kacey and I used to hide little messages to each other in there. It never got fixed. You can't tell anything is unusual when you look at it."

"All right." Tyler leaned forward on his bed. "Describe it to me."

"It's left of the fireplace itself. In the second row of tiles." Stacy closed her eyes and envisioned it. She and Kacey hadn't used it since her older sister went away to college. "Third from the end. There's a little bit of a pit under it. A few inches deep."

"Big enough to hide a flash drive."

"We need to get back there."

"It's risky." Tyler stood and paced the small room. "Even if no one who wants to kill us is there, the police could be. Your house was an active crime scene."

"I know," Stacy said through clenched teeth.

"I'm in a bind. I don't want to bring you with me, and I also don't want to leave you here. Both are bad."

"I can get the drive while you check out the house."

"You told me the hiding place. I don't need you to come along."

Stacy crossed her arms. "You're trying to keep me alive, right?"

"Yes," Tyler said.

"My chances are better with you than alone in a hotel room . . . even if you leave me a gun again." When Tyler again fell silent, she continued. "I'm going either way." She held up the burner phone and shook it. "This stupid thing won't take Uber, but I can get a cab."

"You're determined to go, aren't you?" Tyler stopped pacing and frowned. Stacy's response was a stare. Let the man have a little of his own medicine. "All right. If I can't talk you out of this, we'll try to do it as sensibly as we can. There's a lot more downside than upside. So here's how it's going to work. I'll get us a car. We'll drive up, not park near your place, execute our search, and leave. I don't want to spend one extra minute in the house. We're exposed the entire time we're there."

"All right," Stacy said. "Let's get what we need. Then, we'll find my sister."

20

Tyler did leave Stacy with the pistol again, but he planned only a brief outing. He would hotwire another car. With the warmer temperatures and melting today, they didn't need an SUV. Still, he would take what he could get. He left the hotel and walked about two-thirds of a mile to a shopping center parking lot. Piles of snow dotted the landscape. They would take a while to melt. A few people parked their vehicles near them. Tyler wanted to find something old enough to break into easily and not be trackable. He found a good target behind a small snow bank.

The white pile would serve to hide him from the stores in front of him. Tyler approached a Maxima from the late 'nineties. He walked around the perimeter. It was gray, a color which wouldn't stand out much. Automatic transmission. All four tires inflated. The car looked to be in good repair save for a few spots of rust on the trunk. Tyler took out the hanger he'd used to steal the Blazer the day before. A quick look around showed no one paying attention to him.

Within a few seconds, he sat behind the wheel. An equally short time later, he'd gotten the Nissan started. Tyler backed it out of the spot, left the shopping center, and returned to the hotel. He texted Stacy before pulling up, and she walked out of the side door a minute later. They got back on the road. This time, Tyler avoided the lot where he'd just snatched the Maxima. It took a couple extra minutes, but they soon picked up I-95 and drove toward Cecil County.

The Chaplains' neighborhood would be the issue. Only one road provided ingress and egress. There would be few places to hide from the cops or a hit squad. "You know any of your neighbors?" Tyler asked.

"All of them," Stacy said. "Why?"

"Any of them out of town?"

"I don't think so."

"Any yards we could cut across? I'd like to avoid parking near your house if I can help it."

"I think we can manage," Stacy said. "Stop at the first home. I'll take it from there."

"I still don't like this," Tyler said. He'd dressed for stealth in a black sweatshirt, dark blue jeans, and thin black gloves. Stacy's more colorful attire meant she'd be easier to spot, but at least the residents up here knew her. "It introduces a lot of risk. The reward is high if the flash drive is still there. I'm concerned someone might've found it already. It doesn't seem impossible to discover the loose stone by accident."

Stacy sighed. "It's not foolproof. We'll have to hope for the best. I don't know how we'll find my sister any other way." She paused and showed a small smile. "Our parents never found the spot."

"Or they never told you they did."

"Has Lexi ever called you a killjoy?" Stacy asked.

"She probably thinks it's my middle name," Tyler said.

He exited the highway a few minutes later. Snow and slush still lined both sides of the ramp, but road crews did an admirable job keeping the bulk of it clear. The Maxima provided a steady ride. Despite the car being over two decades old, the owner clearly took care of it. Tyler almost felt guilty for swiping it. Maybe he would have a chance to return it when all this was behind them.

They approached the community entrance. Tyler made a U-turn immediately before the development's lone road and eased the car to a stop on the snowy shoulder. "We're getting out here?" Stacy wanted to know.

Tyler nodded. "It's a little more of a walk, but it makes our presence less obvious. What if the goon squad comes back, and they happened to notice the car parked in a driveway which had been empty before?"

"I don't know how likely that is."

"Probably not very," Tyler admitted. "If it happens, though, it introduces more risk. They might be ready for us. They might call in another team and surround the house. I'm trying to keep the upside above the downside here."

"All right." Stacy sighed and opened her door. The snow crunched under their feet. Tyler used trees to help him up the small hill leading into the community, and Stacy did the same. They emerged onto a narrow patch of grass. Stacy pointed at the first house. "There's the one I wanted to use. We can get into their backyard and make our way to my house. I doubt anyone would see us."

Tyler scanned the road and the area they'd just left. No people or cars. He stayed low and dashed across the street. His shoe slipped a bit on an icy patch, but he maintained his balance and kept going. Soon, they crouched inside a yard surrounded by a white wooden fence. It looked to be five feet high. Easy to hide by keeping low. "I don't see anyone," he whispered. Tyler drew his pistol and led the way through the gate. They crunched through crusted snow behind other fences. The sounds would normally be a cause for concern, but no one seemed to notice them. Soon, Stacy opened the gate to her yard, and they slipped inside.

"Lot of police tape," Stacy said in a hushed tone. She was right. It covered the perimeter of the rear door and also formed a giant X on the diagonals. The entrance from the deck to the yard featured two rows blocking it off.

"It's easy enough to cut," Tyler said. "Give me your key. I'll go first." Stacy handed him her keyring with a trembling hand. Tyler tried to give her a reassuring smile. "It's all right. We'll be in and out quickly." Her demeanor seemed unchanged. Pep talks and most soft skills weren't in his wheelhouse, and this served as the latest reminder. Tyler stepped over the tape onto the deck. He cut the yellow plastic around the door and tried the key. Gun back in hand, he moved slowly inside.

The place had been ransacked. A combination of people looking for the flash drive and the police searching the rooms, Tyler figured. Even with divergent goals, both groups worked similarly. Cops executing a search warrant or investigating a multiple murder left equally as big a mess as a hit crew desperate to find a missing device. Tyler cleared the kitchen and the rest of the first floor. He did the same upstairs where the mess persisted. If anything, it was somehow worse. Turning out someone's bedroom always felt like an invasion of privacy. The Chaplains being dead did little to soothe Tyler's unease.

The lower level was similarly empty of people trying to kill them. Tyler sent a quick text to Stacy, and her footfalls descended the steps a minute later. "Did you find it?" she said.

Tyler shook his head. "I didn't want to steal your thunder. It was your idea. You should be the one to do it."

Stacy walked up to the fireplace. She dropped to her knees and ran a hand over the tiled stones. A tear slid down her cheek as her fingers dug in under the balky one and lifted it. Her hand disappeared inside and emerged a second later holding a small black flash drive. She replaced the stone and stood. "We got it. Now, we just need a computer."

"We need to get out of here first," Tyler said. "There are a few steps before we find something to plug the drive into."

They walked back up the steps. Stacy moved ahead of Tyler and surveyed the scene. Her head wagged from side to side as she took it all in. "I can't believe this is my house," she said in a pained whisper.

"It will be again," Tyler told her.

Stacy started to say something but stopped. "There's an SUV outside."

"Shit. Get down." She sank to all fours as Tyler approached the front window. He peeked out the gap in the curtains. Three men dashed up the driveway. They were talking but not loudly enough for him to hear. These guys were dressed just like the first crew. If they were smart, one assailant would cover the back and cut off their escape there. Even if they left via the walkout basement, he could shoot them from the deck above.

"Give me the flash drive," Tyler said. When Stacy frowned, he added, "The worst-case scenario is they kill me and take you. This way, they don't also get the drive." He held out his hand, and she placed the drive in it. Tyler dropped it down the front of his pants. "No guy will search there. Now, go upstairs and hide in a bedroom . . . not yours. Stay up there until I come and get you."

"But—"

"Go." She did. Tyler moved into the dining room as he heard someone work on the front door lock.

Donald felt this whole excursion was futile. Edgar and Francis thought so, too, but they remained quiet about it. Collecting a check was more important to them than questioning the validity of the work. Donald would do the job. He was being paid well for it after all, and the rote search of a house came in well below waterboarding when evaluating the crimes they'd all committed.

As they approached The Manors of Rock Run, a gray Maxima sat on the opposite shoulder. No snow covered it. Donald slowed to get a better look. The Nissan made fresh tire tracks going in, but it was empty. Why would someone park a car there? Did it break down? "Looks like an old model," Edgar said from the passenger's seat. "I wouldn't worry about it."

"I guess," Donald said, though he wondered how recently the Maxima assumed its current spot. Did the girl and her savior come back? Being too suspicious wouldn't help the team. Donald steered the Suburban up the road. Lingering snow and slush crackled under the tires. The street needed another plowing or a couple days of solid melting to be clear again. He guided the Suburban to a stop in its original tire tracks.

The three men got out and locked the SUV. As they approached the driveway, Francis said, "Someone's inside. I think it's the girl."

"Shit," Donald muttered.

"She's gone now." They moved faster. "I think the guy's with her."

"Gives us a chance to kill both of them," Edgar pointed out as they put their backs to the garage. "Raburn will give us a nice bonus."

"One problem at a time," Donald said. "Remember, this asshole took out alpha team by himself."

"Let's go quickly, then," Francis said. "I'll cover the back.

You two go in the front. We're better than alpha team. Let's prove it."

Donald nodded. "All right." Francis sprinted toward the rear of the house. Edgar produced a snap gun. Donald kept his pistol trained on the front door as Edgar went to work on it.

21

E dgar's snap gun bypassed the lock quickly. Donald heard his own pulse in his ears. This was supposed to be a simple operation if a pointless one. Search the entire house for a flash drive which may or may not still be inside. They weren't supposed to encounter anyone else. County deputies had come and gone. The younger sister showing up here was an unexpected bonus, but her driver and protector being with her dampened any enthusiasm Donald could muster.

"I'm in," Francis' voice said in his earpiece. "I'm coming in via the basement." A different tactic, and it might be helpful in catching John Tyler off-guard. Edgar nudged the front door open. Donald stayed low and moved in first, sweeping the entryway with his pistol. All the lights in the area were off, though a little sun made it past the windows and curtains. As he and Edgar slowly advanced, Donald realized the place looked the same as when he last came.

They cleared the living room. Other than their own quiet movements, Donald couldn't hear anything. The girl, wherever she was, didn't make a sound. Neither did Tyler, but this was to be expected. They knew his background, and alpha team already made the mistake of underestimating him. "Lower level is clear so far," Francis whispered over the comms. Donald didn't want to answer and give away their location.

Edgar moved first toward the dining room and kitchen. He crouched at the corner and leaned around. A single gunshot blew his head apart, and his lifeless body sagged to the floor. Donald backed up and put down a volley of suppressing fire as he retreated to the stairs. "What's going on?" Francis demanded. He kept his voice quiet, but Donald heard the urgency.

"Edgar's down," Donald replied. He heard soft footfalls approaching. Getting the drop on a man like Tyler seemed impossible . . . at least by himself. "Francis, I need a distraction." Donald barely heard his own voice. He hoped it came across in the other man's earpiece. "We have to do this together."

No reply came. Donald saw a distorted reflection of Tyler in a vase. It was impossible to judge his position based on it, but he'd probably emerged from the dining room and edged his way into the main area. Donald took a deep breath and readied himself for the confrontation. Tyler would take his time. He knew the layout of the house by now, and he'd be expecting two more men. Another footstep drew nearer.

Then, Donald heard a clattering sound from the basement.

The advancing footfalls stopped and moved in the opposite direction. "All right," Francis said, "he knows I'm down here now. I'm going to try and get up the stairs before he makes it. Be ready to back me up."

Donald didn't care for the plan, but they didn't have time to debate it. "Roger," he said, holding his position. When he could no longer hear Tyler move, he stepped out from the staircase and padded toward the dining room. The entrance to the basement lay off the kitchen. If Francis could gain a good position before Tyler opened the door, the two of them might be able to take him out. It was a risky proposition, but they weren't getting a better opportunity any time soon. Their adversary was cautious. He would take his time getting into position.

It was something they could use against him.

Donald crept across the dining room toward the arch leading into the kitchen. He held position there. Tyler was good. Donald couldn't even hear him moving across the tiled floor. He turned his head away and whispered, "He's closing in." A couple seconds later, he risked a quick peek into the other room. Tyler stood at the door to the basement. He didn't give any indication he knew Donald watched. The retired soldier stood to the side of the door and opened it.

A gunshot barked, and a bullet slammed into a cabinet.

Tyler disappeared inside the door. Donald followed. He heard the telltale sounds of a struggle and quickened his pace. The entry remained open. Francis and Tyler grappled near the top of the steps. Both their guns had already fallen down about halfway. Tyler turned as Donald filled the doorway and brought his pistol to bear. Despite being engaged with Francis, the man managed to sweep his arm out, knocking Donald's hand high and wide. His shot blasted a hole in the ceiling, and the report rang in his ears. Tyler flinched, too, and Francis capitalized by elbowing him in the head.

Donald kicked him in the chest, knocking him down all the steps and onto the floor below.

"I'm glad you showed up when you did," Francis said, gulping large breaths. "Otherwise, I might be down there." He moved past Donald. Tyler lay on the basement floor clutching his knee, his face twisted in pain. Donald took a shot, but he missed. Tyler rolled to his left. Two more bullets followed him before Donald lost sight of the ex-army guy.

"He's injured," Donald said to the panting Francis. "Let's finish him off."

Francis shook his head. "Screw him. We should get the girl."

Donald nodded his agreement, and the two sprinted through the house and up to the second level. They found the girl in her brother's bedroom. She stared at them with wide eyes as they walked in. "You're coming with us," Francis said. "Make it easy on yourself."

"Go to hell," Stacy said. She tried to run between them, but Francis kneed her in the midsection when she approached. When the girl bent in half, Donald shoved her to the ground. Francis knelt over her and punched her hard in the face. Two more hammer blows knocked her out. They picked her up and carried her downstairs.

"I'll back the car up," Francis said. He was smaller than Donald, who could carry the young woman on his shoulder with ease. Francis reversed the Suburban up the driveway. Donald checked for nosy neighbors before moving as quickly as he could to the SUV. He tossed the unconscious girl in the back and climbed in the passenger's seat.

"I still think we should've gone downstairs and killed Tyler," Donald said. "For Edgar."

"I have a better idea," Francis said. "Stranger in the house. Girl missing. Dead guy inside." He grinned. "I'm sure the county cops would love to hear all about it."

As they drove out of the community, Francis dialed 9-1-1.

22

Tyler tried flexing his knee, and it hurt more each time. The gunshots from above thankfully missed. If the two guys chose to come down and finish him off, he didn't know how much resistance he could've offered. Footsteps moved around upstairs. He tried to stand but fell over again. Tyler crawled closer to the living room furniture. He used the side of the couch to pull himself to his feet.

His knee could take little of his weight, so he limped to the steps. Tyler grimaced, took a deep breath, and painfully scaled the stairs. He picked up his own pistol and another along the way. Despite moving with a severe limp, he cleared the main level. The footfalls he heard a couple minutes before must have been the two surviving assailants leaving. Their SUV no longer sat in front of the house.

It meant they probably took Stacy with them. Tyler needed to check on her to be sure. He grabbed the railing and hauled himself up each step until he reached the top story. Stacy wasn't anywhere to be found. Fresh drops of blood marred the carpet in her brother's room. She must have hidden here and been hauled away. Tyler scanned the area for anything useful. A lot of soccer trophies sat on two sturdy shelves. Team photos hung on the walls. Stacy's brother wore a heavy knee brace in one of them. Tyler searched the closet and found it.

It would cover his leg from the lower thigh to the upper shin. Metal sides helped with support and stability. He'd seen football players and wrestlers wear similar models. The brace fit well with a little adjustment. Tyler flexed his leg and found he could move a little easier with the extra support it provided. Lights outside caught his eye. He peeked out of the blinds and saw three county police cars pulling up in front of the house. "Shit."

Tyler limped into a different bedroom, this one facing the rear of the property. A deputy emerged from behind the garage. He couldn't get out the front or back. The cops would be very interested in the dead body on the main level. No way even a trained operative could sneak past them. "Shit, shit, shit," Tyler muttered as he moved between rooms. The smallest bedroom held what he wanted: a door to the attic.

It was the least bad option. The police and forensic teams would be here a while, and Tyler would need to hide up there the whole time. He'd also have no way of knowing when they actually left. The clock ran short, however. He pulled the rope, and the two-part ladder dropped down. Tyler extended it and climbed as quickly as he could with his balky knee. From above, he pulled the apparatus back into place, closing the door again.

If the police were thorough, they might also pull the cord and try to gain access. He couldn't let it happen. Tyler moved quietly, trying to walk on the thick wooden beams to keep the noise down. The Chaplains used their attic for additional storage. Tyler employed the faint light of his phone screen to find a length of string tying a bunch of old college course catalogs into a pile. He undid it and used it to bind the two parts of the ladder together. His father taught him how to make good knots. No one pulling from below would be able to extend the steps. Tyler had to hope it would be enough to discourage a curious deputy from coming up.

He settled into a spot where he could keep an eye on the door to the house but be out of sight of someone trying to peer into the darkness. A little bit of light came in via a small window facing the street. From below, Tyler heard people moving around and a bunch of indistinct chatter. He held his position. Patience was a virtue Tyler tried to instill in young soldiers. Some of them listened. Others didn't. The ones who heeded his advice tended to survive more often than those who ignored it.

It took over an hour, but someone finally approached Tyler's position. He heard a deputy moving around the room. "I have an attic entrance here," he said.

"Copy," came a reply.

"I doubt anyone's up there, but I'm going to have a look."

TYLER FROZE. If the deputy pulled the access panel, he wouldn't be able to deploy the ladder. This alone may not prevent him from coming up. It would take more effort, however, and Tyler hoped he would categorize the stairs as nonfunctional and move along. Light poured in from below as the small door opened. Sure enough, wood clattered as the deputy tried to pull the ladder to its full length. Tyler tied a good knot. Now, he needed the string itself to be strong enough.

The deputy yanked a few more times. Tyler readied himself for the man to climb up anyway. After another futile moment, he said, "Looks like it's inaccessible. Ladder's broken. I don't think anyone could make it up here."

"Roger that," another male voice replied.

Tyler let out the breath he'd been holding when the panel returned to its normal position and darkness prevailed. Outside, an engine fired to life and drove away. Tyler scooted closer to the window, kept his body below it, and peeked over the bottom pane. One police car left the scene. Three others remained along with a white forensics van. Tyler inched away from the window and flexed his knee, which stiffened the longer he remained up here. He resumed waiting. No one else tried to gain access to the attic.

After another half-hour, a second police car left the property. The third accompanied the white forensics van about twenty minutes later. One vehicle remained. From his vantage point, Tyler couldn't tell if anyone sat inside it, and he didn't want to run the risk of exposing his position to get a better look. He scooted closer to the attic entrance and listened. Nothing. He gave it another ten minutes before easing the access door down. Thankfully, it didn't squeak.

Tyler kept the string in place. He climbed down half the ladder, hung from the bottom rung, and dropped a foot to the floor, landing on his good leg. If a deputy remained in the house, he or she was nowhere to be seen. Tyler crept down the main stairs. He hugged the wall at the bottom, peering in both directions. The coast was clear. If someone remained in the car, they were probably sitting on the house to see if anyone returned. Tyler kept low and padded into the kitchen.

The coroner took the body on the main level away. One more down. Tyler hoped he would be able to make these losses count, but he needed to find Stacy and her sister. He went down to the basement. No one waited for him there, either. Tyler slipped out the back door, moved across the yard at a crouch, and slid the gate open barely wide enough to slither through. He closed it behind himself and reversed the course he and Stacy took a few hours ago.

Navigating the hill back to the Maxima on a balky knee proved a challenge. Tyler took it slowly and used trees to support himself. As he approached the car, he bit off a curse. Someone cut both tires he could see. He looked at the other side and found them slashed, as well. The clock ticked on Stacy and Kacey, and Tyler couldn't afford this setback.

Maintaining radio silence would have been his preference, but the situation no longer supported this. He took out his burner phone.

LEXI'S PHONE vibrated on her grandfather's kitchen table. She looked at the number—her dad's burner. He would only call if he needed something important, and this didn't bode well for Stacy. She answered with a lump in her throat. "What's up?"

"Stacy and I went back to her house to find something," he said.

"You what?"

"I tried to talk her out of it. She's almost as stubborn as you are."

"Dad, what happened to Stacy?"

"They took her. I got tossed down the stairs and hurt my knee. I have what we came for, though, and I think it'll be useful."

"You all right?" Lexi asked.

"I'll be fine," her dad said. "Let's focus on the people who are missing."

"What do you need?"

"Transport out of here for starters," he said. "They cut the tires on the car I . . . uh, borrowed."

"Why don't you come to Grandpa's? It's not a terrible drive from there, and this is a pretty secure location."

"Good call. I only have this basic phone, though. No Uber or anything. I'll need you to book me a ride."

"Where are you?" He gave her the address of the first house in the community. "All right," Lexi said. "I'll feel three times my age, but I'll call you a cab."

"Tell them to hurry," her dad said. "I'll pay extra. Still have cash from before."

"Will do." She hung up and searched for taxi companies servicing Cecil County and Bel Air. A few choices filled her screen, and she dialed the one with the highest rating. A short conversation got her dad a ride. She sent him a text. *Chesapeake Taxi, 10 minutes.* He replied with a quick confirmation.

"My dad's coming," she said when her grandfather walked back into the room.

"You're awfully popular today," he said.

"Stick with me, Grandpa. I'll up your social game in no time."

The old man snorted. "Definitely something I don't need at my age."

Alex Anne chuckled from the living room. "You all are certainly an interesting family."

Lexi smiled at her friend's observation. "You have no idea."

23

———

Stacy woke up and felt herself getting bounced around. It took a second for the cobwebs to clear. She'd convinced Tyler to return to her house to look for the flash drive. She gave it to him when an SUV rolled up, and she hid in her brother's room. Soon, a couple of men barged in and beat her. Was Tyler dead? She'd feel awful for Lexi. As consciousness returned, Stacy realized she lay in the very back of an SUV, and she could barely move. Ropes covered her wrists and lower legs, but she must have been tied down to something she couldn't see.

Stacy did the first thing she could think of: she screamed.

"Shut up," a man said from the front. She screamed again. "I told you to shut up. Don't make it any harder on yourself."

Rather than work against the rope, Stacy stopped struggling. She scooted toward the side wall, and the slack in her bonds allowed her to almost sit up. She could see over the rear seat, at least. One man drove the SUV, and another sat in the passenger's seat. It was hard to tell from the backs of their heads, but she reasoned they were the same two who grabbed her a short while ago. They'd come with three, though. "How's your friend?" she asked in a taunting tone. "That's what . . . four dead now?"

"You're very annoying," the driver said. His voice matched the one who'd told her to shut up.

"And you might be on borrowed time."

The passenger scoffed. "We're not worried. The guy protecting you is dead."

Stacy's heart sank. She'd hoped they managed to overpower Tyler but left him alive in their haste to grab her and leave. Another girl would be without a father. How could she face Lexi after something like this? Tyler had only tried to help, and in doing so, got himself killed. She couldn't let these two assholes see how it affected her, though. Being meek and submissive wasn't going to keep her alive. "I don't believe you," she said with as much defiance as she could muster.

"Believe what you want."

"You're still down four friends."

"Coworkers," the driver said. "We didn't even know their real names. Let's not pretend we were all on the same bowling team."

Stacy lapsed into silence. She wondered if anyone would see her sitting up in the rear of an SUV and be concerned enough to call the police. A glance around them told her it was unlikely. Everything outside looked darker than it should have been. Tinted windows. They also traveled a narrow county road partially covered by lingering snow and slush, so the odds of seeing other vehicles were small.

After a few minutes, the SUV drove up a long driveway toward a large manor. The house was three stories tall, and trees covered much of the right side of the property. Even in a rural county, an estate like this would cost a lot of money. Whoever ordered Stacy and her sister kidnapped must have been rich. It made sense. Kacey targeted powerful people, and they were the ones with the big bank accounts. A garage door at the rear of the building slid open, and the driver steered the large vehicle inside.

The two men up front got out. The larger one held Stacy in place while the smaller man—who still looked like he could've played football in college—undid the rope anchoring her. Her hands and feet remained bound. The big guy then carried her over his shoulder. Despite her struggles, she couldn't wriggle out of his grip. They walked into the house and down a flight of stairs. Stacy bonked her head when the man made a turn at the bottom. He didn't apologize. She figured he did it on purpose.

The other guy opened a door. Kacey shot to her feet and stared with wide eyes. The large man dropped Stacy into a chair and sliced her bonds with a sharp folding knife. Kacey hugged her younger sister as the two hired goons left the small room. Stacy cried as she squeezed Kacey tightly. "I didn't think I'd ever see you again."

"Me, either," the older sister said, her voice cracking.

"Where the hell are we?" Stacy looked around. Gray stone walls marked the borders of their space, which might have measured twelve feet per side. It was about the size of an average second or third bedroom. Instead of a closet, however, this room featured a couple basic metal folding chairs, a large sink, and a set of storage shelves. A drain in the floor marked the approximate center, and the area around it still looked wet. "What do they do in here?"

"You don't want to know." Kacey leaned close to Stacy and whispered in her ear. "They might be watching or listening."

The two pulled apart. "Who's doing all this?" Stacy asked. She didn't care if someone saw or heard what she said. Spying on a couple of women didn't even crack the list of the worst things the mastermind could have done.

"Richard Raburn." Kacey scowled when she said the

name. "He's a state senator. Wants to be something bigger, and he thinks my article could hurt him . . . which it probably can."

"All this over something you wrote? Our family is dead."

Kacey nodded. "I know. It's hard to believe how far some fragile men will go." Her voice grew louder as she talked. If Richard Raburn were listening, he'd certainly get an earful.

Stacy dropped onto one of the chairs. It felt like sitting on a rock. "What's our plan to get out of here?"

"We don't have one," Kacey said. "Raburn's already waterboarded me twice." She put up a hand when Stacy started to speak. "I'll live. I'm not giving him what he wants." Kacey sat beside her younger sister and leaned close enough to whisper again. "How have you survived this long?"

"Lexi's dad. He drove me from the airport and was there when three guys circled back for me. He took out another earlier." She paused and sighed. "It's sad, but I think they got him."

"They told you he was dead?"

"Yeah," Stacy said. "I feel awful."

"These guy are all assholes and liars," Kacey said. "I'm not sure I'd believe them."

"If he's alive, he's going to keep looking for us."

Kacey mustered a smile. "Let's hope he is, then."

IT TOOK LONGER than ten minutes for the cab to come. After fifteen, Tyler grew antsy. He hated running into delays while the clock ticked for Stacy and Kacey. He was about to take out his phone and tell Lexi to scrap the whole thing when a silver Camry with a Chesapeake Taxi logo on its side pulled to the curb. Tyler climbed into the back and slammed the door. "You're late."

"Sorry, sir," the slender Asian man behind the wheel said. "Roads are still rough in a few spots." He pulled back onto the road.

"You have the address where I'm going?" Tyler asked.

"Yes."

"Good. Drive fast to make up for the delay, and I'll tip well. In cash."

The guy nodded in the rearview. The Camry rode on a good front-wheel drive platform, and the driver fed it enough gas to make the ride interesting in a few spots. Still, he made it out of Cecil and into Harford County quickly. As they approached Zeke's community, Tyler spotted a convenience store on the corner. "Pull in there," he said. "Wait for me. I won't be long."

"The meter will be running," the driver pointed out.

Tyler got out and limped into the shop. Moving around made his knee feel a little better, but even with the brace, it was at way less than a hundred percent. Whatever. It would need to be enough. He snagged the last pack of disinfectant wipes, paid, and got back into the cab. The ride to Evergreen Acres took only a few minutes. Tyler did the talking at the security checkpoint, showed his ID, and the cab drove to the front of Zeke's building.

"Twenty-six dollars, sir," the driver said, switching the meter off.

"Sure." Tyler opened the package of wipes and ran one over the rear of the passenger's seat and any surfaces on the door he might have touched.

The driver frowned at him. "I appreciate it, but you don't need to clean the car for me."

"I'm doing it for both of us." Tyler handed the man four twenties. "Keep the change. You never saw me if anyone asks."

"Who might ask?"

"The kind of people you don't want to answer." Tyler opened the door, climbed out, and wiped down the rest of the interior and his seat. "You a good poker player?"

"I do all right."

"Good. You should be fine, then. Thanks for the lift." Tyler closed the door and walked into the building. He took the elevator to Zeke's floor and knocked on the door a moment later. The old man opened up.

"I was wondering when you'd make it."

"Cab was late," Tyler said. "Plus, I didn't want to leave a trace." He tossed the package of wipes onto his father's bare coffee table.

Zeke grimaced. "Your daughter has been waiting for you. Her friend, too."

"Her friend?"

As if on cue, Lexi and Alex Anne walked into the living room. The singer closed the distance to Tyler at a run and hugged him. "Good to see you."

"You, too," he said. "How have you been?"

"Getting by a day at a time."

"How's therapy?"

"Some sessions are harder than others. You were right . . . it's worth it."

"Good." He smiled and patted her shoulder.

"We need to get Stacy and her sister," Lexi said, quashing the brief reunion.

"I have the flash drive her abductors are looking for," Tyler said. "Get the Patriot laptop, and we'll see what it holds."

24

"And at what point did you think putting the drive down your pants was a good idea?" Lexi grimaced as she looked at the small black device.

"When we noticed three men advancing on the house," Tyler said. His laptop sat on the coffee table. He, Lexi, and Alex Anne all shared Zeke's couch. Other than the furniture and a TV, the living room was the most spartan Tyler ever saw. "Even if they got me, a bunch of macho guys like them wouldn't put their hand in another man's shorts."

"Gross, Dad."

"Maybe, but I'm right," Tyler said. "Besides, I already cleaned it with one of those wipes."

"Not enough." Lexi wrinkled her nose. "Never enough. It touched your junk."

"I'm not a leper for Christ's sake." Tyler picked up the device, pushed the ebony switch on the side with his thumb, and extended the USB connector. He popped it into a port while Lexi continued looking at the drive as if it dripped poison. "There." He waved his hand at the computer. "Do your magic."

Lexi and Alex Anne shared a giggle. "You probably do think it's sorcery," his daughter said.

"More like witchcraft," Zeke said from his recliner.

"How's your knee?" Lexi asked while she opened the Windows control panel.

"So-so." Tyler flexed it. The outline of the brace remained visible past his black jeans. He'd need to wear it for a while despite the unusual feeling of his pants fitting tighter on one side. The extra support mattered. "Been a while since I took the express route down a flight of stairs." He looked at the screen again. "I thought this thing ran Linux."

"Virtual machine. For basic things like this, I think Windows is easier." Tyler offered a nod as if he understood any of what his daughter told him.

"You're lucky they didn't finish you off," his father said.

"I probably am." They'd tried, at least. The first bullet came the closest. Whoever fired wasn't a very good shot.

Zeke whistled a tune. Tyler soon recognized it as "Anchors Aweigh," and he rolled his eyes. "Shoulda taken someone from the navy with you. We're used to helping the army out of tough spots."

"Do you think Stacy's still alive?" Lexi asked.

"I don't know," Tyler said, glad to talk about anything other than his father's barb. "My guess is yes. Whoever took her wants Kacey to talk, and maybe the idea is her younger sister provides some incentive. He doesn't need them both alive long-term. So long as Kacey holds out, I think they're both okay."

Lexi's phone rang. She picked it up long enough to see the number, muted it, and set it down again. "I've got the flash drive setup." She double-clicked on its entry in Windows Explorer. Another folder appeared along with a text document. Lexi tried the folder first, but it produced another box asking for a password. "Any idea, Dad?"

"None."

She tried the text file next. Its contents displayed without incident.

The LAST NAME of the target opens the folder.

"I take it we don't know who this is?" Lexi said.

Tyler shook his head. "I'd been trying to get it out of Stacy, but she was in the dark, too."

"If we want to get Stacy and Kacey back alive, we need to come up with it."

"Yeah, I know," Tyler said.

"Two girls, Richard. We don't need them both."

"I'm aware." Despite Raburn's agreement, the hard expression on his wife's face didn't ease. Miriam remained a beautiful woman in her forties, but when determination mixed with ambition, it made her look angry and severe.

"What are you going to do about this?"

"One of them knows," he said. "Probably both. Now, we have two people to get information from. If Kacey won't tell us, maybe seeing her younger sister get tortured will give her some motivation."

"It had better," Miriam said. Her palm slapped the arm of the beige leather sofa for emphasis. "We need to know everything she knows. Everyone she talked to. Maybe you should have the men bring in her editor."

Raburn extended the matching recliner. They didn't use the sitting room much, but it made for a nice spot to go over their plans without the hired men listening in. "Let's not get ahead of ourselves. She may not have told him anything yet. I'm not adding to the body count unnecessarily."

Miriam narrowed her eyes. "You and I don't always agree

on what's necessary." When Raburn didn't say anything, she continued. "What about the man at the house?"

"He was injured. Donald and Francis thought the girl was the higher-value target, so they brought her. I think it was the right call."

"They left him alive, though," Miriam said. "He's taken out four of our men so far. Don't worry. I've already informed the company we need more."

Raburn sighed. "I don't always agree with your bloodlust."

"You know I'm right."

"Maybe," Raburn said. "Getting a few more guys was a good call at least. We have no idea if this John Tyler even knows anything."

"If he does, he's going to come for you." Miriam jabbed her finger at her husband. "For us."

Raburn snickered and spread his hands. "You think he'd have any success trying for us here? Come on. The man may be skilled, but he's not making it to the front door."

"Have we checked his house?"

"Yes." Raburn bobbed his head. "Empty."

"I hope you're right," Miriam said. "Let's get the girls to talk quickly. Then, it won't matter. We can be done with them both." She paused and sneered. Another expression which twisted her pretty face into something ugly. "Unless you don't agree with my bloodlust again."

"In this case, I do," Raburn said.

"WE NEED to use whatever Stacy told you, Dad."

Lexi sat with her fingers hovering over the keys. Her right knee bounced. With Stacy now gone, too, it became personal for Lexi. Tyler understood the feelings and the nerves all too well, but he also knew talking her down wasn't in his wheelhouse. "I'm not sure it's a lot to go on," he said, "but we can try. The last time we talked about this whole mess, she told me she was sure it was a Maryland state senator."

"Good. That narrows it down . . . to . . . " Lexi trailed off.

"Forty-seven." Tyler smirked. "How much am I over-paying for your college? Do they still teach political science?"

"Yeah, yeah." Lexi opened a browser, and it displayed a list of Maryland's senators—forty-six and one recent vacancy due to illness—a few seconds later. She scrolled through the names and pictures. "It's hard to believe one of these people killed my friend's family."

Tyler recognized a few of the names. He'd even voted for one of them. "Politicians are just like anyone else, Lexi. Some good . . . others bad . . . a few willing to kill for what they want."

"Any of the names jump out at you?" she wanted to know.

"Some but only because I've heard of them before. None in context with what we want."

Lexi sighed. Her knee bobbed up and down again. "Did Stacy tell you anything else?"

"A few things." Tyler searched his memory. The young woman gave him information in fits and starts. She didn't know much, and she'd undergone a huge trauma. He couldn't fault her. "Something about a vacant lot in Cecil County."

Lexi frowned. "That's it?"

Tyler spread his hands. "What was I supposed to do? Interrogate a girl who yesterday saw most of her family dead?"

"No, no." Lexi stared at the screen. "Of course not. It's not much to go on is all."

"People only care about vacant lots if they were supposed

to be something else," Tyler said. "Maybe it was a failed development project or just a crappy land deal."

"Seems pretty frivolous to murder and kidnap over it."

"People get killed for less." Tyler shrugged. "Every day. If you can find anything about empty lots up there, it will help us reduce the pool from forty-six."

"I'm on it," Lexi said. She ejected the flash drive, closed Windows, and returned to a Linux prompt. "Easier to do on the main OS."

"Like I always say."

Lexi grinned and rolled her eyes as she worked. Tyler understood the basics of what the former Patriot Security laptop could do, but the red team guys who developed it gave it a lot of capabilities he didn't even begin to grasp. Lexi picked it all up very well, and she'd used the computer to help him out a few times. "I wish your internet was a little faster, Grandpa."

Zeke harrumphed. "Comes with the apartment. I don't need anything else."

After a couple more minutes of typing and searching, Lexi said, "I might have something. Several years ago, a bunch of people invested in a lot which was supposed to be developed. It never happened."

"Who was in charge of it?" Tyler asked.

"Miriam Nicholls."

He frowned. "Name's not familiar."

"No, it isn't," Lexi said. "She's not a senator or affiliated with the state government in a meaningful way. Nicholls is her maiden name. She's the wife of Richard Raburn. He's been in the senate for years, and he's on a bunch of committees, including law enforcement."

"He might be the one. His position could give him influence over the police. Easy to quash an investigation when your hands are on the checkbook."

Lexi switched to another tab on the browser. "There are rumors he has designs on higher office, too. Like in DC."

"Keeping a bunch of money from a shady land deal could help the coffers," Tyler said. "Put the drive back in. I think Raburn is our best chance."

25

The LAST NAME *of the target opens the folder.*

Lexi and Tyler looked at the contents of the text file again. Her fingers hovered over the keys. "I guess Kacey wanted the name in all caps."

"I agree." She double-clicked on the folder. The password box appeared again. Lexi typed *RABURN* and pressed Enter. The directory opened. Tyler clapped his hands loudly, causing Lexi to jump and the computer to fall onto the plain gray rug covering much of the living room floor. "Sorry, kiddo."

"It's all good." She picked it up and set it atop her lap again. "Maybe a little warning if you're going to make noise so close to me."

"Sure," he said. It was unusual for Lexi to be so jumpy. The past couple months had been hard for everyone, but her more than most. The traffickers Tyler went up against to save Alex Anne also targeted his daughter, and she'd been forced to pull the trigger a few times to save herself. She talked to a therapist on a regular schedule—something Tyler encouraged her to do—but needed time to process everything. Her best friend being kidnapped would only add to her stress. "Can we make copies of this?"

"If we have something else to put all these files on," Lexi said. "Grandpa, do you have a flash drive?"

"A what?" Zeke said. Lexi turned up her hands.

"I have one," Alex Anne said. "You never know when you might need to record some music and take it with you. Hang on." She dug around in her bookbag and produced a hot pink model.

"Pink," Lexi commented with a grin as she accepted it. "So much for not being a pop princess anymore."

Alex Anne chuckled. "My dad bought it for me. You can delete whatever's on there. It's old material by now."

Lexi connected the colorful drive, wiped its contents, and formatted it. Tyler actually understood what she did. He'd done similar work with floppies years ago in the army during the heyday of MS-DOS. It might have been the last time he really understood how computers worked. "Will the files be encrypted after you make duplicates?" he asked.

"Yes," Lexi said. "Otherwise, it would be really easy to get around. We might be able to change the password on the other drive. We could decrypt them if you think there's value in it. Might make it easier if someone else needs to see them."

Tyler bobbed his head. "Let's do it. We need to get a copy circulating." He looked at the contents of the Raburn folder. Dozens of files and subdirectories filled the screen. "Lots to go through, though. Maybe we can split it up. Dad, you still have a computer?"

"Sure," Zeke said, "for all the good the blasted thing does. It's in my bedroom."

A couple minutes later, Lexi handed Tyler the pink flash drive. "Of course," he said as he watched her amused smile. "I'll start from the bottom and work up." He took it down the hall to his father's bedroom. He'd never been in this part of

Zeke's unit before. The last time he'd been in the old man's bedroom came after Tyler bought the house he currently lived in from his father a decade ago. It felt strange to walk into it. Like he was a kid sneaking in while his parents were away.

The computer was a desktop model from several years ago which sat on the floor under a small desk. A monitor—thankfully a flat screen—keyboard, and mouse took up most of the surface area. Tyler powered the old PC on and looked around the room. Zeke left all his furniture behind when he moved from the Baltimore house. Tyler kept some of it but donated the majority. His mother had picked it out years ago. Here, everything fit his father's simple tastes. Plain white paint on the walls. Medium brown for the dressers and bed frame. Even the little desk matched.

While Windows loaded, Tyler got up and limped to the long chest of drawers. Four large photo frames sat in the middle of it. The first was of Zeke and Tyler's mother on their wedding day over fifty years ago. Beside it was their twenty-fifth anniversary picture. It was the last major milestone she'd live to see. His father's last official photo from the navy was in the third frame, *Master Chief Tyler* engraved at the bottom. The final picture was of Tyler himself on the day of his promotion to warrant officer. He never knew his dad took any snapshots of the ceremony. Seeing the collage made his eyes well, so he turned away and returned to the desk and its mediocre chair.

The operating system loaded with no password required. "I shouldn't be surprised," Tyler whispered to the empty room. Once he closed all the annoying apps which launched at startup, Tyler popped in the pink device. After accepting the password, its contents displayed in a new window a few seconds later. He scrolled to the end of the listing and worked from there. A few pictures showed the empty lot from various angles. The last was an overhead shot. Based on the scale of the houses nearby, the vacant area could have been developed into something sizable and profitable.

Tyler heard an approaching footstep just before Zeke came in and asked, "How's your leg?"

"Good enough."

"Is it?"

He changed the subject. "I might be in here a little while. This computer is an old relic."

"Yeah, well . . . it ain't the only one."

Tyler pivoted in the chair. "Dad, I—"

"Forget it." Zeke put up a hand. "I'm seventy-six years old. I'm long past the point I give a shit if people apologize to me." He paused and took a breath. Tyler couldn't recall the last time he saw his dad need to steady himself. "Yeah, I'm an old relic, too, but I don't want to be the kind who has to bury my son. I wasn't always the best husband or father. You've done a lot better than I ever could."

"I'm not so sure," Tyler said.

"I am," his father said. "I know you're big on helping people. Maybe you think it's some kind of penance. I don't think you need to atone for anything, but I'm glad to see you do this kind of stuff. Just don't go off injured and get yourself killed."

"I won't."

"Good." Zeke offered a small smile and nod before leaving the room. Tyler stared after him for a moment before turning back around and focusing on the task at hand again. He continued from the bottom of the file list. Several people invested in a project tied to the lot, and all of them lost their money when the contract fell through. Tyler wondered if Raburn ever planned to do anything with it. It would have been easy to find a crony to sign an empty agreement and then fail to take action on it.

At the time, Raburn was about to complete his first term as a state senator and sought re-election. His coffers were low, and a couple news articles at the time expected a strong primary battle. His re-election had been far from certain. The infusion of cash allowed him to augment his staff and buy ads. In the end, he won a narrow primary victory and then romped in the general election, and he'd been a constant presence in the state legislature since.

His career and his more recent aspirations got built on a foundation of tainted sand, however. If Raburn sought national office, something like this coming to light could sink him. Outside of his own district, he'd need to appeal to voters across the state, and many of them wouldn't want to elect someone shady.

It definitely provided enough motivation to kidnap and kill.

KACEY'S HEART thudded in her chest.

"You're tough," Richard Raburn said. "I'll give you that much." He glanced at Stacy and smiled. "I wonder if she's cut from the same cloth." The younger sister now sat in the uncomfortable chair, her wrists and ankles bound to its frame. Raburn stalked closer to her and leaned down. "Perhaps you'd like to tell me something and save yourself the agony?"

"Go to hell," Stacy said. "You kidnapped my sister and had my family killed. I'm not telling you shit."

"Suit yourself." Raburn shrugged and moved a few steps away. "Donald."

The large man tipped Stacy's chair back to where it rested against the sink. He put a towel over her face, held up a jug of water, and poured. Stacy coughed almost immediately, and

Kacey watched helplessly as her sister thrashed against restraints she'd never break. She gagged and sputtered as Donald kept the liquid coming, only stopping when the massive bottle ran empty. He pushed the chair forward again and removed the towel. Stacy spat out a mouthful of water, gasped, and cried.

"No," Raburn said, "I don't think she's as strong as you." He smiled like a predator. "She doesn't have it in her."

If Kacey could have moved, she would have clawed his eyes out. Ropes held her to a different chair, however.

"I'm not . . . telling you . . . anything," Stacy said around her own ragged breaths. Donald refilled the bottle from the sink. His large hand gripped the handle with ease. It must have held at least three gallons.

"One of you will. It's a matter of time. Once you give me what I want, of course, I don't need to keep both of you around. I might not have use for either of you."

Kacey realized this possibility as soon as Stacy turned up. If they got her to crack, the group wouldn't hesitate to get rid of the uncooperative older sister. They also wouldn't need Stacy anymore. Either the girls stayed quiet and both of them lived while being waterboarded daily, or one of them spilled the details to Raburn, and both of them would die.

It was an impossible choice.

With the jug full, Donald slammed Stacy's chair back into place. She grimaced as her head hit the edge of the sink. The large enforcer put the towel over her face again, and Stacy screamed. Her cries of anguish soon turned to coughs and desperate chokes as the water rushed in again. A fit seized her, and Kacey wondered if she would be able to keep breathing.

Maybe the choice wasn't so impossible after all.

"Fine!" she said. "I'll tell you. Just stop torturing her."

Donald continued until Raburn nodded his assent a

couple seconds later. Stacy's chair returned to normal, the sopping wet towel fell onto her lap, and she sobbed as she tried to draw in enough air. Once she stopped choking, Kacey continued. "I've been looking into you for a couple weeks, you prick."

Raburn flashed another vicious grin. "Sticks and stones. What do you have?"

"A lot. I have the entire land deal you and your wife used to fund your second senate campaign." Raburn's face twisted, but Kacey didn't let him get a word in. "There's more, of course. No one's only a little dirty. I've got enough to sink you from any office you want to run for."

"Who else knows?"

"Just me."

"Do you expect me to believe your editor is in the dark?"

"He doesn't know you're my target," Kacey said. "He just knows I'm digging up dirt on a prominent state senator."

"And where is this dirt?" Raburn demanded.

"On a flash drive."

"Don't tell him!" Stacy said.

"I have to." Kacey shook her head. "I have to. It's under a loose stone around our fireplace in the lower level. Left side as you're looking at it. I think it's in the second row. It'll be obvious once you start trying to move them."

"Take Francis and check it out," Raburn instructed Donald, and the paid lackey replied with a short nod. "You two had better hope we recover this drive." Raburn stared at both of them before he left the room and slammed the door shut behind him.

"It's not there," Stacy said in a whisper so quiet Kacey barely heard her. "Lexi's dad has it."

Kacey didn't know what this meant for their survival, but she didn't like it.

26

———

"Thanks for the flash drive . . . even though it's pink." Tyler grinned, and Alex Anne pulled him into a hug. Lexi removed the encryption which made Tyler's future plans for the data easier.

"Good luck, Mister Tyler," she whispered while they hugged. "I wish you could walk away from trouble . . . mostly for your daughter's sake."

"Not how I'm wired."

She nodded, said goodbye to Zeke, and left. Though he noticed it earlier, Tyler pointed toward the duffel bag in the corner of the living room. "Did you two take her to the range?

"She loved it," Tyler's father said.

"I'm sure it's a good story. You'll have to tell me about it when this is all behind us." He dropped back onto the couch beside Lexi, glad to take the weight off his knee. "How are we making out?"

"I've uploaded everything to my Google Drive," Lexi said. "I sent you the link. If you want to share it with anyone, just forward it to them."

Tyler mostly understood what she told him, so he bobbed

his head. "Good. Let's make sure we know as much as we can about Raburn, too. Not just what Kacey put together. I didn't see anything in her dossier which would suggest he has two hit squads at his beck and call."

"I'm on it."

"Thanks, kiddo." He got up and walked down the hall. Zeke's bathroom featured a large medicine cabinet. Many of the residents probably needed the ample space. His father didn't. A couple prescription bottles sat inside along with a bunch of common over-the-counter medications. Tyler found a bottle of Advil, shook out four tablets, and dry swallowed them one at a time. He wouldn't get a chance to tend to his knee until he dealt with Richard Raburn, so managing the symptoms would need to be good enough for now.

Tyler hoped he didn't need to run or get into a protracted fight anytime soon. Alex Anne was right—he couldn't walk away from trouble. He'd never been able to. In moments like these, however, he wished it didn't find him quite so often.

DONALD SPOTTED the police car in front of the house as they drove in. "I guess our last time here made them cautious," Francis said from the passenger's seat. "What with finding another body and all."

"It's a complication we don't need," Donald grumbled. Even if he pulled to the curb now, they'd already rounded the bend before the first house. Anyone inside the sheriff's office sedan would probably see them and their Suburban.

"I got an idea," Francis said. "Keep going. Drive to the end."

Donald steered the SUV past the Chaplain house and its guardian. He kept an eye on the mirror, but the man in the cruiser didn't pay them any mind. They passed about sixteen houses on each side before the road ended at a cul-de-sac. "What are we doing?"

Francis pointed to the house on the right side of the circle. "Looks like no one's home there. Stop in front. I'll get out and act like I'm knocking." Donald stopped the Suburban, and Francis climbed out. He walked up the steps, and as far as Donald could tell, he knocked on the door. After a moment of no response, the other man turned around and got back in. "There. Looks like we were trying to visit the homeowner."

"I'll go around the bend and stop after the last house," Donald said as he drove back down the street. When they went around the curve, and the police car disappeared from view, Donald stopped. They climbed out and moved behind the row of houses. At the Chaplain home, both men checked for any other deputies before slipping through the gate. Francis cut the new police tape away and used a snap gun to pop the downstairs lock. They walked into a darkened basement.

Francis smoothed the curtain back over the sliding door before flipping a light switch on. Four bulbs in the ceiling fan glowed, providing enough illumination to search the area. Donald checked out the fireplace. He found the loose stone after a few seconds and lifted it. Most of his hand fit into the hollow beneath it, but he pulled it back empty. The flashlight feature of his cell phone confirmed it. "Nothing here. The bitch was lying." Francis didn't say anything. "What? She told us it would be here, and it ain't."

"She might not be lying, though."

"What do you mean?"

"You tossed Tyler down the stairs when he and I were fighting," Francis said. "He rolled away from the gunshots. We left him down here."

"Didn't look like he could walk," Donald said with a shrug.

"Even if he couldn't, reaching the fireplace from the steps isn't far. If the girl told him about the hiding place, he could have crawled here and made it outside while we were snatching her."

"Son of a bitch."

"Let's get out of here while we can," Francis said. "We've already been over the house. No point in risking it again."

"We're gonna have to call the boss," Donald pointed out.

"I know. He won't be happy. Maybe you're right, and the girl lied to us to buy some time. But if she didn't, John Tyler could have what we need."

"I want to kill him." Donald pulled the curtain back, and the two men walked outside. "I can't believe I missed him three times."

"We'll get him," Francis said. "He's one man. He'll give us what we want, and then you can take as many shots at him as you want."

"I like the way you think," Donald said.

TYLER SENT the Google Drive link. Having another copy was always a good goal, but someone else needed to be in the loop. He forwarded the info to Captain Leon Sharpe of the Baltimore Police Department. Tyler and Sharpe served together in the army, and the man rose through the ranks of the BPD after his discharge. Even in a world where state and federal entities forced Baltimore into new-school policing, Sharpe thrived as an unapologetic old-school cop.

As soon as the email left his outbox, Tyler called his old friend at his office. He got connected after a quick chat with the secretary. "Check your email, Leon. I sent you something important."

"All right." In a few seconds, his deep voice came back on the line. "Who the hell is Richard Raburn?"

"State senator," Tyler said. "I know he's way out of your jurisdiction, but I figure you know the right people to contact if shit gets sideways."

"Tyler, exactly what are you planning?"

"At the moment, I'm not a hundred percent sure. Here's what I know. Raburn is shady. A reporter has been working on a big exposé. Somehow, he found out. A hit squad kidnapped her and murdered the rest of her family. Except for a younger sister who happens to be Lexi's friend and sat in my SUV on a ride from BWI while all this was happening."

"Jesus." Sharpe blew out a deep breath, and a loud, violent hiss filled Tyler's ear. "You really landed in it this time."

"I know. The link I sent you contains everything the reporter put together."

"Do I want to ask why I need it?" Sharpe demanded.

"You know why," Tyler said. "I'm going after Raburn."

"The reporter still alive?"

"As far as I know." Tyler paused a beat. "He has the other girl now, too. I . . . feel responsible."

"Of course you do. Look, why not let me call a few people? We can investigate the right way."

"I don't think it'll work," Tyler said. "I don't know where he is yet, for one thing. He's also on a bunch of senate committees, including law enforcement. I'm sure he has some influence he could exert."

Sharpe grunted. "I guess he could shut things down. At the very least, someone might tip him off."

"Right. This is why I want to go after him myself. The girls probably can't wait for long. He doesn't need either of them once he gets what he wants, but keeping both of them even short-term introduces risks."

"All right. I'll stand by. What's the timeframe?"

Tyler looked at his watch. "It's almost seventeen hundred now. If you haven't heard from me or Lexi by noon tomorrow, send the data to everyone you can. Cecil County sheriff. State police. Any reporters you're friendly with. Folks you know in state government."

"I got it," Sharpe said. "I hope I hear from you before then. Sounds kind of final."

"Yeah," Tyler said, "I hope so, too."

"What are you going to do now?"

"I want Raburn to focus on me instead of the girls. I'm going to call him and offer a trade."

"You know this is poking the bear, right?" Sharpe said. "People get eaten for this kind of shit."

"Sure. Some end up with bear pelts on their wall. Don't tell me you're going to bet against me, Leon."

"Never. Just be careful. If I have to eulogize your dead ass, I'm not gonna be nice."

"Fair enough," Tyler said. He broke the connection and asked Lexi to use all her knowledge of the Patriot laptop to find the best direct number for Richard Raburn.

27

Tyler pondered the best way to threaten a powerful state senator.

Regardless of whether Raburn took the deal, there would be a response. He'd probably send goons to Tyler's house. They would find it empty, and the security system would monitor everything they did. A law enforcement action would be more difficult. The senator's goons might stop looking at Tyler's home. The police would check everywhere, including Zeke's residence. He'd be no good to Stacy and Kacey in jail, and a man like Raburn could ensure he stayed there long enough to matter.

In the end, Tyler decided to wing it. He punched in the number Lexi gave him and waited. A gravelly voice answered after the third ring. "Who is this?"

"Senator Raburn?"

"Yes. Who are you?"

"I'm a man who has something you want."

Silence filled the line for a few seconds. "John Tyler," Raburn eventually said, his voice dripping venom.

"The same. I know you might want to trace this call, so

I'm not going to stay on long. I have the missing item your hired killers have probably been searching for."

"I don't know what you mean."

"My mistake. Never mind, then." Tyler ended the call.

"What are you doing, Dad?" Lexi asked from her spot on the couch.

"He needs to have this conversation," Tyler said. "Even if I were full of shit, he would need to talk to me long enough to figure it out. I also don't want him to have any of his cop friends try to trace the call." Sure enough, Raburn's number appeared on the burner phone's simple screen a few seconds later. "Hello, Richard."

"Don't call me Richard."

"Fine. Hi, Dick."

Raburn sighed into the phone. Tyler smiled. Despite living a long time and experiencing success, some men remained easy to provoke. "Let's say I know what you're talking about. The missing item and all."

"All right," Tyler said.

"What do you propose to do about it?"

"I think a simple trade is in order."

"I'm not sure it's as simple as you think."

"Uncomplicate it, then," Tyler said. When Raburn didn't reply for a few seconds, he hung up again.

"Make sure you don't get Stacy killed," Lexi muttered.

"He's not going to do anything to her because I clicked off." He stared at his temporary phone. "He'll call back. Besides, this is all helping me stay off a trace. I don't want a bunch of Raburn's stooges in uniform coming here."

Lexi crossed her arms. "Me, either."

Raburn called back, and Tyler picked up. "Did you find a way to make things less complex, Dick?"

"I don't trust you, Mister Tyler."

"Feeling's mutual. I don't trust any politician, especially ones who send hit squads to do their dirty work."

"I'm willing to listen to your proposal," Raburn said.

"It's easy," Tyler told him. "I give you the flash drive, and you release the girls unharmed."

"What if they've already been hurt?"

Tyler clenched his fist hard enough to make his phone creak in protest. "Then, I'll cram the flash drive down your goddamn throat before I kill you in front of your wife."

Lexi frowned from the sofa, and Tyler took a quiet breath. Sometimes, he was easy to provoke, too. "No need for threats," Raburn said. "I understand your offer. How do I know you haven't made copies of whatever's on the drive?"

"You don't," Tyler said.

"So we come back to me not trusting you."

"Think of it as insurance. If something happens to the girls, or you try to come after them in the future, I go public with everything, and you're finished."

"You could do it anytime you wanted," the senator said.

"True. I guess you're going to have to trust me a little. It seems I need to do the same. I have to believe you'll be willing to return the girls unharmed."

"I'll think about your offer," Raburn said, and he hung up.

Tyler slipped his phone back into his pocket. "Now we wait?" Lexi said.

He nodded. "Not much else we can do. Keep digging up dirt on this asshole. I want to know as much about him as possible. He's down at least four men right now. Where are they coming from? How many more does he have?"

"I'll work on it." Lexi picked up the laptop again.

Tyler looked at his phone screen and waited.

∽

THE TWO ADDITIONAL men arrived at John Tyler's house about twenty minutes later. It ended up being a lot faster than Donald and Francis could have gotten there. When dealing with a man like Tyler, time mattered. He'd already taken out Adam, Baker, Charlie, and Edgar. Raburn knew one more reinforcement would be coming—the best, in fact. Luring Tyler to his house with the promise of saving the girls would be easy. Raburn scoffed. In the end, his adversary was just another soldier who couldn't let go of his past glory days.

His phone rang a few minutes after the initial text. "Patrick and Quincy reporting for duty."

"Excellent." Elite Security Services came through yet again. The arrangement had proven very beneficial. Score one for Miriam. "To whom am I speaking?"

"This is Patrick, sir."

"Tell me what you see, Patrick."

"No one's here," he said. "Looks like the place has been empty for a couple days. Two newspapers out front. It's clean inside."

"Have you gone through it yet?" Raburn asked.

"Not in depth."

"It's possible no one has stayed there, but it doesn't mean the owner couldn't have popped in long enough to drop something off. I'm looking for a flash drive. I've been told it's a solid black PNY model, two hundred and fifty-six gigs."

"We'll look, sir," Patrick said.

"Good. Tear the place apart if you need to. Ransack it. I don't care. This man is our enemy. Let him know we were there."

"Do you want us to torch it when we're done?"

Raburn pinched the bridge of his nose and took a calming breath. "Of course I don't want you to burn it down. We don't need the attention and response a blaze would bring."

"You're on the law enforcement committee in the senate, right?" Patrick wanted to know.

"And you think it would let me sweep an arson under the rug? Never mind the firefighters who would also respond. What if wind spreads the fire to his neighbor's house? Just search the place. Leave the thinking to me." Raburn ended the call and shook his head. He felt glad to have more bodies on duty. He would need them for John Tyler's inevitable visit. Sometimes, however, he wished they came attached to better brains.

A minute later, he made another call. His contact in the state police picked up right away. "Hello, Senator."

"Good afternoon, Captain Jensen."

"Thanks for your donation last month," the man said. "It put our fundraiser over the top."

"I was glad to do it." Raburn didn't tap into his own money for it, and it bought him a little more goodwill than simply being a powerful figure in Maryland politics afforded.

"What can I do for you today?"

"Captain, I'm in a bit of a situation. It's something I wanted to resolve for myself, and I tried. I don't think it's going to work out, so I'm reaching out to you."

"I'm happy to do what I can," Jensen said.

Raburn smiled. "Thank you. I was hoping it wouldn't come to this, but I'd like to file charges for harassment and assault."

"Do you know the identity of the person who harassed and assaulted you, Senator?"

"I do," Raburn said. "His name is John Tyler."

28

———

About forty-five minutes passed before Tyler's burner rang. He recognized Raburn's number and walked into Zeke's bedroom to take the call. "Well?"

"I accept your trade, Mister Tyler."

Too easy. A slimeball like Raburn would have something up his sleeve, especially when allowed almost an hour to put it together. "Fine," Tyler said. "Tell me when and where."

"I want some assurances from you first," Raburn said. "And I don't want to hear how I'm not in a position to negotiate. Two lives are on the line, and they're under my control. I think I have plenty of leverage here."

"I wasn't going to say otherwise."

"Good. I want you to destroy any other copies you made of whatever's on the flash drive. Delete them from your computer. Whatever you did, undo it. I want to be sure I'm getting the only copy."

It took much of Tyler's willpower to avoid laughing. He would never comply with this demand, and on some level, a man like Raburn must have suspected it. The contingency with Leon Sharpe would remain in place. Still, he said, "All right, I agree."

"Excellent. If you want the girls, you're going to come to me. I'm not delivering them anywhere."

"I understand," Tyler said. He kept his voice neutral. Let Raburn think he was winning. The illusion of control would be important. "You still haven't told me when and where."

"Patience, Mister Tyler." Raburn took his time. He was enjoying this. Tyler guessed it felt like being on the senate floor and engaging in some procedural debate—boring to normal people but enthralling to folks like Raburn. "My wife's family has owned an estate for several years. You'll find it in Rising Sun. I'll text the coordinates to you. Come in two hours, and be sure you're alone."

Tyler looked at his watch. The sun would be setting then. He wanted to get there early and scout around. The problem with agreeing to meet Raburn on his turf was conceding home-field advantage. A good half-hour of prep time would allow Tyler to take it back. "All right. I'll be there."

"Remember," Raburn said, "just you. No police, no posse." The senator broke the connection. A text came in a moment later. Tyler used Zeke's computer to view the coordinates in Google Maps. He spent a few minutes looking at the 3D view of the landscape. In such a rural area, some details and parts of the estate were missing. Still, partial information remained better than nothing at all.

Tyler slipped his phone back into his pocket and returned to the living room. "I'm going to get the girls. Dad, do you have a vest I can use? Maybe with a rifle-fire plate?"

"Sure," his father said. "Far end of my closet. You want to take some rifles?"

"No. I think I'll need to stay as mobile as possible. Maybe a shotgun."

"Need a pistol?"

"I took a Glock from someone earlier. Perfectly good gun."

"Where are you going?" Lexi asked.

"Some estate Raburn's wife's family owns," Tyler said. "I'll be back as soon as I can." Lexi stared at him but didn't say anything. Tyler knew what she was thinking. *It's a trap. It's foolish to go alone.* Both were probably true. This would be his best—and probably only—chance to get the surviving Chaplain sisters back alive, however.

Whatever the risks, he meant to take it.

LEXI CROSSED her arms on the couch. As much as she wanted Stacy back, her father setting off alone wasn't the way she wanted it to happen. He returned to the living room a moment later, a bullet-resistant vest strapped around his torso, and a shotgun in his left hand. "Dad, why don't I come with you?"

He shook his head. "Raburn told me to come alone."

"But I—"

Her dad put a hand up. "I appreciate it. I don't know what surveillance capabilities he has on the property, though. If Raburn spotted me dropping you off somewhere, what do you think he's going to do to Stacy and her sister?"

She nodded, forced to acknowledge his point. "I don't like you going there by yourself. You're still limping."

"I'm fine," he said as he lifted his knee to bend it a couple times. "Between the brace and the Advil, I'll be all right. Dad, you know anyone who has a car I can borrow?"

"Plenty of people," her grandfather said. "Let me make some calls." Lexi's grandfather got up and walked down the hall. Her dad dropped onto the sofa at the opposite end from her.

"I still don't like this," she said.

"Me, either. I'm getting there early to scout around."

"Please be careful, Dad. You know this is a trap of some sort."

"Hence, why I want to get there before Raburn expects me," he said. "If I can catch one guy on patrol and kill him, it might change their plan entirely."

"Call if you need help," Lexi said.

Her grandfather walked back into the living room. "Geoffrey in the next building said you can take his Continental."

"You don't know anyone who has a Camaro?" her dad said.

"Take what you can get," Zeke said. "It's pretty new. Nice car. He's going to meet you downstairs in a couple minutes. You . . . might want to put the gun in a bag. I didn't tell him you were driving an hour to shoot a bunch of people."

"Good call." He left and returned a minute later with a green duffel matching the one Zeke carried to the range earlier. It felt like yesterday at this point. With the shotgun stowed, her father headed for the door. "I'll be careful. See you all in a few hours, I hope."

Lexi shot to her feet and hugged him tight. "Don't get yourself killed," she whispered as she squeezed. "I can't handle Mom being my only parent."

He held on until she let go. "I'll be all right, kiddo. Experience and treachery can overcome a lot."

"You got spare magazines?" her grandfather asked.

"Did you raise me?"

"Good luck, then."

Her dad left. Lexi stared at the door for a minute and then sat back down on the couch. "I don't like this, Grandpa."

"I don't, either. You heard him, Alexis. They might be able to see you if you went along." He paused and smirked. "Or if you followed him. Your dad's done this kind of thing plenty of times before. He could raid a compound in his sleep at this point.”

“He was younger then,” Lexi said. “He had a team, and he didn’t have a limp.” She sighed. “He feels responsible for Stacy ending up with Raburn, but speeding off into danger isn’t the way to solve it.”

“What do you have in mind?”

She opened the Patriot laptop again. “I want to know where he’s going.”

“You think this is your fault, too, don’t you?” Zeke said.

Lexi bobbed her head as she logged in. “I was going to pick Stacy up originally. When the weather turned, Dad insisted on going. I could’ve pushed back, I guess, but he’s driven in bad conditions way more than I have.”

“Don’t beat yourself up over it. He made his choice. It’s not on you.”

“Thanks, Grandpa.” She thought back to what her dad told her. *Some estate Raburn’s wife’s family owns.* It made sense for the senator to do his dirty work at a place which couldn’t easily be connected to him. Depending on the actual owner-ship, it might not even be traceable to his wife. Proprietary holdings were one of her least favorite things to untangle. Wills, deeds, trusts, and the like made her eyes cross after a while. Still, if she could find the right property, maybe she could drive up there and help her father. Whether the stub-born man wanted it or not.

“You find something, let me know,” Zeke said. “I’ll go with you.”

“He’ll hate us both, then.”

“Let him. The army always needs the navy to save its ass, anyway.”

Lexi started her search for Miriam Nicholls. The only house in her name was the one she owned with her husband. Lexi cracked her knuckles. This could take a while. “Get your bag ready, Grandpa. I'll let you know when I have something."

GEOFFREY WAS ALREADY DOWNSTAIRS when Tyler reached the lobby. His age was hard to gauge, but he looked at least as old as Zeke. His clothes fit like he bought them when he weighed forty pounds more, and his suspenders were probably necessary. Geoffrey was slender to the point of being gaunt. It didn't seem to bother him much, as his kind face split into a large smile as Tyler approached. "You must be Zeke's boy," he said in a strained voice.

"I am."

"You dressed for war?"

The green duffel and exposed vest certainly lent the appearance. "Never know when one might break out," Tyler said. "I like to be prepared."

"I understand." Geoffrey handed Tyler a set of keys. "Both my boys were in the Air Force."

"Army . . . to my father's constant consternation."

"Bah." Geoffrey waved a dismissive hand. "Your dad's a little full of himself sometimes."

Tyler smiled. "Maybe more people should tell him. He might actually listen." He held the key fob up. "Thanks for letting me borrow the car."

"Anytime."

The dark blue Continental sedan sat in the lot in front of Geoffrey's building. It occupied one of the many handicapped spaces at the sidewalk. According to a badge near the trunk, a 2.7-liter turbocharged engine powered the car, and it featured all-wheel drive. Tyler remembered when American luxury cars had big V8s under the hood and sent their power to the rear axle. Those were the days. He unlocked the door, set the duffel on the passenger's seat, and fired up the engine.

It let loose a satisfying sound when he revved it. Tyler backed out of the spot and drove away from the retirement community. It wouldn't be a long drive to the destination. He plotted the route on his father's computer. Major roads would get him almost all the way there. Tyler guided the sedan up Route 1, across the Conowingo Dam, and into Cecil County.

A few minutes later, he spied a police car coming the other way. It whizzed by on the left. Tyler remembered Raburn's involvement with law enforcement across the state. Would siccing the cops on Tyler be part of his trap? In the rearview, the cruiser's lights came on, and it made a U-turn. "Shit," Tyler muttered. They'd never be able to trace Geoffrey's car to him. Raburn must have gotten the word out and circulated his picture.

By Tyler's guess, he was ten minutes away from the estate. He didn't know the roads well, so evading his pursuers wasn't an option. The Continental's turbo V6 might be able to gain him some ground, but an advantage the police enjoyed was superior numbers. Still, he couldn't let them take him out of the situation. Raburn could have Stacy and Kacey killed while deputies wasted time with questions they didn't need to ask. Tyler didn't pull over as the flashing lights drew closer in the mirror.

Captain Casey Norton of the Maryland State Police read yet another email. As his responsibility increased, his time in the field decreased in proportion. While he'd been a captain for a few years now, the state added task after task to his workload. Most weeks, he felt grateful for the overtime. Some days, however, he wanted to be out in the field with the men and women who reported to him. Reading reports at this desk never felt the same no matter how well they were written.

A knock snapped him back to the here and now. "Captain?" Trooper Leslie Green stood at his door. Norton waved her in, and she handed him a piece of paper. "Came in a few minutes ago. Thought you'd want to know." He took the sheet and looked at it. It was a new complaint for harassment and assault. Norton was about to ask why she brought him something so mundane when he saw the complainant's name.

Richard Raburn.

"Son of a bitch," he grumbled.

"I know you don't like him, sir."

"You're really underselling my disdain for him. I don't

care how good a game he talks in Annapolis. He is *not* our friend."

"This came to us," Green said, "and it also went to Cecil, Harford, and Baltimore Counties as well as the BPD."

"Pretty wide net." Norton frowned and kept perusing until he found the alleged perpetrator's name.

John Tyler.

"Any action on this?" he asked.

"None yet, sir."

Norton nodded. "All right. Thanks. I want to look into it." Green walked away. Norton knew Tyler a little. They'd crossed paths before. He thought the man was a wild card and likely to harm any investigation he might stumble into by going off book. He'd almost done it with a band of sex traffickers, but Norton had to give him credit for resolving it all at the end. Tyler didn't seem the type to bother with a state senator, and if he got mixed up with Raburn somehow, Norton would believe him over the senator.

He closed his email and researched the complaint. Raburn called it in himself. He filed it with Captain Jensen. This raised a flag. Jensen was fine, but few reports for common crimes came to high-ranking officers directly. A trooper would be far more likely. This meant Raburn contacted Jensen directly. They probably enjoyed a good relationship, and the captain wouldn't ask a lot of questions of a senator who claimed to be the best friend to law enforcement. When the police had an ally—even someone like Raburn—they tried to keep him or her on their side.

A little further investigating showed Tyler's cell phone offline for a while but nowhere near Richard Raburn before. Jensen could have performed such a basic check, but he accepted the senator's claims and filed the report. Norton called up the complaint on his computer. He added comments questioning the legitimacy and officially rescinded it with a note instructing the state police and all other law enforcement agencies to disregard it as invalid.

Someone like Raburn would try to use it to jam up Tyler somehow. Even getting him off the street for a couple hours could make a difference. If Raburn and Tyler were indeed at odds and cruising toward a showdown, Norton hoped his actions came in time. He'd be rooting for John Tyler.

As much as it pained him, Tyler pulled to the side of the road. Trying to outrun this police car would only bring more. He wasn't going to get into a shootout with a deputy, but he also wouldn't let some corrupt yokel on Raburn's payroll delay him. The man who stepped out of the cruiser was tall and lean, and he wore mirrored sunglasses. "You know why I pulled you over?" he said as he approached. When Tyler didn't answer, the cop said, "Are you John Tyler?"

"Did I win a prize?"

"Are you?"

The deputy's right hand rested on his belt near the hilt of his service pistol. A quick check in the mirror showed no one else in the police car. Not many cars traveled the road in either direction, so there would be few witnesses to whatever went down. If Tyler needed to, he could throw the door open into the cop's body and then deal with the situation from there. He slid his right foot over to brace it against the short wall next to the accelerator. "I am."

"License and registration."

Tyler dug out his wallet and handed the deputy his license. As he reached for the glove compartment, he hoped old Geoffrey didn't keep a gun in the car. Thankfully, he didn't. Tyler found the registration inside the leather folder holding the owner's manual. "Here you go."

"This isn't your car," the deputy said as he looked at both items.

"He's a friend of my father's," Tyler said. "My car got hit in the snowstorm yesterday."

A grunt served as the only reply before the cop walked away. He would run Tyler's license through the computer in his cruiser. If Raburn tried to delay him with some bullshit complaint, it would be in the system. Why do a one-eighty otherwise? Tyler slipped his gun from the back of his waistband and stashed it under his left leg. He wouldn't shoot first, but he also wouldn't allow himself to become a target if Raburn offered to sweeten the pot beyond a simple arrest.

The Dodge's door opened, and the cop approached again. He handed the license and registration though the window. "Must have been an error in the system. You have a nice day, Mister Tyler."

"Uh . . . yeah, you, too."

As the deputy walked away, Tyler put the MVA card back in the glove box. He wondered what happened. A glitch didn't explain his getting pulled over in a vehicle no one could connect to him. Raburn must have done something. Tyler maintained a few friends in law enforcement. Maybe one of them saw the complaint or whatever it was and tossed it out. Regardless, Tyler wasn't going to be delayed anymore. He pulled back onto the road and sped up when he saw the county cruiser turn around and head the other direction.

Stacy and Kacey couldn't keep waiting.

～

RABURN SEETHED AS he held his phone. "What do you mean my complaint against Tyler got tossed out?"

"I don't know how else to explain it, Senator," Captain

Jensen said. "It's no longer active in the system. Any state agency who pulls from us will disregard it."

"How did this happen?" Raburn demanded.

"Someone else saw the document."

"A name, Jensen. Give me a name."

"Casey Norton. He's a fellow captain. Good guy."

"Great," Raburn said through clenched teeth. He hadn't heard Norton's name in a while, but he didn't share Jensen's opinion of the man. "I'll be sure to send him a fruit basket. Can't you do something about this?"

"Norton's notes indicated your complaint was without merit," Jensen said. "He added a few details . . . cell phone locations mostly."

"I didn't think anyone would scrutinize my report so much." Raburn paused for a small sigh. "Perhaps I've misplaced my support of the state police all these years." Jensen didn't say anything. Not surprising. Raburn put him in a bad position, and he chose silence over badmouthing his employers or the senator. "Never mind, Captain. I'll consider all this later. Good day." He broke the connection. The criminal complaint was always a bit of a gamble. A patsy like Jensen would be happy to file it, but if someone investigated it—or Tyler—it wouldn't hold up. Still, he expected it to buy him more time.

Now, he needed to get the men ready to change tactics.

Raburn walked downstairs. He opened the door to the small room where the Chaplain sisters remained captives. The younger sister, her face, hair, and sweatshirt wet, blubbered and sobbed in the chair. The older one tried to keep her composure, but the red eyes spoiled her resolve. Donald filled the large water bottle again while Francis watched the girls. "Change of plans," Raburn said. "You two come out here. Lock up behind yourselves."

A moment later, both men joined the senator in a

different area of the basement. He kept his voice low in case one of the girls tried to overhear. "John Tyler will be coming," he said. "I tried to delay him, but it's not going to work." His phone vibrated, and he checked the message. "Two more guys just arrived. With Hong and Isaac, we have six. Francis, you go upstairs. Gustav is still here. Keep an eye on things. Cameras should allow you to see most of the property. Donald, you'll join Isaac, Patrick, and Quincy at the top level."

"Why up there?" Donald wanted to know.

"Tyler's smart. He'll use his training. The best way to approach the house is from the trees. He'll think they protect him."

Donald frowned, and the corner of his mouth twisted down. "Don't they?"

"Nominally, perhaps," Raburn said. "My wife's great-grandfather built this place originally. He was a bootlegger, and he knew people might come for him. There are shooting lanes through the trees. From the top-floor windows, you should have line of sight."

"All right." Donald and Francis both headed for the stairs. Raburn tested the lock on the spare room door before he followed them. The defense plan was almost as old as the property. Miriam's granddad used it at least once following his father's death. It had been tested, and landscapers carefully maintained the trees to ensure any shooters who needed to man the top story kept line of sight. Raburn smiled.

Let John Tyler come. He'd never reach the house alive.

30

As usual, Tyler arrived early. After the delay with the county cop, he pushed the Continental hard to make up for lost time. The Nicholls estate proved easy enough to find. Tyler left the car at the side of the road, took his supplies, and made his way to the fence. He could have driven a little farther and gone through the motorized gate, but why announce his arrival? The black metal fence didn't offer a lot of footholds, but Tyler managed to get over it.

The enemy always needed time to set things up. Arriving early allowed him to scout an unfamiliar area, see what steps Raburn and his men were taking, and maybe even disrupt them. The property was massive. Mostly flat, it extended as far as Tyler could see. A wooden split-rail fence separated it from the closest neighbor. Whichever company built it around the perimeter made their money for the entire year.

Tyler kept close to the barrier as he surveyed the landscape. It was probably a farm in years past. The open spaces and level ground would enable the owners to plant a variety of crops. A modern storage shed could have been an old barn before a renovation. Tyler eyed the massive house through the trees. It looked way too modern to be original. Three stories of brick extended above the earth. Windows marked major rooms, and there were a lot of them. Even with lower prices in the rural counties, this house and lands would be worth millions of dollars.

The neighbor's grounds featured a hill with some pines on the other side of the fence. It would be hard for anyone to see what went on here. Raburn chose this setting well. It was remote by both location and construction. A large patch of trees provided cover as Tyler observed the house. He parked himself behind a big one at the back. A door lay just around the back corner of the house. He would be able to see anyone using it to exit. Enough light remained to see into some of the windows, also. There was no movement anywhere.

Tyler's hands clenched and unclenched as he waited. He was overdue to sit down and paint. Years ago, when his third Veterans Administration shrink recommended the program to him, he scoffed. She insisted he try it. Some mumbo-jumbo about getting out what's in your head and working through the PTSD. A few sessions made him a believer. Tyler had never been a skilled artist, but quality wasn't the goal. He stored a few mental pictures of the property in case he wanted to paint them later. Walking out of here with Stacy and Kacey remained the priority.

A car drove through the gate. Two men sat in the front seats. The sedan moved past the house and parked behind it. Tyler watched as two guys who could have stepped off the football field got out and walked inside. They were dressed like the initial group at the Chaplain house. He was tempted to move closer and shoot them, but then he'd reveal his presence. Another car followed, and two guys dressed like security guards climbed out and went into the house. For now, he didn't want anyone to know he was here. Raburn sent for reinforcements. He would need them.

Even with the trees, however, the house would be difficult to assault. Shooters—and now there were at least four—could station themselves at any number of windows. They could afford to play the long game. Tyler would need to emerge from cover at some point, and their long guns would give them an advantage over his pistol or shotgun. Maybe he should've brought the rifle his father suggested. He kept low and moved behind a different oak. A brief glint of light caught his eye.

Tyler looked up and stared into a security camera.

So much for catching them unaware.

LEXI TRIED to pull apart Richard Raburn's life.

Her dad's former company laptop helped. It featured all kinds of apps and programs to enable this kind of research. She'd come to understand how some of them worked, but a few remained mysteries. Maybe she'd need a couple semesters of computer science to help her make better use of it. Raburn was fifty-four years old, and his official bio said he'd always been interested in leadership roles. In Lexi's experience, this made him an ambitious prick who enjoyed having power over other people. She'd known a few in her high school days. Ready smiles put most people at ease and hid their true motivations.

Sure enough, Raburn sought higher office. Rumors swirled he wanted to make a run at the United States Senate. It would represent a big uptick in pay, responsibility, influence, and prestige. All things he would value. Men who sought power were so predictable. Raburn's legislative history as a Maryland delegate and then a senator proved mixed. He talked a good game and always made himself available to the press and anyone willing to hear him speak. As someone who advanced legislation, however, he ranked around the middle of the pack.

Richard Raburn and his wife, the former Miriam Nicholls, owned a home in Port Deposit and a condo in Ocean City. The latter would be too far away. Their residence was nice. Large enough to hold a couple captives. Nothing in Raburn's history suggested he was an idiot, so he wouldn't hold Stacy and Kacey at his home. Too many chances for people to see what was going on. He wouldn't take the risk.

Where were they, then? Maybe his wife owned a property on her own. A detailed search showed she did not. She never had, in fact. Miriam went from her parents' house to college to living with her husband. Following her mother's death, Miriam sold her childhood home to someone outside the family. There was no indication she maintained contact with them. Stacy and Kacey wouldn't be there, either.

"How goes the hunt?" her grandfather asked.

"I'm oh-for-two."

"What are you going to do when you solve this problem?"

"I don't know," Lexi said. "I guess it depends what we're looking at." She paused. *What we're looking at.* Her dad disappeared down the hall when his phone rang. He spent a few minutes in there. Long enough to punch in an address, look at a map, and get directions—which he'd need to do on the PC thanks to his limited burner phone. "Grandpa, can you check your computer? I think Dad used it to learn where to go. Pull up Google Maps and see if there's a recent entry."

Zeke clapped his hands and stood. "I'm on it." While her grandfather walked away, Lexi kept searching. Miriam Nicholls sold her parents' house. Her mother and father bought it thirty years before. They didn't inherit a property. Lexi didn't know the best way to search for something going back generations. County records would get less precise the farther back she went, and this assumed they were digitized and online in the first place.

Her grandfather returned a minute later. He handed her a small sticky note with two coordinates on it. "He put it into Bing Maps. Probably figured we wouldn't check past Google."

Lexi wasn't convinced her dad could be so crafty when it came to technology, but she took the small piece of paper. "Thanks, Grandpa." The data resolved to an address, and the map showed a sprawling estate.

"Big place," Zeke said.

"Yeah, it is." A large house sat in the front half toward the left side. Trees surrounded it, and expanses of green lay beyond. "This is a lot of land. Probably a farm years ago. Who the hell owns it?" She searched and discovered it belonged to an entity called the MN Trust. Another minute revealed Miriam's grandfather named Marshall established the trust years ago. Lexi didn't know the ins and outs, but Miriam's parents weren't mentioned as beneficiaries. When she turned twenty-one, Miriam Nicholls gained the ability to use the house including as a primary residence if she wanted. Lexi found nothing to indicate she ever actually lived there. The MN Trust still owned the property, and this made it untraceable to Richard Raburn and difficult to tie back to his wife.

The perfect location to stash a couple captives.

"They have to be here," she said. "It's the best option. No one could tie this place to Raburn." Lexi switched to a 3D view to try and get the lay of the land.

"Looks easy to defend," her grandfather said. "At some point, whoever wants into the house has to come out of the trees. A couple guys with long guns would be all you'd need."

"Dad's not equipped for a proper assault."

"No. He should've taken the rifle. Even then, he'd be one guy in the woods. I think his odds would be pretty slim." Lexi frowned in concern. "Look, I'm not the building raider your dad is. Most of my time was at sea. I'm sure he has a plan, but even he would tell you the operation would be a lot easier with a team . . . like he used to have."

She flipped the laptop shut. "I'm going. He can't do this alone."

"Wait just a minute," the old man said. "There's no way your dad would want you anywhere near this operation. Above all else, he'd want to keep you safe."

"He's not here to make that call," Lexi said. "Besides, he always tells me I'm an adult. This is my choice."

"Shit." Her grandfather frowned and shook his head. "You're not going by yourself, then. I'm coming with you."

"You think he'd want you there anymore than me?"

"Probably," Zeke said. "Besides, I'm seventy-six years old. I'll be living on borrowed time soon enough." He stood. "I'll get us a couple rifles and vests. You bring your pistol. Be ready to go in three minutes."

Lexi smiled.

31

Raburn spared a small smile for his reinforcements. Out of all of them, he'd only worked with Hong before. The young Asian man was an expert in martial arts, and Raburn had never seen anyone move faster. He would be an excellent bodyguard against a middle-aged retired soldier like John Tyler. The other three in black were new to him but all came from Elite Security Services, so he knew they'd been vetted carefully. Isaac, Patrick, and Quincy all could have played linebacker in the NFL. The other two came from a different company. No time to vet them. He'd be hoping for strength in numbers. "We're going to have an uninvited guest soon," Raburn said. "He's after me, my wife, and two people we're keeping downstairs. The details aren't important right now. Here's what matters—he shouldn't be allowed to reach the house."

"Understood, sir," Isaac said. Unlike the other two from ESS, he was a blond. Their black sweaters and chinos matched. Only Isaac's platinum hair and Hong being Asian broke the illusion of the gang being related.

"Four of you will take positions at windows on the top

level. It'll give you line of sight into the trees. My ancestor carefully set things up so he'd be able to shoot at people who tried to steal from him. The man who's coming here is named John Tyler. He's retired special forces, so don't take him lightly." The four exchanged glances among themselves. "He'll be badly outnumbered and on unfamiliar ground, however. If he manages to make it to the house, we'll deal with him inside. All of you have walkie-talkies and earpieces. Keep chatter to a minimum. We don't want to tip off the enemy."

"When are we expecting him?" Hong asked in a slightly-accented voice.

"I don't think we'll have to wait too long," Raburn said as he glanced at his Rolex. "He's due here in about forty minutes. I want to be ready."

The communicator on Raburn's hip crackled. "Senator, he's here," Gustav said. "I just spotted him on a camera at the edge of the trees."

"He's early." Raburn grabbed his walkie-talkie and pushed the button. "You heard the man. Donald, upstairs to your window. Francis, go outside and keep an eye on him. If you get a shot, take it." He released the switch and pointed to the uniformed pair. "You two, take the front door for now. Hong, you're with me. The rest of you, upstairs. You'll find rifles waiting for you. I presume you're all good shots."

The group bobbed their heads as they filed out of the kitchen. Tyler came early. He probably wanted to get the lay of the land. A man like him wouldn't want to get into a battle on unfamiliar ground if he could avoid it. He'd soon have four men with rifles to contend with, however, and the trees wouldn't be the shelter he expected.

Raburn smiled again. Tyler would never reach the house alive. Once he was dead, the Chaplain sisters could join him. They'd have no choice but to talk. He'd even let them see Tyler's corpse for a little extra motivation.

THE ACCORD SURGED past eighty-five as Lexi passed a slow-moving SUV.

"Don't get pulled over," her grandfather said from the passenger's seat. "If we're going to help your dad, we can't afford the delay."

"I know." She backed off the throttle, settling in at seventy-five. Ten above the speed limit. Probably all right. If she saw a police car, she'd slow down more. "I just want to get there while it still matters."

Zeke didn't answer. Lexi picked up her phone, found Rollins' number, and called him. Her father's friend answered quickly. "Hello, Lexi. Everything all right?"

"Not really. My grandfather and I are driving to Cecil County to help my dad. He's wading into a bad situation, but I couldn't talk him out of it. You know him."

"For a long time, yes." He sighed. "I'm afraid I can't help you tonight. I'm working for someone in Calvert County."

"Shit," Zeke grumbled. "Way too far."

"I don't know what kind of support you need," Rollins said. "There's a PI I work with sometimes. He helped us with the tech when your dad and I went to Texas to take on the cartel."

"This is more of a compound raid," Lexi said. "From what I can tell, it doesn't look like an easy one."

"C.T. isn't your guy, then. No one's better at storming a building than your dad, Lexi. He taught other people how to do it."

"I know," she said. "Thanks anyway, Rollins." She broke the connection. "I can't think of anyone else who's close enough. They're all in Baltimore or south."

"What about the guy who started working at your dad's shop?" her grandfather asked.

"Ortiz? He seems capable. Doesn't really have a history with Dad, though. I don't think they've seen each other since the interview. Besides, I think he lives in Catonsville or somewhere like that."

"He wouldn't make it in time."

"No." They sped by the exit for Belcamp. The bridge across the Susquehanna River would come in about ten miles, and then they'd be in Cecil County. Lexi eyed the map on her car's primitive GPS. It showed twenty minutes remaining. She wanted to cut the time down but needed to balance getting there quickly with not attracting the attention of the police. A little more gas brought the coupe up to seventy-eight.

"I think it's down to us," Zeke said.

"We'll be enough." Lexi tried to fill her voice with confidence. She'd never done something like this before. Her concern for both her father and her missing friend—plus the sheer size of the Raburn compound—spurred her to action.

Her grandfather nodded in the passenger's seat. The small vote of confidence made her smile. She pushed the Accord up to eighty.

TYLER COULDN'T WORRY about the camera. He would lose the element of surprise at some point, anyway. Doing so this early wasn't part of the plan, but he would adapt. Besides, just because he showed up on a video feed somewhere didn't mean anyone sat and watched it and also didn't mean an immediate response would follow. Tyler flexed his knee and scampered as best he could to cover behind another tree.

No camera this time. A lot of oaks and maples covered the flat expanse of ground. Tyler enjoyed a good view of the large house from this spot, also. Concern pulled his brows into a frown. He still didn't see anyone, so he moved to a position behind a large oak toward the front of the home. Still a good view. It meant anyone inside could see him, as well. There were plenty of windows for shooters to use.

This might be harder than he expected.

Tyler moved through the small forest for another few minutes, confirming his recent suspicion. These were old, tall trees. Whoever planted them years ago did so strategically. Anyone assaulting the house would expect to have cover. The sheer size of the trunks would provide some, but movement would be difficult. Too much visibility from the main building. If he didn't want to get pinned down—and he absolutely did not—Tyler would need to be selective and careful.

He considered advancing on the house before the defenses were ready when he heard another footstep.

It came from behind his position. Tyler put his back against the tree and looked to the left toward the edge of the property. No one was here. He checked to the right. One of the guys he saw at the Chaplain house picked his way through the grove. On the whole, he wasn't bad. He might have managed to sneak up on a lot of people. Tyler kept an eye on the man as he took a cautious path.

Shooting him would be easy but would also draw a swift response from anyone inside. Tyler edged around the trunk to the left as the other man drew nearer. If the fellow kept going, Tyler could get behind him and take him out quietly. It took a couple minutes. The guy moved without hurry, which was the smart approach. When he skulked past the tree, Tyler completed his circuit of the trunk.

He matched the taller guy stride for stride as they approached a sturdy maple. When his quarry went to take a step, Tyler surged forward, grabbed him by the hair, and slammed his head into the wood. It didn't turn the lights out, but the man grunted and tried to blink away the cobwebs.

Tyler didn't give him the chance. A hard elbow to the jaw bounced his skull off the maple again. When his foe stumbled and fell to his knees, Tyler drew his knife. Before the other man could recover, Tyler drove it through his ribs. Blood burbled around his mouth as Tyler twisted and withdrew the blade. The larger man sagged to the ground as crimson liquid stained the grass and dirt around him.

Tyler cleaned his knife on the dead man's sweater. He took two spare magazines from the guy's belt. The distinctive sound of a rifle cocking made Tyler dash to cover. His knee barked, and he rubbed it as a bullet slammed into the tree he stood behind. It was a large one, at least, and it lined up with the front of the manor.

More bullets blasted into the wood. These came faster. Something semiautomatic. Probably an M4 carbine. It would be good from this distance. Tyler drew his pistol. He was badly outgunned. He couldn't make a run for the house. His current inability to run presented a problem, but a bigger one was the fact he'd be exposed. These guys wouldn't even need to be good shots to kill him. Even though Tyler had just taken out one of the enemy's forces, it didn't feel like much of an achievement as a hail of bullets pinned him where he stood.

32

Zeke readied his duffel as Lexi approached the destination. The Nicholls estate sat in a rural area of Cecil County. Most properties were farms which stretched for acres. As she stopped outside the fence, Zeke frowned. "I ain't getting over it." He looked at the iron barrier. In his younger days, he probably could have scaled it. Now, he needed an easier way. Zeke thought back to the map Lexi displayed on the laptop. The neighbor's property wasn't fenced where it bordered with Raburn's. "Back up a little. I'll go at it from the side."

Lexi put the Accord in reverse and backed up about fifty yards. Zeke got out and crouched. "Be careful," he said. "Do as we discussed. Don't get involved directly unless you really need to. Your father would kill me if anything happened to you."

"I will, Grandpa," she said. Zeke nodded and padded onto the grass. The trees thinned as the edge of the property neared before thickening again right before the border. He already heard shots. Other than the Nicholls place, the nearest house would be a third of a mile away if not farther. Even if anyone heard the gunfire, they might not think much of it in an area dominated by farmland.

Zeke took his rifle out of the duffel and tossed the bag down. He still used the weapon handed down from his father —an M1903 Springfield bolt-action model. It was good out to at least a thousand yards—he wouldn't need most of the range today—and the .30-06 rounds meant someone didn't get up if he hit them anywhere near a vital area. Zeke stayed low and moved through the trees. He saw his son standing behind a large oak. Four men in the upper floor windows took aim on his position. Tyler was basically pinned down and wouldn't be able to do much until at least half his assailants ran empty.

This was the situation Zeke worried about. The house was easy to defend and hard to assault, especially for one man. After sending a quick text to Lexi apprising her of the situation, he found a level area of the grove and stretched out on the ground. His son's eyes flicked in his direction as Zeke studied each of the four shooters in the building.

TYLER CHIDED himself for not bringing a rifle.

He could have used one here. Getting a shot off would have been perilous, but at least he'd be holding a gun with a good chance of hitting its target. The shooters firing on him were about two hundred yards away. Tyler was very good with the M11, but such a distance with a handgun required a fair bit of luck, too. He'd figured the trees would provide better cover, and he wondered how many people buried under the earth here once shared the same thought.

A chunk of the trunk behind him splintered from a rifle

round and pelted his face with bits of wood. Tyler wiped his face and blew small pieces out of his nose and mouth. He held his pistol out toward the windows and squeezed off a few rounds. Nothing changed. He needed time to take aim from a long distance, but the four men raining gunfire on him would never give him the chance.

Moving to his left would be a death sentence. Going to the right would still be risky. He needed to try. Tyler took a step from behind the trunk, lined up the nearest man in the house, and fired twice. One round hit the house, and another shattered the window near the gunman. Not bad for a first attempt. Tyler pivoted back to cover. He wondered how many more bullets the tree could absorb. It was thick and sturdy, but the men upstairs unleashed a barrage.

Someone clicked empty. Tyler pivoted out again and emptied the magazine at the closest window. He hit it with most of his shots, and the man who stood there disappeared from view. Tyler didn't know if he hit him or if the man simply dodged away from the bullets. He'd find out soon enough. A round whizzed over his head as he took up his position behind the reliable oak and reloaded his gun. If he survived this, Tyler resolved to plant a similar tree in his backyard.

"Give up!" one of the men shouted as the gunfire eased. "We have you pinned down."

"Step out, and we'll make it quick," another called.

"You guys get paid by the word?" Tyler said. He refused to take the bait. Let them hoot and holler. He would use the patient approach which had served him well so many times over the years. One of these men would run out of ammo. Then another. They didn't seem smart or patient enough to coordinate, and different windows likely meant each occupied a separate room. Two shooters would be a lot easier to contend with than four. If this happened, Tyler could get closer and reduce the numbers. Then, his pistol and shotgun would become a lot more relevant.

The brief reprieve ended when Tyler didn't fall for the simple trap, and the shooting resumed. A few more bits of wood hit him as the rifle rounds blasted into the tree. He might need to move soon, and he hoped another break in the action would allow him the opportunity. As he listened for the telltale sign of someone running out of ammo, he saw motion in front of him. On the other side of the fence in a copse of trees on the neighbor's property, someone moved. Were they trying to get him in a crossfire? How did he miss someone moving across the property and over the barrier?

For the first time in the encounter, Tyler felt exposed.

Lexi looked at her phone as she drove past the manor. Her grandfather texted her. She wondered how many he'd sent before today. *Your dad is pinned down. I'm going to help. You make sure you're safe.* Even with the windows up, she heard the shooting. "Come on, Dad," she said to the empty car. "Don't get yourself killed. Be smart like I know you are." She kept going, pulling to the side of the narrow road about a hundred yards past the house.

Her grandfather might not be enough help, and she didn't know anyone else who could get here on time. Out of options, she dialed Captain Leon Sharpe of the Baltimore Police. After expressing the urgency of the situation to his secretary, she got connected to the man himself. "I don't like what it means if I'm hearing from you," Sharpe said in his deep but rhythmic voice.

"My dad's in trouble. I think he told you about the situation?"

"More or less."

"Well, it's gone to shit. I realize we're an hour outside your jurisdiction, but I didn't know who to call. Raburn has his hooks in law enforcement. I figured you'd know some people he can't push around."

"As a matter of fact," Sharpe said, "I do. Where are you? Don't tell me you're with your dad."

"Of course not," Lexi lied. She gave him the coordinates from memory. "It's a fancy house in Rising Sun. Plenty of land. Not much around, so it's perfect for keeping people prisoner and shooting at the rescuers."

"I'll make a couple calls." Sharpe paused. "If you were on scene, I would tell you to get to a position of safety . . . away from all the shooting."

"Good thing I'm not there, isn't it?"

Sharpe grunted an acknowledgement and hung up. He knew the right people to contact. Cops Raburn didn't know and couldn't try to intimidate with his committee assignment. Lexi checked her Glock 19, made sure she carried two extra magazines, and got out of the car. Her grandfather and Sharpe wanted her to keep out of harm's way, and her dad would tell her the same thing. She would. A pistol wouldn't be much good on the other side of the house. She'd been forced to use lethal force to defend herself a few months before, but it was a close-quarters situation. Lexi pushed aside thoughts of finding a new therapist to focus on the here and now.

Her research told her a bootlegger built this place. There would be non-obvious ways out. Secret doors. Tunnels into the yard. She scaled the fence, dropped into the grass on the other side, and moved deeper onto the grounds. There were plenty of good places to hide over here. Trees. A large shed. An old barn. Her grandfather could help her dad, and the two of them could deal with a lot. The situation would get worse for Raburn and his wife. When it grew bad enough, one or both of them might try to bolt and escape into the expanse of the property. She would take care of anyone who panicked enough to run for it.

33

____

Zeke watched as Tyler spun out to the right and blasted the closest window with a hail of bullets. He was impressed at how many hit the target. The man inside scrambled back once the glass broke. Through the scope, Zeke could tell he was all right. His son would have no way of knowing. Thankfully, he was smart enough to pivot back into cover. His situation hadn't improved any, however, and he couldn't change it much on his own.

The eyes found Zeke again. The old man tried to see the situation through his son's perspective. He was pinned in place by four well-armed shooters who would cut him to ribbons if he moved. Now, he needed to worry about someone else on the other side. A crossfire. Zeke didn't want Tyler to be concerned about it. He whistled the opening bars of "Anchors Aweigh" as he sized up the four gunmen.

From his position, his best shot would be against the second man from the right. None of the quartet acted like they took notice of him. They would soon enough. Zeke knew they wouldn't be able to see him easily, and the time of day removed common issues like the sun glinting off a scope or barrel. He put the shooter in the crosshairs, released the breath in his lungs, and squeezed the trigger in a quick, fluid motion.

The window blew apart as the .30-06 round blasted through it and into the upper chest of the man standing behind it. His weapon tumbled from his hands as he stumbled backward and fell out of Zeke's sight. The gun clattered to the ground near the base of the house. For the first time since he arrived, quiet prevailed. The other three assailants looked around, trying to find the new shooter. Zeke hunkered down and lined up another one.

Casey Norton returned to his office and set his 9MM in the top desk drawer. The voicemail light on his phone pulsed a bright red. He looked out into the area beyond his door. Anyone who might normally field his calls and take messages had left for the day. Norton checked his cell and saw nothing. He pushed the button, frowned when he heard Leon Sharpe's voice, then brightened when he learned the call was about Richard Raburn.

Norton dialed the Baltimore captain. "Hello, Leon," he said when the other man came onto the line.

"Casey. Got a live one for you."

"So I hear. Raburn's landed in the soup, it seems."

"Didn't think you'd be disappointed to learn of it," Sharpe said.

"Not at all," Norton confirmed. "The son of a bitch. Your message didn't go into a lot of detail, so what's going on?"

"I'm not sure I have the complete story. Raburn is about to be exposed. There's a journalist who found the skeletons he wanted to keep in his closet. It seems he had her family murdered and abducted the girl to learn what exactly she knows."

"Holy shit." Norton had disliked Richard Raburn for years. Some twenty-five years ago, the then-delegate dated Norton's mother. Despite being a teenager, young Casey knew firsthand Raburn was a slimeball. Thankfully, his mother came to her senses after a few months, but it was enough time for the man to be completely tainted in Norton's eyes. The senator trying to paint himself as a champion of law enforcement only served as the latest indictment of his character. Still, he wouldn't think Raburn capable of kidnapping and murder even in the name of his political career.

"Yeah," Sharpe said. "I think you met John Tyler a few months ago. He ended up involved in this mess."

"Of course he did."

"He didn't seek out trouble here."

"He didn't walk away from it, either," Norton said.

"The man isn't capable of it." Sharpe let out a dry chuckle. "Never has been. I don't know exactly how he got involved, but he's trying to rescue the reporter and her younger sister. I'll email you the coordinates. It's a big house owned by the family of Raburn's wife."

Norton checked Outlook and found the message Sharpe sent. He clicked on the coordinates, and Google Maps resolved them to an address in Rising Sun. "I'm a long way from there," he said, "but I know some troopers who are closer."

"Pick them carefully," Sharpe said. "Raburn has a long reach."

"I will. I'll contact the sheriff, too. Thanks, Leon." Norton hung up, called a state police corporal he knew to be trustworthy, and told her to take a team to the Nicholls estate. They'd be leaving from Perryville, so they would get there well before he did. Norton fetched his gun and hat and jogged down the stairs. As he fired up his car, he called Kenneth Roth, the sheriff of Cecil County. "Ken, I've got a situation in Rising Sun."

"What's going on?"

Norton provided as many details as he knew. "I've sent a few troopers there already. They just left. This is a . . . delicate matter considering it involves a sitting state senator who's spent years cozying up to guys like you and me." Norton drove away, activating his flashing lights and getting on the gas.

Roth snorted. "Son of a bitch. He's my senator, and I can't stand the prick."

"We both know yours isn't the prevailing opinion," Norton said.

"Yeah. I'm sure some of my deputies fell for his bullshit. Hell, I think a few have even done security work for him in their off-duty hours."

"I hope none of them are there now."

"Me, too," Roth said. "Don't worry. I'll hand-pick a few I trust. We'll deal with everyone at the old Nicholls place . . . no matter who they work for."

"Speaking of which," Norton said, "there's a civilian on scene working against Raburn. He has something to do with one of the girls who's supposed to be held there." He paused. "If it comes to it, I'll vouch for him."

"Will he stand down?"

"No."

Roth sighed. "Jesus, Casey. This really is a situation."

TYLER BRACED for the thought he'd be caught in a crossfire. The person in the trees on the neighbor's property represented the easiest target. He was closer than the four men in the house, but no bullets flew from his direction yet. How this newcomer took up a position there unnoticed still gnawed at Tyler. Even so, he needed to act. He scanned the copse and raised his Glock.

Over the sound of the gunshots from his six, he heard whistling.

He recognized it as the opening bars of "Anchors Aweigh," the official song of the US Navy. He remembered what his father said recently. *We're used to helping the army out of tough spots.* If Zeke made it here, it meant Lexi must be nearby, too. Tyler hoped she stayed out of harm's way. It was one thing for his dad to put himself under the gun. He was a combat veteran. Lexi was a college student, and even if the guys on the top floor got the better of him, she needed to keep living her life.

A shot rang out from the other trees. Glass shattered, and a rifle fell to the earth. Tyler peeked from behind the tree. The man second from the far end no longer stood at his window. The other three stopped shooting and scanned the area. The telltale sound of a bolt-action rifle readying another round broke the quiet.

Definitely his father.

One of the gunmen fired a shot into the other trees, but Tyler knew immediately it came nowhere close to the mark. Zeke wouldn't make himself an easy target. Regardless, he was outnumbered three to one by men whose guns fired a lot faster. He looked to his right. The man he'd fired at before also searched the neighbor's property for the new arrival. None of them were paying attention to the man they'd been trying to kill.

"Nice discipline, guys," Tyler whispered. He focused his front sight at a spot above the window casement, took a deep breath, and squeezed off six rapid-fire rounds. Four hit the mark. A spray of blood preceded the gunman's rifle tumbling from hands which could no longer hold it, and the body soon followed it out the remnants of the window. Tyler popped back into cover as the two surviving assailants opened up on him again. One round blasted through the wood and raised a line of blood on his left arm. Tyler grunted and gripped it. A graze. He'd been lucky, but he couldn't count on it—or the oak—to hold out forever.

He hadn't advanced on the house at all, but with an assist from his father, he'd taken out half the upstairs defense force. Raburn couldn't have many men left. If Tyler got Stacy and Kacey out of this hellhole alive, it would be worth the barbs from his father about the navy rescuing the army again.

34

With their numbers cut in half, the snipers grew more cautious. They could no longer afford to pelt Tyler's position with bullets and hope for the best. Now, thanks to Zeke's arrival, they were forced to fight a two-front war. A few rounds still thunked into the tree behind Tyler. No more made it through. He didn't want to move yet even though he felt he needed to. He also didn't want the men upstairs to figure out where his father was.

The shooting stopped for a moment. Another blast rang out from Zeke's direction. Glass broke, but Tyler didn't hear a rifle clatter to the ground. Maybe the gunmen decided not to be such sitting ducks. Tyler peeked out to his left. No one stood at a window. He eyed a large tree about thirty feet to his right and at least fifty feet closer to the house. Still no shooters. He probably wouldn't get another chance like this again soon.

Tyler took off at a sprint. His left knee complained, and he quickly found himself unable to put his full weight on it. The trunk he would use for cover now seemed farther away. Tyler had never been a fast runner, but he felt exposed moving at less than full speed. He saw a man come into view at one of the upstairs windows. A shot from Zeke's position chased him back into hiding. Tyler made it behind another large oak and paused for a breath. His heart raced and not completely from the exertion.

A memory came to him of raiding a compound in Afghanistan. The team took the ground and killed the opium traders and their hired mercenaries, and they only succeeded because one of the men on Tyler's team sniffed out an ambush. If he hadn't, they would've been caught in a crossfire and put in a very bad spot. Instead, three soldiers took care of the small—but well-armed—second force while the rest shot and killed everyone inside.

The men on the top floor did not get an advance warning.

Tyler meant to keep them on their heels. Before he could, the two gunmen opened fire on the neighbor's trees. They sent a dozen or more rounds screaming toward Zeke, whom Tyler couldn't see. He took it as a good sign. Zeke knew how to conceal his position and roll right or left after firing if needed. Undertaking the operation at dusk helped. He hoped his dad would return fire when the barrage stopped, but he didn't.

Was he all right? Tyler's pulse quickened again. He hadn't always enjoyed a good relationship with the old man—neither of them were particularly easy to get along with—but they'd been in a solid place for a while. His dad showing up here to help him free the Chaplain sisters represented the nicest thing he'd done in a long time. Tyler whistled the opening of the navy chantey, sending an off-key "Anchors aweigh, my boys, anchors aweigh" toward the neighboring trees.

"Farewell to foreign shores, we sail at break of day" chirped back at him—on key even, because of course it would be. His father was all right. Tyler took a quick look at the house. A new wave of bullets tore out chunks of the tree. He had an equally good shot at either remaining man. While he didn't know Zeke's exact position, the first guy he shot at had been toward the far end. Tyler held up his hand, pointed to his left twice, and then held up three fingers. He didn't know if his father could see him, but if he did, he would understand.

Tyler counted to three in his head, dropped to a crouch, and leaned around the tree to his left. He sighted above the man in the far window and fired five shots as a loud report accompanied a much higher velocity bullet blasting the window to bits. Several red spots covered the shooter's torso. The automatic weapon fell from his grip as he sagged against the frame. His body settled half in and half out, with his left arm flopping against the exterior of the building.

A single gunman remained. And now, for the first time, the shooter upstairs was the one outnumbered.

"IT'S NOT GOING WELL, SIR," Gustav said.

Raburn watched the action unfold on the tech wizard's multi-screen setup. He could never stare at such a monstrosity all day, but he would admit its utility for situations like these. Thanks to cameras in the trees and on the eaves, he could follow the action, and he shared Gustav's grim assessment. Someone arrived to help Tyler. This much was clear. Another reminder of it came when several rounds peppered Quincy at his window. The poor man didn't even fall out when he succumbed to his wounds.

He was the third sniper to fall. "Donald, pull back," Raburn said into his walkie-talkie. "Tyler has some help. You're a sitting duck."

"I thought I had a bead on the other guy," he said. "Don't

know where he is. This has been really hard. You made it sound easy."

"It will be," Raburn said. "You and Gustav will help defend the house now. You go outside near the front."

It took a few seconds, but Donald eventually said, "Copy that."

"I'm not a shooter," Gustav said before Raburn could conscript him.

"You are today," Raburn told him. "You knew the job when the company sent you here."

"Yeah." He crossed his arms. "Do my usual."

"Consider these other duties as assigned."

Gustav stood. He wasn't built like a fighter. He was slender, which alone didn't disqualify him. The same description could be applied to Hong, but he was wiry where Gustav could only be considered scrawny. If he'd built up good reflexes, he did so playing video games. "I know how to handle a gun." He shrugged. "I guess I can pitch in."

"There you go," Raburn said. "I'll put in a good word for you with Elite."

"If I survive," Gustav said miserably.

"Get a gun from downstairs. Your choice. If you're worried about being accurate, get a shotgun. If John Tyler walks up to the door, unload on him."

"I hope he doesn't get past Donald." Gustav left the room and headed to the first floor. Raburn hoped Tyler didn't make it to the house. He couldn't count on a geek to muster much of a defense, though he could get lucky with a shotgun. Still, if Tyler made it inside, it would be down to Hong to stop him.

Raburn smiled. He very much wanted to see Hong beat John Tyler to death, even if it meant he got past all the other defenses. Let him come.

No more shots came. Tyler took a cautious look over his shoulder and around the trunk. He couldn't see a figure in the window. "You got eyes on anyone?" he called toward his backup man.

"Negative," his father said. "I saw him leave the room. This asshole must be redeploying his men."

"Hold your position," Tyler said. "I'll come to you. Cover the house just in case." He waited a couple seconds, then stayed in a crouching gait toward the property line. No shots rang out in either direction. The going proved a little slower than Tyler wanted. His knee protested. He still felt the sprint of a few minutes ago every time he took a limping step. Not surprisingly, he didn't spot his father as he first approached. The old man was still too good to be detected easily even by a trained operative. His dark pants stood out from the grass and pine needles on a third look. "Hi, Dad."

"I wanted to see if you'd find me."

"Thanks for coming," Tyler said.

"Thank your daughter. She insisted and drove." He held up a hand before Tyler could say anything. "I told her to keep herself out of the action. She was going to drive to the other side of the house."

"What's over there?"

"Hell if I know," Zeke said. "A bootlegger built this place ages ago, so she thinks there might be some hidden ways out. The grounds are a lot more expansive on the far side."

It made sense. The house definitely sat off center, and there was a lot more real estate to its right. A tunnel dug over a hundred years before could lead to an old barn or dump someone out in the middle of a group of trees. Raburn chose this place well—or more accurately, his wife did, and he agreed to it. "He can't have too many guys left," Tyler said. "I'd taken out a few already, and we just picked off three right here."

"We did." His father nodded, and a grin split his aged features. "Once again, the army gets its ass in a bind, and the navy sails in to bail it out."

"Yeah, yeah," Tyler said. "I thanked you already. I'm sure you'll hold this over my head for a while, but you're not getting much more out of me today." He took out his burner and sent a quick text to Lexi. *Your grandfather and I are both fine. I'm headed toward the house. Stay vigilant for runners.*

"You all right?" Zeke jutted his chin toward the blood on Tyler's arm. "You ain't moving too well."

"I'll survive." He pointed to his arm. "This was just a graze. I took a tumble down the stairs before. Knee still hurts. I have a brace on it, which helps, but I'll make do." He adjusted the brace, which had slipped around to the side a little. "I've fought better enemies when I've had worse problems."

"Where you want me to be?"

"You and Lexi checked the property out, right?" The old man nodded. "Hell, you probably got a better look at it than I did. I wanted to get on the road. Put yourself wherever you think you can help the most."

Zeke bobbed his head. "All right. I'll probably move farther down and cover the back door." He fixed Tyler with his gaze. "You be careful in there."

"Don't get all sentimental on me," Tyler said. "The navy can't take credit for rescuing the army if it spends the second half of the battle weeping in the trees."

"Go to hell," his father said with a chuckle.

Tyler patted his dad on the shoulder. Then, he crouched and moved quietly toward the front of the house. However diminished Raburn's forces, he still didn't expect this to be easy. The senator would have kept a couple men back—his best, probably. Tyler would be ready.

STACY WAS tired of feeling afraid.

Ever since she walked into her house and saw her mother, father, and two younger siblings shot dead, she'd been in a constant state of fear. A few moments had been worse than others. When the two men in dark coats came into the store. When she and Mister Tyler went back to the house to find the flash drive . . . and two men burst through her brother's bedroom door to grab her.

The torture.

The only positive had been confirming Kacey was still alive.

For the past few minutes, she'd heard gunfire, and she knew Kacey heard it, too. "What do you think's going on?"

"I don't know." Her older sister shook her head. "I would say it's the cops, but Raburn's big on cozying up to law enforcement. I can't see him ordering a shootout." She paused. "What about you?"

"I think it's Lexi's dad."

Kacey frowned. "You'd better hope some of that gunfire is him shooting back, then."

"No," Stacy said, "*we* had better hope. I think he's our only way out of here alive. It's only a matter of time before this asshole gets what he wants."

"I can hold out," Kacey said, but the small tremor in her voice gave her away.

Stacy went along with it. No use arguing the point. "Even if you can, I don't think I could." The recent memory of feeling as if she were drowning, and it would never end, rushed into her mind. She remembered something Mister Tyler told her —"Everybody breaks."

"Let's not worry about it right now, huh? We should try to get out of here." Kacey looked around the room. Her eyes were red from crying, and her clothes were still wet, but she kept herself focused on what mattered. Stacy had a long way to go if she wanted to be as composed as her older sister. *My only sister now.* She fought back tears as she searched the area from her spot. There wasn't much in the room. No one was careless enough to leave a knife lying around. The shelf was crowded on the lower levels, but Raburn wouldn't keep captives in here if he also provided a means of getting free.

"I think I see something," Kacey said after a moment.

"Really?"

"Second shelf up, back left. I think it's a box of ceramic tile."

"So?" Stacy said. "Probably left over from redoing a floor."

"Ceramic tile breaks," Kacey said in a patient tone. "When it does, it leaves a sharp edge." She scooted her chair about two inches closer. "I know it's a lot. I need to grab one, drop it or smash it, and hang onto a sharp edge." She shrugged as much as her bonds would allow. "Right now, I don't see another way out of here. We should take advantage of Raburn and his asshole squad being distracted."

"You're right." Kacey got the chair to move again. She was closer to the shelf. Still, it would take a couple minutes just for her to get into position. "Can I help?"

"I don't think so." Another inch or two nearer.

Stacy heard footsteps come down the basement stairs. Kacey stopped moving, and the sisters looked at each other. "Who do you think it is?" Stacy whispered.

"I don't know."

The footfalls came closer. Stacy's heart pounded. Would Raburn decide to cut his losses and simply have them killed? Would he waterboard them nonstop until someone cracked? Fear gripped Stacy again, and despite her best efforts to appear strong in front of her sister, her eyes welled.

36

Lexi heard footsteps approaching her position.

She put her back against a tree and slipped her Glock from its holster. Whoever drew closer did a good job of keeping quiet. What if it was her dad looking for her? She didn't want to give herself away by saying anything, though. Another couple steps. Then, she heard a whispered voice. "Lexi? You over here?"

"Grandpa?" She stepped out from behind the trunk. Zeke padded to her. Lexi studied his face. Other than a wrinkle line or two, it hadn't changed much in the last five years. He didn't look sad, which was good news. "How's my dad?"

"As stubborn as ever," he said, standing against a nearby tree to reload his rifle.

"How did it go?" she asked. It felt a lot like talking to her father. She understood where he got his reticence.

"Three snipers are down. The fourth abandoned his post. Probably called back by Raburn. Your father's going into the house to get the girls."

"I want to go, too. Stacy's my friend."

Her grandfather put up his hand. "I get it . . . but there's no way your dad would want you to. We're presuming there's not a lot of resistance left in there, but we don't know. This senator could have a dozen men. I don't want you going in there, either."

"What about you?"

Zeke scoffed. "I'm too old for full frontal assaults. Listen. We can both do some good out here. You said this was a boot-legger's house, right?" She nodded. "There are probably escape tunnels into these woods."

"I was thinking the same thing," Lexi said.

"If things go wrong in there, the senator and his wife are going to cut and run. No matter how cozy he thinks he is with the cops, they're going to haul him away for this."

"Not if my dad shoots him first."

Her grandfather smiled. "We can only hope. He may not stick around long enough. I don't know where any tunnels are going to empty out, but they won't be too close to the main building." He pointed to the wooded area behind the house. "There's a shed back there. It would be a pretty long passage, but who knows? I'm going to take up a position to watch it. I think you should stay about where you are. Keep as much of the building in sight as you can."

"I will," Lexi said. She was already a few hundred feet from the house. "I doubt anyone's running out the front door. Not with the cops on their way."

"Be careful," the old man said. He ducked under a branch, stayed low, and moved farther into the woods. Lexi quietly stepped thirty or so feet to her left. She stood against a large maple about five hundred feet from the house and waited.

T YLER MOVED through the trees again. Zeke left his post to find Lexi. It was unlikely anyone would appear in one of the windows again. It didn't go well the first time. Still, Tyler prepared for the possibility. He moved from trunk to trunk, pausing and taking cover for a couple seconds before continuing. When he cleared the last tree, he dashed to the main building as quickly as his knee would allow and put his back to the bricks.

So far, the coast was clear. Raburn would keep a few guys back to protect him, but he couldn't have more than a handful left. Tyler inched closer to the front. As he neared the edge, he stopped and stole a glance around it. One of the uniformed guys walked a perimeter in front of the raised porch. He moved toward the far end. Tyler stayed low and crouched from sight. He pondered the best way of taking the guard out. He lost the element of surprise a while ago. The men inside would be expecting him. No need to keep things quiet.

The sentry stopped at the far corner of the house and turned back. Tyler watched his every step. The man didn't even keep a pistol at the ready. What did he expect to do if someone went at him? As he closed to within a hundred feet, Tyler saw the telltale lines of a vest under the man's jacket. He'd need a headshot, then. Seventy-five feet. Tyler stepped out into the open and stood. The guard's eyes widened, and he reached for his gun as Tyler split his forehead with a shot from the Glock. The body sagged to the ground.

Tyler slipped forward and swiped the dead man's spare magazine. He noticed an earpiece and took it, too, fitting it in his own ear. He heard chatter about the shot outside. Someone asked the fallen man to check in. Tyler crouched at the porch and waited to see if anybody else came to look. After a ten-count, he stood and walked up the stairs. The newness of the wood marked the porch as a recent addition or renovation. It ran the entire length of the building. A swinging bench hung from beams toward the other end.

The door remained unlocked. They were practically rolling out a red carpet. Tyler stood to the side, threw it open, and waited. A hail of bullets streamed past. When the shooter's gun clicked empty, Tyler stepped into the doorway and shot the other uniformed man. A slender fellow who looked like he belonged sitting at a computer came into the main room holding a shotgun. No vest. Tyler put two in his chest, and he dropped to the wooden floor.

Tyler stepped inside. Despite the age of the home, renovations made its interior look modern. Hardwood floors. Crown molding. He'd barely started clearing the first floor when someone sprang out of hiding and kicked the Glock from his hand. The next kick took Tyler flush in the chest and drove him backwards. He stayed on his feet. A wiry Asian man glared at him and advanced.

37

Casey Norton pushed his state police cruiser over ninety miles per hour.

He zoomed onto the shoulder when he needed to, but most drivers signaled a drift to the right at the approach of his lights and siren. Other troopers would be close to the Nicholls estate by now, but Norton remained about twenty minutes away. Maybe a little less at his current pace. The scene could be a minefield, and he wanted to keep things under control. He called Sheriff Roth. "Ken, what's the ETA on your deputies?"

"About ten minutes. This place is pretty remote even for Cecil County."

"All right," Norton said. "I think a few of my people might get there first."

"We'd appreciate them waiting," the sheriff said. "I'm grateful for the assist, but this is a county matter, and Raburn represents us." He paused. "Whether we like him or not."

"I'll tell them to wait for you. However, if they hear gunshots or the like, they're going in. We're not going to stand around while people get killed."

"Understood," the sheriff said and hung up.

Norton shook his head. This wasn't the time for territorial pissing matches. He scrolled through his contacts and called Corporal Sutherland. "I need your ETA."

"Seven or eight minutes, Captain."

"Make it seven," Norton said. "The county's coming, too, including the sheriff. They want us to wait for them."

Sutherland chuckled. "I hope you didn't say yes."

"I placated him, but I don't care about his pride or where this is happening. We're heading into a bad situation. You take charge at the scene. If you hear anything—and I mean *anything*—from the house, treat it as someone being in danger. Go in."

"Roger that," Sutherland said.

"We expect there will be hostages," Norton said. "Two women, both under twenty-five, and we don't know what condition they'll be in. When you hang up with me, make sure you request an ambulance."

"Wilco."

"One more thing." Norton sighed. "There's a civilian on scene. He's there to rescue the girls. His name is John Tyler. Retired military, about fifty, average height."

"How the hell did he get involved?" Sutherland wanted to know.

"I heard he knows the captives," Norton said. "I've run into Tyler before. He doesn't let things go. If he believes he can get the girls out of there, he's going to try. He's one of the good guys, though I can't say I endorse his methods . . . or his meddling."

"Understood. I'll make sure the civilian stands down."

Norton snorted. "Yeah. Good luck. I'll see you when I get there." He gave his car a little more gas. Maybe he could make it to the estate in fifteen minutes. Between Raburn's schemes and John Tyler's tendency to shoot first and skip the questions, he wondered what kind of scene he'd be rolling up on.

TYLER EXPECTED MORE resistance inside the house. A few guys with automatic weapons at least. He might still encounter such a defense force. At the moment, however, the Asian guy who stepped out of hiding and kicked the pistol from his hand was enough to contend with. Tyler overcame the shock of the man's initial attacks and blocked his next kick. He took a defensive stance, presenting his left side to his opponent. Not putting all his weight on his left knee represented a perk of this pose.

His adversary was fast. No time to bring the shotgun to bear. Three punches came in rapid succession. Tyler turned them all aside. He'd fought martial arts guys before. The Taliban and their supporters used some. It had been about a decade, and Tyler was younger then—and he'd stood on two good legs. The longer this fight went, the more it favored his foe. After blunting another punch, Tyler launched one of his own.

The Asian man's speed saved him a hard blow to the face. He caught Tyler's wrist, pulled down, and turned his hips. Tyler left his feet, flipped over his opponent, and came down hard on his back. An upraised foot offered no time to recover. He rolled to the side and avoided the hard stomp, though the Remington stayed behind. Tyler kicked his adversary behind the knee, and he tumbled to the ground. Unfortunately, he got back to vertical right away.

Tyler was still on his knees when the next kick came. He crossed his forearms and blocked it, then lashed out and punched his foe flush in the family jewels. He grunted and went down again. Tyler scrabbled to his feet and booted the other guy hard in the ribs with his right leg. He went for another, but his opponent enveloped his ankle in his left arm. Tyler's left knee suddenly had to take all his weight, and it buckled. He crashed to the wooden floor again.

His adversary grinned like a predator.

The younger man regained his feet, grabbed Tyler's left leg, and twisted. Tyler howled in pain as his knee got wrenched. He used his right leg to kick at his foe's arms and knocked one free. Another booted the second one away. It still left Tyler in a bad spot. He turned enough to put his left leg under him so his enemy couldn't grab it again. Not much else was going right at the moment.

"You're old and crippled," the guy said in a slight accent. "Why'd you even come?" He tried to give Tyler a solid punt to the ribs. It was predictable, though. Tyler caught his foe's foot, grabbed the other leg, and pulled. The younger man crashed to the hardwood. Capitalizing would have been nice, but it took a fair bit of effort for Tyler to get back to his feet. His left knee felt worse than ever and would take little of his weight.

His opponent stood at the same time. "You're not bad, old man. But now, you die."

He launched a flurry of blows. Tyler fell into a defensive rhythm as he blocked them. His forearms stung from the effort as he waited for an opening. He found one when his opponent overcommitted to a wild left cross. Tyler grabbed his arm, pulled the man along, and shoved him face-first into the nearby wall. He followed up with an elbow to the back of the other man's head, bouncing his skull off the drywall. It didn't knock him out, but it stunned him. He lashed out blindly as Tyler backed away and looked for an advantage.

He limped through an opening into the kitchen. It featured a door, so he closed and locked it. A look around revealed no other way in. Once his enemy recovered, it wouldn't keep him out for long. Most household doors yielded to good kicks in the right spot. Tyler hobbled to the counter. A full block of knives sat near the stove. He could use one. Kitchen knives weren't balanced for throwing, so he'd need to use it in melee. This ran the risk of his adversary taking it away and using it against him. In Tyler's condition, the odds were not in his favor.

A loud bang came from the door. "You won't keep me out for long, old man!"

"How ancient do you think I am?" Tyler muttered as he looked around the rest of the space. He spied something he could use, and he grabbed it while he still had time.

RABURN UNLOCKED the door in the basement, and his wife and Donald followed him in.

The girls managed to move their chairs around. No matter. They wouldn't find anything they could use to get free. Raburn still needed information from Kacey. He didn't want to appear desperate, however. She and her sister must've heard the gunshots. Upstairs, Tyler breached the front door and currently tangled with Hong. He didn't know how it would go, but things in general went very poorly today. Miriam encouraged him to cut his losses and run. Raburn couldn't bring himself to do it.

Not without a final effort to get what he needed.

"I'm going to have what I require soon," he said, looking between the sisters in turn. "If either of you want to tell me now, I'll spare your life."

"Life," Kacey said. "Singular."

"Yes." Raburn nodded. "Whoever talks will live. The other will die."

"Screw you." Stacy snorted. "We're not ratting each other out for you."

"When my needs are met, you'll both become expendable."

"So be it," Kacey said. "Personally, I think you're full of shit. If you really got what you wanted, you'd be ordering us shot right now."

She'd seen through his bluff. It always carried some risk. He probably should have figured neither would throw the other under the bus. With two strangers or acquaintances, maybe. Not this pair of sisters. They were the only survivors of their family thanks to Raburn, and Kacey just declared they wouldn't give him anything.

"You foolish tramp!" Miriam moved around her husband and slapped Kacey hard enough to turn her head. "You're both going to die down here."

Raburn gave the girls his best hard stare. "Say goodbye to each other."

"Piss off," Stacy said. Miriam slapped her, too.

"Have it your way," Raburn said. "Donald will stay here with you. If either of you try something . . . or a rescuer comes for you . . . you're both dead."

"I hope you're happy with all the trouble you've caused us," Miriam shouted at them.

"You murdered our family," Kacey said. "How about checking your privilege, Karen? And screw off while you're at it."

Before Miriam could hit either of them again, Raburn grabbed her arm, put another hand on her waist, and steered her toward the door. She jerked free of his grip and stomped from the room. The senator spared a final glower for the girls before following his wife.

38

Tyler twisted the cap from the bottle of cooking oil. He moved closer to the door and poured the contents on the floor. The color more or less blended in with the beige tile. Attackers could see it but only if they stopped to look for it. He tossed the empty bottle across the kitchen. It clattered to the floor as the door burst into the room from a mighty kick. The Asian man glowered and stalked forward. "I've wasted enough time with you," he said. "Time to die."

"Get on with it, then." Tyler stood just past the puddle. He made a show of raising his fists to keep his adversary's eyes up. His left leg still wouldn't support him well, but he hoped it wouldn't matter for much longer. His foe took a step forward. One more would put him in the oil. The man let out a yell and surged ahead.

His eyes went wide as he never found the traction he expected.

His feet moved wildly as his arms flailed. Tyler's opponent skidded across the floor and toppled forward, crashing headfirst into the freestanding island. A large spot of blood marred its white surface. Tyler walked around the long way to avoid the pool of oil. His enemy groaned but made no attempt to get up. It could have been a ruse to lure him close. Stacy and her sister couldn't wait forever, though.

Tyler limped close to his fallen foe, who barely seemed to register his presence. "I think you need to learn some respect for your elders," he said. An incoherent groan served as the only response. Tyler bent down, grabbed the Asian man in a headlock, and snapped his neck. The body fell to the floor, its head rebounding off the tile. Lifeless eyes stared back at Tyler. He hobbled from the kitchen and picked up his pistol and shotgun from the living room. He still didn't know where Raburn or the Chaplain sisters were.

The rest of the house was quiet. Tyler put one hand on the railing to help pull himself up the stairs to check out the upper levels.

KACEY COULDN'T TRY to get free with Donald in the room.

The plan to smash a piece of tile and use a shard to cut her bonds had been a good one. She didn't know if it would actually work, but there was no way Raburn's pet goon would allow her to make the attempt. For his part, Donald stood silently near the door. Kacey grew more interested in what happened on the other side. Raburn and his wife argued.

"There's no reason to stay, Richard," she said. "None."

"Of course there is. We get everything we wanted."

"I'm not sure it's even possible anymore. How many of your men are dead? Is Donald the last one left?"

"Hong is upstairs," Raburn said. "John Tyler might have pulled off an upset outside, but there's no way he gets past Hong. The guy's a straight-up killer."

"I'm not very confident in your predictions anymore," his

wife said. "We had the girl we needed. Then, you wanted to get the sister, too. And why? Simply because she got away the first time? She might never have figured all this out." Stacy smirked at the mention of her situation. "You took on a lot of risk, and it hasn't paid off."

"We can still come out on top, Miriam."

"Oh, bullshit! Look around. How do you come out of this ahead? Even if that Tyler man dies upstairs, how is this going to look? I know this is a remote house, but if someone heard shooting and called the cops, we're screwed."

"You know I—"

"Do you think your committee assignment in Annapolis is going to get you out of this?" she said. "Really? Don't be delusional, Richard. There are a bunch of bodies outside. I'm sure there are a few more in here by now. You've kept two girls captive down here, and if they live, they'll tell the police every little thing that happened to them." She snorted. "You lucked into finding the reporter was on to you in the first place, and all you've done since then is piss it away."

"How did he find out?" Stacy asked.

"Quiet," Donald barked.

Kacey ignored him. "I don't know. I've thought a lot about it, but I really have no idea."

"Your editor?"

"No way." Kacey shook her head. "He's way too old school to give up a reporter or a source."

Stacy frowned. Her cheek still showed red from where Miriam Raburn slapped her. A realization came to Kacey. "When she hit you, she didn't say anything."

"So?"

"So she called me a stupid tramp," Kacey said.

"You're no tramp," Stacy said.

"Thanks." Despite the situation, Kacey had to smile at her younger sister defending her honor. "I'm not. I've barely even dated since I finished college. But recently, I've been seeing Lamont . . . and he works in Annapolis." Donald's face twitched at the mention of the man's name. Kacey knew she was on to something. "I don't know how or why, but he must also work for Raburn. Or at least feed him information for money. It's the only explanation that makes sense."

"Quiet," Donald said again.

Stacy ignored him this time. "He seemed nice enough when I video chatted with the two of you."

"I think he might have sold us down the river," Kacey said. She lapsed into silence. The argument in the basement continued.

"Just because you want to stay on a sinking ship doesn't mean I have to," Miriam said.

"What the hell are you talking about?"

"I know this house, Richard. Things you don't. You stick around. See how it goes for you. I'm leaving."

"Miriam, wait," Raburn said. One set of footsteps moved away, and then a door opened and closed somewhere else on the lower level. Raburn shouted in rage a few seconds later.

"Serves him right," Kacey said. "Prick."

"Let's hope he doesn't take it out on us," Stacy said.

Donald didn't speak, but the wolfish grin on his face told the sisters he'd be happy to dish out whatever pain his boss commanded.

Miriam Raburn stalked from her husband. The damned fool. If he didn't have enough foresight to abandon ship now, he and his career were doomed. All they'd worked for . . . gone. A part of her hoped he would come to his senses and make a run for it. Another wished he wouldn't. Miriam would be better off with a man who could make tough decisions.

Who would stick it out most of the time but cut and run when the chips were down. Voters had short memories. A few news cycles and another scandal or two, and they'd forget why they were supposed to be outraged.

If she needed to, Miriam could divorce Richard and start over. She'd find another man whose ambition matched her own. Maybe he'd be more malleable than Richard. A little younger would be nice, too. Miriam smiled as she opened the door to the laundry room. The washer and dryer occupied one end. The rest held several storage shelves. One, the lightest and most rickety of all, remained empty. Miriam pulled it away from the stone wall. She remembered helping her grandfather paint it white.

It was the first time she learned of the tunnel.

Bootleggers always needed a way out, he told her. Sometimes, politicians and their wives did, too. With the rack out of the way, the trap door cut into the floor was obvious. Miriam lifted the iron ring and grunted as she twisted it. She lubricated it every six months in case they ever needed to use it. It still took a fair bit of effort, but Miriam guided the ring through the ninety-degree turn and unlocked the door. She set her feet and lifted. It was heavier than she remembered, but she probably hadn't opened it for a decade.

When a nearby flashlight failed to turn on, Miriam used the app on her phone to help her get down the first few stairs. Once her head cleared the floor, she reached up, grabbed a handle, and pulled. The trap door slammed shut above her, showering her head with dust and dirt. She coughed as she made her way down the rest of the steps. There were eight in all. At the bottom, a tunnel about six feet tall and four feet wide led away from the house. It smelled musty. Many of the stones had cracked over the years. Miriam didn't want to think about how many rodents and snakes crawled in here at various times.

Thankfully, she didn't encounter any. She would have kept going—escaping the house and the deteriorating situation inside remained the priority—but the presence of vermin would have tempted her to turn back. Miriam wished she carried a proper light. The app used her phone's flash to simulate one, but it didn't produce a focused beam. Still, it was better than nothing, and slow progress counted, too.

The underground passage went on for what felt like miles thanks to the darkness and odor. In reality, it probably covered about a seven hundred feet. A significant achievement at the time her ancestors built it. If she got out of this with her holdings intact, Miriam resolved to update the tunnel. Her next husband would pay for it. He just wouldn't know about it.

A set of cinder block steps going upward loomed ahead. Finally. Miriam coughed as the smell of dampness grew stronger. She stopped about halfway up the stairs and used her light to see the metal escape hatch. No one used this in a long time. Miriam shook her head. She didn't even know if it would open. The locking mechanism here was similar to the one at the other end. It took a minute and a lot of effort, but she turned it enough to unlatch it. A hard shove threw the door open.

Miriam stepped out into the trees. She could see the house in the distance. There were plenty of places to hide on the rest of the property, and if no cops were here yet, she could use the time to get away. Miriam closed the hatch. Its dull brown color allowed it to blend in with the forest floor. As she walked away, she noticed a woman standing nearby. Who the hell was this?

Miriam made a run for it, but the mysterious figure matched her stride for stride.

39

Tyler moved pistol-first into a bedroom. It was the third one on the second level and the largest. One of them served as Raburn's office. He spent a minute looking through things there but found nothing of interest. No one occupied any of the spaces here. When he was outside, Raburn's men fired from windows on the top story. It struck him as unlikely anyone would remain there. Raburn would have redeployed his men after three of them died. Still, leaving potential enemies on your six doomed an operation to failure. Tyler limped up another set of stairs.

The ceiling was a few inches lower. He wondered if this entire floor was originally an attic and got converted to more usable space over time. Another bedroom served as an office. Lavender curtains matched a rug on the floor in front of the desk. The fake plants, color scheme, and wall photos made this one Miriam Raburn's. Her husband's had been much more plain and Spartan—much like Tyler's office or Zeke's entire apartment. Tyler looked around the work area for a moment but didn't see anything noteworthy. The drawers were locked, and he didn't want to take the time to jimmy them.

Two unfurnished rooms faced the woods, and their windows served as the shooters' nests. The one's corpse remained in the window, Tyler nudged it as he approached, and the body fell to the ground below. He thought about picking up a rifle but didn't have much need for it in the house. His pistol and shotgun would be good enough. Tyler took the stairs back to the main floor. Raburn must have held the girls in the basement.

He verified no one took up a position on the main level while he nosed around upstairs. No sirens approached, either, though he couldn't count on this to remain true indefinitely. Someone was bound to hear or see something amiss eventually. A door off the dining room led to the basement. Tyler stood to the side and pulled the knob. A hail of bullets ripped through the opening. The barrage stopped a couple seconds later. It wasn't enough rounds to run a full magazine out. The shooter probably hoped Tyler would think he was empty, come down the stairs, and get filled with lead. He nudged his gun inside the doorway and fired a single shot downstairs.

Another torrent of bullets blasted into the ceiling above the jamb.

~

Lexi kept an eye on the forest.

It was a lot of ground. Plenty of trees for someone to hide behind. A few derelict buildings could help, too. She would see someone leaving the house, however, and so far, nobody made a run for it. Lexi hoped her dad was all right. She still felt this whole mess was her fault. If she'd just picked up Stacy as they planned . . . No, she chided herself. The factors beyond her control would've played out the same way. The hit squad's grim work remained the same. If anything, her dad picking up Stacy worked out well. He was better equipped to handle a team of killers than she would've been.

A metallic *thunk* from the trees drew her attention. It was the wrong sound to come from a verdant setting. Lexi kept low and padded closer. She unholstered her Glock and moved toward the noise. Something popped up from the ground. Lexi stood behind a nearby tree and peered around its trunk. A slender arm raised a hatch, which blended in well with the dirt, grass, and stray leaves. A woman climbed out and let the hatch fall back into place with a similar solid *thunk.*

She turned in both directions. Enough light came through the canopy for Lexi to get a decent look at her. Brown hair, slightly above average height, slender, probably in her forties. Miriam Raburn. The wife decided to cut and run after all. Lexi wondered what this meant for the senator's fate . . . and her father's.

Lexi stepped out from cover. Miriam Raburn turned in her direction. She stood motionless for a moment before taking off at a run. "Oh, no, you don't," Lexi said. She holstered the Glock and took off after the senator's wife. The terrain reminded Lexi of some of her cross country races in high school. They did their fair share of running on pavement or wooded trails, but sometimes, the girls made their own path. She remembered picking through the trees to catch up to a rival her junior year. Chasing after Miriam Raburn felt similar.

For a middle-aged woman, she set a pretty good pace. A lot of people could go fast initially, however. The key was how long they could maintain their speed. In Miriam's case, it wasn't very long. She slowed after about a quarter-mile, and Lexi gained significant ground on her. Like her father, she'd never been the fastest runner. Endurance was her hallmark, and it allowed her to maintain her speed and catch up to the older woman.

Miriam knew the woods better, though, and a branch to the face made Lexi stumble and almost knocked her prone. She resumed her pace quickly enough. An old barn loomed in the distance, but she knew she could catch her quarry in time. When she closed the distance to a couple feet, Lexi lunged forward and tackled Miriam Raburn. The older woman landed on the ground with a loud grunt.

She recovered quickly and shoved Lexi off. A strong grip on the bottom of Miriam's sweater held her in place while Lexi regained her feet. "Get off me," the senator's wife said. She threw a punch. Lexi turned and let it hit her on the back of the shoulder.

"You murdered my friend's family," she said.

"Grow up, girl. Richard and I have plans for this state."

"I hope they involve dying in prison." Lexi kicked Miriam Raburn in the stomach, bending her in half. She followed it with a boot to the face, dropping the other woman to the ground. To her credit, Mrs. Raburn lashed out with a kick to Lexi's leg. It didn't put her down, but it staggered her long enough for Miriam to get back up.

She threw another punch. Her technique was poor, however. Rather than a straight right, it looked more like a loose hook. Lexi blocked it and did the same with the follow-up. "Your friend's family didn't matter," Miriam Raburn said. "Her whore sister got in the way."

Lexi deflected another wild strike and answered with a solid left to Miriam's jaw. A hard right dropped the older woman to the ground again. When she tried to get up, Lexi kicked her hard in the ribs. "Stay down," she said as Miriam groaned. "Or get up. It won't go well for you if you do, but if you're willing to take a beating, I'll give you one. Someone needs to."

"You're as big an idiot as your friend," the senator's wife said. She rose to one knee, and Lexi delivered a hard side kick flush in her face. Miriam fell prone and didn't try to move again.

40

W hile the barrage ripped the ceiling above him apart, Tyler switched weapons. He stuffed the pistol into his waistband and brandished the Remington shotgun. It wasn't the same model he used overseas, but it was close. A good, reliable weapon. Perfectly adequate for clearing a trigger-happy idiot from the bottom of a staircase. Tyler brushed drywall dust from his hair and face, and he heard the telltale click from the basement a second later.

He stepped to the side and pivoted to face his adversary. The large man at the bottom of the stairs frowned at his automatic weapon. He tried pulling the trigger again with a predictable result. Tyler placed the front bead on the man and fired. The slug shredded his torso and neck, and a smear of blood trailed the body as it hit the wall and slumped to the tiled floor.

Tyler pumped the shotgun and headed into the lower level. His knee made for slow going, and the Remington meant he couldn't use the railing to steady himself. Once the wall to his left fell away, Tyler pointed his weapon into the open area. He didn't see anyone, and he confirmed the emptiness of the main room a couple seconds later. Other than the corpse of the man he just shot, Tyler found no signs anyone had been here.

He cleared the laundry room, though a shelf dragged away from the wall caught his eye. Something to come back to if the rest of his search turned up empty. The area past the main room was also empty. A single door remained. Tyler tried the knob. Locked. "We're in here," Stacy shouted from the other side. "Help!"

"Quiet!" another voice said. Probably Raburn. He couldn't have any lackeys left at this point.

With his balky knee, Tyler couldn't kick the door open. He didn't have a snap gun handy. The knob didn't look very sturdy, however. He whacked it with the butt end of the shotgun a couple times, and the second blow did the trick. Tyler pushed the door open with his foot and put Richard Raburn on the business end of the Remington's barrel. The man looked a few years older than Tyler. His eyes were beady and unfriendly. How he made it in politics remained a mystery.

Kacey and Stacy sat tied to identical chairs. Water marked the floor around a large basin near the center of the unadorned room. Both young women's clothes, faces, and hair were wet. Two jugs of water sat nearby along with a soaked towel. "You waterboarded them?" he said to the senator.

"I want my lawyer," he said.

Tyler cross-checked him with the Remington. Raburn stumbled into the sink, bounced off it, and fell to the concrete floor. "You must have confused me with someone who gives a shit about your rights . . . Dick." He glanced at the sisters. "If I give you a knife, can you cut yourselves free?"

"Yes," Kacey said.

"All right." Raburn rose to all fours, so Tyler again made use of the shotgun's solid butt stock. He slung the weapon over his shoulder, drew the pistol to replace it, and handed Kacey a small knife. She got to work on her bonds while Tyler kept the Glock trained on the senator. He heard a siren in the distance. "Now's your chance to talk. Why did you need to kill so many people?"

"I'm not telling you anything." Raburn spat a mouthful of blood onto the floor. "I'll be suing you for assault."

"I might as well earn it, then," Tyler said, and he kicked Raburn in the ribs. He used his left leg to avoid putting weight on it. It didn't result in a hard blow, but Raburn still grunted when it found the mark. "No lawyer will get you out of talking to the cops. Tell me . . . why the Chaplains? And how did you know to go after Kacey in the first place?"

Raburn coughed and croaked, "Lawyer."

The sirens grew closer. Kacey freed herself and worked on the ropes holding her sister. Raburn wasn't going to talk. Tyler pondered the poetic justice of waterboarding him. Even if he were inclined to torture someone, he wouldn't have time. The police were too close. Sure enough, he heard footsteps moving around the main level a moment later. "We're down here," he called. "All hostiles subdued. Two women will need paramedics."

LEXI PULLED Miriam Raburn's arms behind her back like she was about to slap on handcuffs. She didn't have any way to restrain the woman, so she put her knee on top of Miriam's wrists. This elicited a grunt of pain and a fresh round of cursing. Lexi took out her phone and dialed 9-1-1. When the operator picked up, she said, "I need to speak to the officer in charge of the issue with Richard Raburn and his wife."

"I'm sorry?" the man on the other end said.

"I'm in Cecil County. It's a property owned by Richard Raburn's wife Miriam Nicholls. Some bad shit has gone down here, and I know the cops are aware of it. So please connect me to whoever's in charge."

"Uh . . . one moment, please, miss."

The line went quiet. Miriam Raburn struggled anew, so Lexi gave her a whack to the head. It put her face in the dirt, and she tried to curse around a brief fit of coughing. Lexi grinned. The woman was at least persistent. It probably helped her and her husband for a while, but—along with their ambition—also contributed to their undoing. Some people were never happy where they were.

"This is Captain Casey Norton of the Maryland State Police," a man said a few seconds later.

"Hello, Captain Norton. I'm on site at the Nicholls estate. I've subdued Miriam Raburn."

"She assaulted me," Miriam said, and Lexi hit her again.

"And you are . . .?"

"My name is Lexi Tyler. I'm the one who called Captain Sharpe, and he probably clued you in."

"You said your last name was Tyler?" Norton asked.

"Yes," Lexi confirmed. "Do you know my father?"

"If he's John Tyler, yes. Sort of, anyway."

"Did you serve together?"

"No," Norton said. "He . . . uh, butted in on an investigation a couple months ago." Norton paused. Lexi waited for the epiphany. "Hang on. You were involved, too. The trafficking ring."

"If by, 'involved,' you mean threatened with abduction and a life of sexual servitude, yes." Norton started to say something else, but Lexi cut him off. "I didn't call you to rehash the past, Captain. I'm at the Nicholls estate. My father is in the house. My grandfather is somewhere on the grounds. He's a senior citizen with a bolt-action rifle. I have Missus Raburn in the woods. We're about five hundred yards from the main building, left side of the house as you look at it from the street."

"I'm not on scene yet," Norton said. "but I'll get word out. Try to hold your position. We have troopers and county deputies arriving right now."

"Better make your call, Captain," Lexi said, and she broke the connection. Miriam Raburn kept struggling. Lexi grabbed her by the back of her bottled brown hair. "You hear that? Cops are here. You and your husband might think you're hot shit, but I'm pretty sure no one's gonna care who you are."

"Help!" Miriam Raburn yelled.

"Shout all you want. They know what you did."

After a few more cries for assistance, Miriam fell silent. Footsteps approached a minute later. Three state troopers and two local deputies approached—four men and one woman. They trained their guns on the scene. "I'm gonna need you to get up, miss," one of the troopers said. Lexi stood and moved off to the side. Two pistols followed her movements, and she took a deep breath. Miriam Raburn stood. "She assaulted me!" The woman jabbed a finger toward Lexi. "She and her father have done nothing but make my life miserable. I want her in prison!"

"Miriam Raburn," the trooper said, "get on your knees. Hands behind your head. You're under arrest for conspiracy to commit murder, kidnapping, and wire fraud. Probably a few more things by the time the state's attorney finishes with you."

"I know the state's attorney," Miriam said. "I'll have your jobs. All of you!"

The lone woman among the responding officers—a deputy—took a few steps closer. "Ma'am, you can either get on your knees voluntarily, or I can help you. I ain't very gentle, so I think you'd rather do it yourself." The deputy was about Lexi's height, though she looked a little more solid. The thought of her tossing Miriam Raburn around was amusing, but it wouldn't come to pass. The senator's wife complied, raising her hands and dropping to her knees as the trooper recited her Miranda rights.

"This is an outrage," she protested as the handcuffs went on.

"We have some questions for you, too," one of the troopers told Lexi.

"I'm sure you do," she said.

TYLER SAT in the living room of the Nicholls estate. The police took his father's shotgun and the Glock he confiscated from one of the Raburn lackeys. He understood they needed facts to establish what happened and build a court case, but he could respond only so many ways to "Why were you here?"

After yet another iteration, Tyler said, "Guys, we've been over this. My answer hasn't changed in the last ten minutes." Three male state troopers and one Cecil County deputy scrutinized him. One of the troopers was Hispanic. The other three were white. All looked a good twenty years younger than Tyler. Still, he wondered how they would have fared in his situation today. "Do you have anything else to ask me?"

"Why shouldn't we arrest you along with Raburn and his wife?"

"Because I defended myself," Tyler said. "I also acted to save other people from potentially lethal harm." All four frowned. "Look, if you want to cuff me and haul me in, I won't stop you. I'm pretty sure the state's attorney doesn't want this kind of egg on his face, though. I know a really good JAG lawyer. No charges would stick, and your agencies would look like jerks for arresting me in the first place."

Captain Casey Norton walked through the front door. Tyler encountered him before. Norton seemed like a straight shooter, even if he suffered from being a little too in love with the rulebook. It was a common affliction among police, especially those who worked for the state. "Mister Tyler is not under arrest," he said. "Through him, we learned meaningful information about what went on here."

"Fine," the deputy said. He closed his notebook and made his way farther into the house. Tyler stood and limped outside. Over a dozen emergency vehicles filled the driveway and parts of the front lawn. About a hundred feet away, Zeke and Lexi stood under a large tree talking to a female trooper. Lexi sprinted over to hug Tyler as he approached. "Thanks, kiddo," he said as he embraced her. "I'm not sure I could've done this one on my own."

"Don't rush off like that again," Lexi said. "I know you felt responsible for Stacy, but you needed a better plan."

"Aye-aye, Captain."

A few cops escorted Raburn out. Norton pointed to his car—the last one in the phalanx—and they shoved the senator into the backseat. Tyler waited a moment and observed what the first responders did. The police were busy trying to process a large house and massive property. The paramedics focused on the Chaplain sisters. No one paid attention to the cars. "I'll be back," Tyler whispered to his daughter. He made his way toward Norton's car, pausing a few times when he thought he'd attracted attention. No one stopped him, however, and he dropped onto the seat beside Raburn. "This isn't a good look in the next election."

"Screw you."

"They're going to grill you. You're a coward, so you'll talk eventually. The question is who you sell down the river."

"I don't know what you mean," Raburn said.

"They've arrested your wife, too." Tyler half-turned in the seat so he could face the disgraced senator. Blood marred his face from the first whack with the Remington. Sitting handcuffed in a police car, he looked defeated. Even the defiance was gone from his voice. "Here's what's going to happen. They'll question you separately. I'm sure you each have a lawyer you can call, but it won't matter much. Whoever talks first will get the good deal. Your wife looks younger than you. I'm guessing she figures she can get out in a few years and graft herself onto some other rich asshole with questionable ethics."

"What's your point?"

"You're going to tell the cops it wasn't your idea," Tyler said. "I only wonder if you'll throw your wife under the bus or someone else."

"Who else do you mean?" Raburn asked. Tyler remained quiet. He learned the value of silence years ago. People got used to the rhythm of a conversation. When a gap cropped up, they needed to fill it, and they would offer additional information. Sure enough, Raburn couldn't resist. "Who are you talking about?" Tyler didn't answer. A few seconds later, Raburn spoke again. "Do you think someone put me on to Kacey?"

Bingo. "It doesn't seem like the sort of thing you'd find out on your own."

"I can't keep track of everything . . . especially not when the legislature is in session. My first job is to represent my constituents."

"Nice speech," Tyler said. "Who was it?"

"Why should I tell you?" Raburn wanted to know.

"Because I'll deal with whoever it is. Your wife might

make the play before you. I'm going to presume she knows because I don't think she'd let you keep her in the dark. If it backfires on her, you can get ahead of her."

"Why do you want to help me?"

"I don't," Tyler said. "If I thought no one would catch me, I'd strangle you where you sit and sleep really well tonight. I just want to get the person who gave up Kacey. Her family got a lot smaller, and someone needs to pay for it."

"Lamont," Raburn said in a quiet voice. "Lamont Williams. Officially, he works for some consultant in Annapolis. Off the books, he works for me."

"Thanks." Tyler got out of the car.

Norton walked up to him and glared. "What the hell are you doing?"

"At ease, Captain. I needed to ask the senator something before you whisked him away."

Norton peered through the window of his squad car. "He'd better be all right."

"He's fine," Tyler said. "If I wanted to kill him, I would've done it before you got here."

"And probably planted evidence to make it seem like he attacked you."

"You can't expect me to give up all my secrets, Captain."

"He's in custody," Norton said, looking again at the rear of his cruiser. "Unless you want to join him, go back with your family."

Tyler headed toward Lexi and Zeke but detoured to an ambulance when he saw Stacy and Kacey sitting on the rear bumper. The younger sister got up and hugged him. "I don't know how you found us, but I'm glad you did."

"Thank your friend Lexi," he said. "I think she owes you a girls' day anyway." He looked at Kacey. "I'm sorry about your family. Raburn said he got the tip from someone named—"

"Lamont," she broke in.

"Yes."

"I figured it out earlier." She snorted and shook her head. "His bitch of a wife gave me the idea."

"I'd like to pay Lamont a visit," Tyler said. "He's going to hear about what happened here and realize his time as a free man is limited. I'd like to get to him before this happens."

"Sure," Kacey said. "I'll give you his address." She paused. "And his access code for the front door."

41

Lexi and Zeke rolled out well ahead of the emergency vehicles. Tyler told his daughter he might need her help tracking down Lamont Williams. Kacey also provided his phone number. Considering the police remained on scene, the young man still had time. It would take a half-hour to get Senator and Mrs. Raburn back to a State Police barracks. They wouldn't let the county host something of such magnitude. From there, the cops would want to make the Raburns sweat, the lawyers would need to arrive, and a bunch of administrative ducks would need to form a tight row.

Call it an hour. It left ninety minutes until someone asked either of them a question. There would be back and forth, protestations of innocence, and some attempted deal making on the cops' part. Tyler figured he had a good two and a half hours until someone uttered Lamont Williams' name in an interrogation room and another thirty minutes on top of it until an enterprising trooper or deputy tracked him down.

Still, he didn't want to spend the time idle. A news van pulled in on the grass. Others would follow. Even if it took a while to setup a TV spot on the evening broadcast, updates would go out via the web and social media. Lamont would learn what happened before long. Tyler climbed back into the Continental and drove away. He put the aide's address into the car's built-in GPS and received a route. Twenty-eight minutes. He could do it in twenty-three.

The big Lincoln lapped up the miles. Its all-wheel drive allowed Tyler to take curves faster than he would've in a rear or front-wheel-drive vehicle. He got onto I-95 and pushed it above ninety. With so many cops at the Nicholls estate, there would be fewer left for things like speed enforcement on the highway. Tyler wished he still had a smartphone to keep an eye on local news accounts.

He exited at Perryville. One of the signs of suburban sprawl was high-rise apartments in cities which would've never had them before. Perryville was such a place. Tyler remembered Aberdeen Proving Ground adding a bunch of jobs over a decade ago. Base realignment and closure—BRAC as everyone called it. The extra thousands of workers needed somewhere to live, and a developer was always ready to gobble up excess demand.

A few minutes later, Tyler pulled into the lot for Susquehanna Sky Tower. It struck him as the kind of pretentious place a young mover and shaker like Lamont would live. The drive to Annapolis would be rough, but a political consultant could work from home at least part time. He circled the lot and didn't see a gray BMW X4 SUV. He backed into a visitor spot in view of the entrance. As Tyler put the shifter in park, Lexi called. "I'm on the laptop."

"Good. I don't see his car."

"According to his phone, he's headed north," Lexi said. "Coming up from Harford County."

"How long do I have?"

"I don't know. Maybe twenty minutes?"

"All right," he said. "I don't have snap gun or any good lock picks on me. Guess I'll do it the old-fashioned way."

"Hang on a minute." Keys clattered over the line. "The property management company has a shitty website. There's a document where I can see who lives in which unit." She paused for a moment. "Lamont's on the top floor. They call them penthouses."

"Of course they do. Adds ten percent to the asking price."

"There are four," Lexi said. He's in the west one. The east is unoccupied." She paused. "Give me a minute."

"Take your time."

After a short delay, Lexi said, "All right, I found who lives in the other two. One's out of town for spring break. The other works nights. I think his floor will be empty when you get there."

"What do you think I'm planning to do?" Tyler asked.

"I don't know. After what he did to Stacy and her family . . . I hope it involves him screaming. A lot."

Tyler grinned. "Good to know his neighbors won't be around, then." The people below him might, however. "Thanks, kiddo. I'm going to head inside."

"Good luck, Dad. Love you."

"Love you, too." Tyler flipped his phone shut, climbed out of the Lincoln, and limped toward the fifteen-story building.

CASEY NORTON DROVE Richard Raburn away from his wife's house. He would have been happy to make the drive in silence. The nearest state police barracks was about twenty-five minutes away. The disgraced senator, however, ruined his plans. "I'll bet you're happy." Norton didn't answer. If he stayed silent, maybe the man would get the hint and shut up.

"I'm sure you've never liked me," Raburn continued after a few seconds.

"You're right," Norton said. "I thought you were an asshole when you dated my mother. You've done nothing since to change my opinion. And don't you *dare* tout your record of working with law enforcement or whatever you call it. You might fool the voters, but you're not fooling us."

"It was thirty years ago, Casey."

"It's Captain Norton to you. I'm glad you found someone who's willing to get dirty. My mother was too good for you."

"I—"

"Shut up." This time, Raburn took the hint. They made the rest of the drive in blessed silence. Norton parked his car, helped the senator out of the back seat, and resisted the urge to ram his head into the door frame. He'd already taken a good blow to the face. The two walked in together, Norton's arm on his prisoner's elbow.

This building hadn't been renovated yet. The paneling and floors were an identical shade of dull brown, and both needed to be cleaned if not replaced. Cubicle walls sprang up in the main work area. More modern facilities featured an open floor plan. The state paid a few consultants to come up with it. When he heard the amount of the check, Norton realized he'd gone into the wrong profession.

He led Raburn to an interrogation room and transferred one of his cuffs to the table rail. "I presume you want a lawyer?" Raburn provided a name, and Norton asked a trooper to make the call. He found an available office with a view of the entrance and sat behind the desk. Miriam Raburn received an escort inside a couple minutes later. She ended up in a room down the hall from her husband. Smart. Norton always liked to put distance between related suspects and then remind them of it. It made walking back and forth more dramatic.

About a half-hour later, a short well-dressed man came through the front door. Someone directed him to Norton. He could smell an attorney a hundred feet away. At least this one wore a nice suit. "I'm Eli Cohen," he said as he stood in the doorway. "I presume Senator Raburn is free to go?"

Norton laughed. "He ordered two abductions and four murders, and I'm sure there will be some other charges in there. He'll be free when he's in a pine box."

Cohen's expression didn't change. "Can I have a few minutes with my client?"

"Sure." Norton waved a hand. "Someone will let you in. He's in room two. You represent his wife, also?"

"No. She has her own counsel."

"All right," Norton said. "I'll see you in a few minutes."

The captain busied himself reading up on Richard Raburn. He checked the online case file, but no one had uploaded any entries yet. Norton sent a text to Corporal Sutherland. *Need to know what the sisters said ASAP. Raburn's lawyer is here.*

Sutherland replied a moment later. *Roger. Standby.* He soon sent a longer message. *Older one is a reporter. She investigated a shady land deal Raburn and his wife made a lot of money on. It funded a senate campaign. She thinks he found out and went after her to keep the story from getting out.*

Norton thanked the man, grabbed a few manila folders to make it look like he carried important documents, and walked down the hall to the interview room. Raburn and his lawyer sat on the same side of the table. Norton stared the senator down before dropping onto a chair opposite them. "You really screwed the pooch this time."

"Senator Raburn tells me he dated your mother thirty years ago," Cohen said. "You have a conflict of interest."

"No, I don't," Norton said.

"You might have it in for him."

"If I were trying to throw him in jail for speeding, you may have a point. This is a lot different, and you know it. We're talking about multiple serious felonies. What happened almost thirty years ago doesn't come into play. Why don't we dispense with the bullshit and try to spend our time here productively?"

"Fine," Cohen said. His expression remained the same. A few years ago, Norton might've tried to provoke him. Now, he was on a path to promotion. Plus, it was late, and he'd rather go home soon rather than after a long dance with a pricey lawyer. "What are you offering?"

"Nothing yet," Norton said. "It'll ultimately be up to the state's attorney. We want to know everything the Raburns did ... and I mean *everything*. Not just the recent stuff." He didn't want to elaborate. Cohen may not have known about the bad land deal. Better to keep him in the dark for now.

"We're happy to sit here and wait you out," the attorney said. He smiled and crossed his arms.

Norton shrugged. "I get paid the same either way."

"Me, too."

"Fine," Norton said. "You should know his wife's down the hall with her lawyer. They're probably having a similar conversation. We don't need the full story from both of them."

"So whoever gives it up first gets the better deal," Raburn said.

Norton nodded. "Usually how it works."

The senator shook his head. "It's exactly how he said it would play out."

"Who? What are you talking about?"

Raburn glanced between Norton and his lawyer. "I need a little time to talk to Eli. There are ... some things he needs to know before we can talk."

"All right." Norton stood. "Take your time. It's not my

prison term." He closed the door as he left the interrogation room. The office he grabbed earlier remained empty. Norton checked his email, read a few updates recently added to the case files, and scrolled through a few hotels he could stay in for his next vacation. About an hour later, a young trooper told him Raburn was ready. Norton returned to the room and took his seat again.

"Senator Raburn has given me the whole story," Cohen said. His face remained inscrutable. Norton wouldn't want to play poker with him. "We're ready to share it with you so long as we're the first ones to do so."

"Nothing from down the hall yet," Norton said. "Talk fast just in case."

The lawyer offered his client a single nod. "It's a lot," Raburn said. Norton flipped to an empty page on his legal pad. "I heard Kacey Chaplain was going to expose a past land deal in an article. The story would damage my career . . . especially my aspirations to Washington. I knew she wouldn't take a bribe, so we hired some men to abduct her and kill her family."

"Who's 'we'?"

"Miriam and I. She was involved with everything. In fact, I didn't want to kill anybody. She was the one who pushed for it. I went along with her. I never thought I'd meet someone whose ambition exceeded mine."

Norton jotted a few notes. "How did you hear about the story?"

"There's a consultant who works in Annapolis," Raburn said. "His name is Lamont Williams. He's been double-dipping for me for a while now. He dated Kacey, and she told him a little about her story. Left my name and details out of it, of course, but he's a smart kid. He figured it out and came to Miriam and me."

"And the two of you hatched a plan which left four people

dead," Norton said. Raburn nodded. "I'll need to know who you hired."

"They were all from a company called Elite Security Services. Miriam's brother runs the outfit. It's a professional operation."

"Based on what I saw at the scene, I think they're going to need to go on a recruiting drive." Raburn didn't take the bait. "I'm also going to want to talk to this Lamont Williams. You have an address for him?"

"Yes," the senator said. "He's local. You can probably pick him up and have him down here quickly."

"Good," Norton said. "Give me his details."

42

The access code for the front door worked. It wasn't even very clever . . . 3-9-7-1. The corners of the keypad starting in the upper right. It probably ranked better than something like 1-2-3-4, but given enough time, an attacker wouldn't even need to be clever to guess the sequence. Tyler often wondered why people created such vulnerabilities in their lives and routines.

The lobby reminded him of the one in his father's building. A large area to gather sat off to the right. To the left, a man in a security guard uniform sat behind a large desk partitioned off from the rest of the space. The elevators were straight ahead. Tyler spotted a camera in the ceiling and kept his face angled away from it as he walked past the desk. "Evening, sir," the sentry said, and Tyler waved.

He pushed the button for the second-to-last floor, noticing the lack of a *13* in the selection. After 12 came 14, then 15, and finally 16. He'd stayed in some hotels which did this and always found it absurd. Superstitious people shouldn't be coddled. Tyler exited on the actual fourteenth floor. In case the guy at the desk paid attention to the elevator, he wouldn't see it go all the way up. He found the stairs and made his way to the top level. A short corridor led to four identical doors, two on each side. All were inscribed with a cardinal direction in fancy script. Another three percent premium per month.

Without any specialized tools, Tyler took an old-fashioned approach. Despite the newness of the building and the asking prices they must have slapped on these alleged penthouses, a simple credit card bypassed the lock in under a minute. Tyler moved inside and locked the door. The apartment was dark. He flipped a switch in the living room, and an overhead light came on.

The supposed penthouse fit Lamont well.

In addition to a massive TV, the young man owned a large stereo which included a turntable, and he kept an impressive collection of CDs and vinyl. The sofa and recliner were tan leather. Tables were a dark brown almost exactly matching the shade of the wooden floors. The kitchen featured all stainless steel appliances. Whoever furnished the place definitely put a luxury spin on it. The bedrooms continued the opulent feel. Despite living alone, Lamont owned a king bed and enough dressers to hold all of Lexi's clothes three times over. Tyler spot-checked a few drawers, and they were full.

He still had a little time, so he searched the place room by room. Sure enough, the top desk drawer in the office held a loaded .357 Magnum revolver. He didn't find any other guns. Tyler turned off any lights he'd switched on, set the gun in the center of the circular dining room table, and sat in the far chair. He kept his left leg straight to ease the pressure on his knee.

Then, he waited.

Tyler's hands clenched and unclenched. He took a few deep breaths. He needed to paint. First, he required ice on his knee and sleep. In the morning, he could sit at his easel. After about ten minutes, he wondered if Lamont would show up.

Someone could've warned him. He might have set up a news alert for Raburn and decided to avoid the area near his house. If he were going on the run, however, he would need clothes and supplies. Easier to grab them quickly at home rather than create a trail of credit card purchases or ATM withdrawals. Sure enough, a key turned in the lock a moment later.

The living room light flicked on again. Lamont soon walked around the corner, stopped and stared. He was a tall, thin black man in a nice leather jacket. A silver necklace peeked out above the collar of his sweater. He probably couldn't see well in the dimness of the area. Tyler chose the farthest chair from the front of the apartment. "Hello, Lamont."

"Who the hell are you? You a cop?"

"Turn on the chandelier and tell me if you think I am." Lamont rotated a dial on the wall, and four bulbs went from dark to bright in a steady progression.

"I'll call the police," he said.

"Good. They're going to be looking for you soon, so you'll be doing them a favor."

Lamont's eyes took in Tyler before moving to the table. He stared at the revolver. "My gun?" Tyler nodded. "I got another."

"No, you don't."

"How do you—"

"Over the years, I've hidden weapons in every reasonable place you can think of. Probably some unreasonable ones, too. This is your only piece." Tyler swept his hand toward the kitchen. "Maybe you'd like a fancy chef's knife from the block in there? I won't stop you."

Lamont sighed. "What do you want?"

"To talk," Tyler said. He gestured toward the chair opposite his. "Have a seat."

"Why the hell would I want to talk to you?"

"Because I'm the only man who's going to offer you a choice tonight."

The words gave Lamont pause. He looked between Tyler and the gun a few times. Finally, he pulled out the dark wooden chair and sank onto it. "What's my choice, then?"

"Not so fast," Tyler said. "First, I want to know why you did it."

"Did what?"

Tyler's hand inched closer to the .357. "Keep dicking me around, Lamont, and I'm just gonna shoot you. By now, I presume you think I don't look like a cop. I probably look like a killer. People tell me I have the eyes for it. There are a few guys at Richard Raburn's estate who could share their experiences if they were still alive."

Lamont didn't say anything. He stared at the gun for a few seconds before meeting Tyler's gaze and answering. "Fine. I know what you're talking about. We got a problem here, though."

"Really?" Tyler flashed a fake smile. "I'd love to hear all about it."

"A middle-aged white guy breaks into a black professional's penthouse, grabs a gun, and thinks he can dictate terms. Typical."

"You asshole," Tyler said. "When you help murder four people and kidnap two others, you don't get to play the race card."

"I didn't kill anyone." Lamont crossed his arms and grinned. "Didn't kidnap anybody, either."

"You don't seem stupid, so you must be trying to project confidence. According to Richard Raburn, you worked off the books for him and his wife. They're two of the most craven and ambitious people I've ever encountered, and I've met people well up in the line of presidential succession."

"What's your point?" Lamont demanded.

"They're going to be fighting each other to see who can rat you out first," Tyler said. "Sure, you didn't pull a trigger or grab anyone from a house. The intel you provided had some direct results, however. I'm no lawyer—"

"Obviously."

"—but I'm pretty sure you'd get charged as an accessory. How well do you think a self-important prick like you would fare in prison?"

Lamont frowned, and his arms fell back to his sides. "I can afford a pretty good attorney, you know."

"How nice for you. Do you think the Raburns can't?" Lamont glared at Tyler but didn't say anything. "At some point, the choices I'm going to offer you will become irrelevant. You need to hear them while you're still in some semblance of control over what happens to you."

"What do you mean?"

"Once the police kick in the door, all bets are off."

Lamont bobbed his head toward the table. "They'll see you sitting there with a gun. I bet your prints are all over it."

Tyler scoffed and held up his hands, which were covered in thin black gloves. "Not my first rodeo, Lamont. Your magnum, your prints . . . especially on the ammo. I don't know if the gun's legit, but I'm sure the cops will have an opinion there pretty quick."

Silence prevailed for a minute. Lamont steepled his fingers and rested his chin on his hands. His deep breaths were the only soundtrack in the apartment. "All right. What are these choices you've been telling me about?"

"Glad you asked," Tyler said. "You have three ways out of here. Choice one is to turn yourself in."

Lamont snorted. "Why the hell would I?"

"Control the narrative. I'm sure a fancy political consultant like you has used the term before. If you wait for the cops to come here, you're on their terms."

"Pass," Lamont said. "What's next?"

Tyler's eyes moved toward the wall to his left, and Lamont's gaze followed. French doors opened to a small balcony. "You go out there and jump. Maybe you'll think about what an asshole you are on the way down. I don't know, and I really don't care as long as you go *splat* at the bottom."

"Wow." Lamont threw his head back and forced a laugh. "I had no idea you were so funny. I can't *wait* to hear the third option."

"It's simple, really," Tyler said. He pointed to the large pistol on the table between them. "Go for the gun." He raised his finger and held it up. "I have to warn you, though . . . I'll be reaching for it, too. I've put it a tiny bit closer to your side of the table. You're half my age or whatever, and maybe you're faster than I am."

"No doubt," Lamont said. His smile looked sincere.

"You should know . . . I've killed a hell of a lot of men in my day. Since my second combat tour, most of them were younger and faster. You want to take the third choice, it's fine with me. There's no going back."

"How do I know the gun's loaded?"

"It is."

"And if I go for it and get it before you, I shoot you?"

"You get to try," Tyler said. "Remember, I'll be reaching for it, too. I might have learned a thing or two about how to disarm people over the years. Still, you'll be holding a weapon, and I won't. The advantage would be yours." Lamont's smile remained. "I wonder if you're a good shot. We're not very far apart, but I'm sure you're nervous. Heart's racing. Breath is coming quick. You fire this gun a lot?" Lamont didn't answer. Tyler kept talking. "It's not a semiautomatic, so you'd have to deal with a hard trigger pull and then a stiff recoil. Even at close range, you'd be an amateur with a lot of factors to overcome."

Lamont stared at the revolver. He looked up at Tyler. "None of these are a good choice."

"This is what happens when you aid in four murders and two kidnappings." Tyler tapped his watch. "Clock's ticking. One of the Raburns is going to give the police your name. Deputies might already be on their way."

"Let me guess," Lamont said. "You want me to jump."

"Actually, I hope you go for the gun. I want to shoot you for what you did to Kacey and her sister. One round in the gut. You can think about it while you lie on the floor in agony. Don't worry . . . I'd finish you off before I leave."

Tyler knew he'd dropped a lot in Lamont's lap. The young man probably expected to pop in, pack a bag, grab some cash, and get going. The last several hours didn't unfold according to any plans he might have made. Lamont stared at the magnum before his eyes lifted to Tyler. Another glare. Maybe he was taking the measure of the man he'd need to beat to grab the gun. "Wasn't supposed to go this way," he said in a small voice.

"It never is."

"I can't do jail. All these options end up with me dead."

"If you're looking for sympathy," Tyler said, "you're really talking to the wrong guy. What's it gonna be, Lamont?"

The young man stared at the table. Tyler blew out the breath in his lungs in case Lamont reached for the gun. After a moment, Lamont stood. He walked to the French doors, opened one, and stepped out onto the balcony. He looked around and shook his head.

With a final glance back at Tyler, Lamont grabbed the rail, vaulted over it, and fell to the asphalt below.

43

After what felt like an endless day and evening helping her dad, Lexi yawned. She'd been up for a long time, and the adrenaline of chasing down Miriam Raburn wore off when the cops showed up. "What a shitshow," her grandfather said as she closed her dad's old laptop.

"It was. Thanks for coming, Grandpa. I'm sure Dad appreciated it, too."

"He did."

"Wow," Lexi said. "He actually told you he did?"

"In his own way." Her grandfather grinned. "I get to hold the navy bailing the army out over his head for a while. It's good for me either way."

Lexi laughed. She didn't understand the relationship between her dad and grandfather. It was probably dysfunctional on some level and had been for years. Both of them were too old and stubborn to do anything meaningful about it. It worked for them, however, and her grandfather's happiness proved it. Her phone vibrated on the coffee table, and it sounded like a power tool against the wood. Lexi picked it up and glanced at the screen. A text from her dad.

Lamont is resolved. I think you can come home.

"He finish everything?" Zeke asked.

"Yep. I think I'll head home and stay in my own bed tonight."

The old man nodded. "I hope I see you again before the next time someone threatens your dad."

"I'm sure you will, Grandpa." Lexi paused. "Besides, that could be next week."

He chuckled and nodded. Lexi packed up, hugged Zeke goodbye, and climbed into her Accord. The late hour meant little traffic, and the trip passed in record time. Someone ransacked the place while they were gone. Lexi was too tired to deal with it tonight. She made it halfway up the stairs to her bedroom when someone knocked on the door. Her dad would have a key. No one else should be at the house at this hour.

On her way to the entrance, Lexi grabbed the pistol her dad kept in the drawer of the small table where he tossed the mail and his keys. She approached the door, stood to the side, and leaned in to look through the peephole. Stacy stood on the porch. Lexi opened up. Her friend ran the couple steps inside and hugged her. Embracing someone with a pistol in one hand was awkward, but Lexi made it work. "You could've called," she said as she locked the door and put the gun back.

Stacy nodded. "I figured I'd surprise you."

Lexi smiled. Her friend had been through the wringer in the last couple days. Her eyes were red and puffy, and bags formed under them. "Well, you did. You sure you should leave Kacey alone?"

"Please." Stacy snorted. "She's not going to do anything. Now, she has another story to write about Richard Raburn.

Hell, at this rate, she might run for his senate seat in a few years."

"Good for her," Lexi said. "What about you?"

A tear slid down Stacy's cheek. "I could use a friend," she said in a quiet voice.

"You've got one." Lexi put her arm around Stacy's shoulders. She realized she would have another friend in therapy. Now, they could form a trio with Alex Anne. "Want some coffee? Beer?"

"Your dad won't care if we raid his brews?"

Lexi shook her head. "Under the circumstances, I think he'll be fine with it." She opened the fridge, pulled out a pair of longnecks, and handed one to Stacy. "To friends." Lexi held her bottle up.

"To friends." Stacy flashed a brief smile, clinked her bottle to Lexi's, and they both took a long draught. "I haven't been here in a while." She glanced around. "What happened?"

"Probably Raburn's men," Lexi said. Stacy grimaced. "Don't worry about it."

"You got a spare bedroom?"

"No. My dad uses it. The couch folds out. You want me to take it? You could have my bed."

Stacy shook her head. "I couldn't put you out. The sofa's fine." She took another drink. "Let's sit down and talk. I think we have a lot of catching up to do."

"I think we do," Lexi said.

Getting out of Lamont's building didn't prove challenging. Tyler rode the elevator down to the second floor, walked toward the back of the building to avoid the guy at the front desk, and took the stairs to the first. Sure enough, a rear exit led to a courtyard and small playground. He limped around the high-rise on a knee which really needed him to rest. Tyler drove the Continental back to Baltimore. It was too late to return it, and he didn't have an easy way home. Without his regular phone, he couldn't summon an Uber for the second time in his life. He'd figure out how to get the car back to Geoffrey tomorrow. When Tyler walked in, he rolled his eyes at the mess. Lexi and Stacy sat on the couch. Two empty and two half-empty beer bottles rested on the coffee table. "Don't drink my last one," he said. "I don't care about the rest."

He chatted with them for a few minutes until it became obvious his presence was superfluous. Tyler bid them good night, limped up the stairs, and grabbed a cold compress from his first-aid kit. He wrapped it around his knee and lay in bed for a while. The pain eased a little. He'd need to make an appointment to get it looked at if it didn't improve after a few days. As he grew tired, Tyler took the cold compress off, changed out of his clothes, and got back in bed. He fired off a quick text to Sara Morrison. *I know it's late. I'm OK. Everyone is safe. Sleep well. Love you.* Sleep came for him a few seconds after his burner phone hit the nightstand.

On most days, Tyler woke up before 7:00 AM. He managed to make it almost to eight. His knee felt a little better, though the trip down the stairs to the kitchen didn't help. He put a pot of coffee on, saw Stacy asleep on the folded-out couch, and smiled. She needed a friend, and Lexi was a good one to have. When the java finished, Tyler poured himself a mug and carried it back to the top floor. He checked his phone and saw a return text from Sara. *Glad to hear everyone is OK. Headed to work. Probably not reachable. Talk later. Love you too.*

He sat in his extra bedroom. Even in his most artistic moments, he wouldn't call it a studio, although Lexi used the term from time to time. Some of his best output from his therapeutic painting program hung on the walls. He always felt self-conscious about it even if his shrink and daughter encouraged him to display the pieces he was most proud of. The rest got bagged and filed in racks sorted roughly by date. Tyler began with plain paper and basic watercolors. He'd upgraded his supplies several times.

After another swig of coffee, Tyler stared at the blank page. He'd always thought talk of the muse was bunk, but he'd come to trust the creative process once he realized he couldn't force it. Tyler picked up a brush and got to work. He paused after a short while, realized he'd painted several trees, and got back to it. When he felt spent, he set his brush down and looked at the easel.

A forest stretched toward the top of the paper. Blood marred the ground where no bodies were visible. A path extended from the trees to the edge of the page. A man led two women along it. Tyler frowned at his latest painting. Soft footsteps approached. He didn't close the door anymore. No reason to hide anything from Lexi. She stopped beside him. "What is it?"

"I'm not sure."

"Looks like where we were last night," Lexi said. She yawned and stretched.

Tyler nodded. "I think this is supposed to be me on the right side."

"I think you're right. You're leading Stacy and me to safety."

"Am I?" he wondered. Lexi frowned, but Tyler continued. "I know she's safe in our living room, but you're going to have another friend in therapy after I got involved. Sometimes, I wonder about the cost of what I do. Even if I don't bear it, someone has to."

Lexi put a hand on his shoulder. "Stacy is alive because of you. If you hadn't looked for Alex, she'd be . . . who the hell knows where? They were already in bad situations, Dad. You didn't make them worse. You might be the only person who could've gotten them out."

He smiled and patted her hand. "I guess you're right."

"I know this is all part of your process," Lexi said, "and I'd never pretend to understand everything you went through in the army. Lots of everyday people walk away from trouble, but *you* can't . . . no matter if it's not your own. I now see it's a good thing, never mind that it makes me and Sara worry about you more than we'd like."

"Thanks, kiddo," Tyler said. "I don't think this is one for the wall, though."

"Probably not the Met gala, either."

"True," Tyler said. "They'd have to abolish their standards first."

"Let it finish drying and see what you think. Besides, don't you need to get to work?"

"Yeah. Ortiz is probably wondering where I am."

"I think he'll understand," Lexi said.

LEXI FOLLOWED Tyler to Bel Air as he returned the Continental to Geoffrey. The old man was happy to receive it, didn't seem to mind it coming back the next day, and asked minimal questions. Zeke must have prepped him. With the Lincoln back in its usual spot, Tyler hopped in Lexi's Accord coupe, and they rode to Special Operations Classic Car Repair together.

Smitty glanced up from the engine of a Trans Am. Other than its desperate need of a paint job, it looked like it could've come off the set of *Smokey and the Bandit*. "You're late," he said. Ortiz bobbed his head in agreement.

Tyler looked at his watch. "Nope. I'm exactly on time." He

followed Lexi to the office. "You finish whatever you were doing in Excel?"

"Mostly," she said. "I think I have one more sheet to setup. Then, all you'll need to do is plug in some numbers, and the formulas will do the heavy lifting. You might want to invest in a real accounting program, especially with two employees now."

"Maybe," he said. He moved a box closer to the desk and put his left leg on it. The brace he took from the Chaplain house helped.

"How's your knee?" Lexi asked as she sat in one of the two cloth chairs on the other side of the desk.

"About the same. Too early to tell if it's better. I'm going to try and stay off it as much as possible. Ice it when I can. We'll see how it is in a couple days."

Ortiz stood in the doorway. "You got a minute, boss?"

"Sure," Tyler said. "What do you need?"

"You all right?"

"Fine. Why?"

"You're limping worse than me, and it looks like you've been in a fight."

"You should see the other guy," Tyler said.

"Is there something going on I should know about?" Ortiz asked.

Tyler took a deep breath. Ortiz seemed like a good guy, and everyone had good things to say about his work. His service record was excellent before an IED forced him into an early exit. "Can I trust you?"

"You in trouble?"

"This isn't the time to answer a question with another one."

"Yes." Ortiz gave a thumbs-up. "You can trust me."

"Good. Close the door." Tyler glanced at Lexi who frowned at him. He put a hand up and flashed her a quick smile. Ortiz dropped into the other chair once they were afforded some privacy. "I had to . . . resolve a situation. Someone was in trouble, not their fault, and couldn't get by without help."

"It involved you getting into a fight?" Ortiz said.

"More than one," Tyler said.

Ortiz inclined his head toward Lexi. "Boss, you sure she needs to know all this?"

"*She* knows everything already," Lexi said.

"I don't have any secrets from her," Tyler added. "Even the stuff the army would redact from my file."

Ortiz put up his hands. "All right. I'm guessing here, but . . . you did more than get in a fight."

"I don't go looking for trouble."

"You just can't walk away from it," Ortiz said.

Tyler nodded, feeling Lexi's eyes on him. "So others have pointed out. Someone killed a few people and kidnapped a young woman. I helped her younger sister. The people responsible are either dead or in custody. Two young women have to put their lives back together, but I think they're going to be all right in the end."

Ortiz didn't say anything for a while. He rubbed his forehead. "Some bad shit. The people who do those things deserve what they get. I would've done the same. Don't worry . . . I'm not going to dime you out. If anyone asks, I don't know anything." He put on a very heavy accent. "*No comprende,* officer."

"I appreciate it," Tyler said.

"Why'd you do it alone?" Ortiz wanted to know.

"I had a little help at the end. I normally have someone I can call for these situations, but he was out of town."

"You need a hand sometime, let me know. I'm no good for chasing anyone down, but I can do other things."

Tyler nodded. "Thanks. I will."

Ortiz stood. "I'll get back to work. The Trans Am ain't gonna paint itself when Smitty's done with it." He left and closed the door behind himself.

"He seems like a solid guy," Lexi said. "Considering you told him what happened, I hope he is."

"He'll be all right," Tyler said. "He's not going to tell anybody. Why don't you go back home? Stacy could probably use the company."

"You gonna be all right with the computer?"

"Can I throw it on the floor if I have a problem?"

"Not this one, no," Lexi said.

"Oh," Tyler said. "I'll do my best, then."

END of Novel #4

THANKS FOR READING *Four on the Floor!* John Tyler will return in a new thriller in early 2023. After he finds an injured street racer, Tyler must confront his deadliest and best-armed enemies yet. Preorder *Forced Induction* via this link: https://books2read.com/forcedinduction

THE END

AFTERWORD

Thanks for checking out this novel! I hope you enjoyed reading the book as much as I enjoyed writing it.

I write mysteries and thrillers with action, snark, and flawed heroes. If this sounds like something you like, you can check out my catalog below.

The John Tyler Action Thrillers

1. The Mechanic
2. White Lines
3. Lost Highway
4. Four on the Floor
5. Forced Induction (early 2023)

The C.T. Ferguson Crime Novels:

1. The Reluctant Detective
2. The Unknown Devil
3. The Workers of Iniquity

4. Already Guilty
5. Daughters and Sons
6. A March from Innocence
7. Inside Cut
8. The Next Girl
9. In the Blood
10. Right as Rain
11. Dead Cat Bounce
12. Don't Say Her Name (Summer 2022)

(Notes: C.T. Ferguson appears in *White Lines*. John Tyler appears in *Don't Say Her Name*.)

While these are the suggested reading sequences, each novel is a standalone mystery or thriller, and the books can be enjoyed in whatever order you happen upon them.

Connect with me:

For the many ways of finding and reaching me online, please visit https://tomfowlerwrites.com/contact. I'm always happy to talk to readers.

This is a work of fiction. Characters and places are either fictitious or used in a fictitious manner.

"Self-publishing" is something of a misnomer. This book would not have been possible without the contributions of many people.

- The great cover design team at 100 Covers.
- My editor extraordinaire, Chase Nottingham.
- My wonderful advance reader team, the Fell Street Irregulars.